Prai

"Smart, deftly written, ar
Lifted is so realistic and
inside Poppy's world, wa
through a school where appearances are deceiving and no one is quite what they seem. A hard-to-put-down, compelling read!"

—Alyson Noël, #1 *New York Times* bestselling author of the Immortals series

"*Lifted* is the story of an imperfect heroine seeking her place not only in school, but in life. Its exploration of the amount of truth behind social and religious stereotypes escalates into a double-dog dare to believe them. A haunting morality tale that will leave you questioning just what it means to be 'good.'"

—Aprilynne Pike, author of the #1 *New York Times* bestselling novel *Wings*

"*Lifted* by Wendy Toliver is an amazing, compelling read, filled with all the realness of being in high school, from humor to love to angst. I haven't met a character so well developed as Poppy since reading *Speak* by Laurie Halse Anderson. At times heartbreaking, at others uplifting, *Lifted* is a book that I absolutely loved."

—James Dashner, author of *The Maze Runner* and the 13th Reality series

Also by Wendy Toliver

The Secret Life of a Teenage Siren

Miss Match

LIFTED

WENDY TOLIVER

SIMON PULSE
NEW YORK LONDON TORONTO SYDNEY

This book is a work of fiction. Any references to historical events, real people, or real locales are used fictitiously. Other names, characters, places, and incidents are the product of the author's imagination, and any resemblance to actual events or locales or persons, living or dead, is entirely coincidental.

SIMON PULSE
An imprint of Simon & Schuster Children's Publishing Division
1230 Avenue of the Americas, New York, NY 10020
First Simon Pulse paperback edition June 2010

For information about special discounts for bulk purchases,
please contact Simon & Schuster Special Sales at 1-866-506-1949
or business@simonandschuster.com.
The Simon & Schuster Speakers Bureau can bring authors to your live event.
For more information or to book an event contact the Simon & Schuster Speakers Bureau
at 1-866-248-3049 or visit our website at www.simonspeakers.com.
Designed by Mike Rosamilia
The text of this book was set in Adobe Garamond Pro.
Manufactured in the United States of America
2 4 6 8 10 9 7 5 3
Library of Congress Control Number 2009938065
ISBN 978-1-4169-9048-2
ISBN 978-1-4391-5747-3 (eBook)

To Mom for her generosity

To Matt for his support

To Christina for her encouragement

To Anna for her spirit

ACKNOWLEDGMENTS

Though it's impossible to thank everyone who helped make this book a reality, I'm going to start with God, as He's blessed my life with some pretty darn awesome people.

I'd like to thank my fabulous agents, Christina Hogrebe and Annelise Robey, for their passion and savvy, and Christina for the perfect title. Wild applause for Michael del Rosario and Emilia Rhodes, my talented and valiant editors. It's an honor and a pleasure to work with all the fine folks at Simon Pulse.

All my gratitude to my stellar critique partners, brainstormers, and readers: Sara Hantz, Marley Gibson, Kwana Jackson, Kay Cassidy, Drienie Hattingh, Angela Bulloch, Christina Nordgren, Shari Cunningham, Marsey Iverson, Nadine Dajani, Aryn Kennedy, Jennifer Evans, Kristin Wallace, Linda Gerber, and Anna R. Haze (who also moonlights as my publicist and party favor specialist). Thanks to the Hetricks for their insights and Dad for the great East Texas details. Thanks to James Dashner, Aprilynne Pike, and Alyson Nöel for their endorsements. I'm lucky to belong to the best and most supportive writing and blogging groups ever: RWA, SCBWI, Eden Writers, Teen Fiction Café, The Buzz Girls, and Rock Canyon.

There are no words to sufficiently express how much I love

and appreciate my entire family. My mom has been with me every step of this journey. She swooped in to save the day on more than one occasion, and if it weren't for her, this book wouldn't be in your hands. Of course, the first thing my boys will do when they see this page is look for their names, so here's to you, Miller, Collin, and Dawson. I adore you crazy kiddos. And last but not least, hugs and kisses and unmentionables to Matt, who believes in me and tells me so every single day.

LIFTED

CHAPTER ONE

"It's hideous."

I slouched in the leather seat and glared at my mom. "You said you wouldn't say anything."

She sighed. "I meant I wouldn't say anything *right then.* Since I was so angry . . . so confused why you'd mess up your pretty face like that."

"I happen to like it." I leaned forward and pulled down the vanity mirror of my mom's Volvo. A beam of sunlight flashed off the new titanium microstud in my nose. I really did like the way it looked. It gave me a dose of exoticness, like this honors student could tear it up on the club dance floor or something. The mirror flipped back into place with a smack.

Mom slowed the car at an intersection by Louie's Café and the Piggly Wiggly and then pulled it up to the Gas 'N' Go. A round man in coveralls jogged over to fill it up. I wondered if he were a bulldog in his former life.

"Can you clean these for me, Poppy?" Mom passed me her sunglasses and rummaged around in her briefcase. I took the glass-cleaning cloth out of the glove compartment and wiped. When I handed the glasses back, her gaze fell on my microstud and she grimaced. "I know your friends back home were into body piercing and tattoos and Lord knows what else—"

"Only two of those guys had tats, Mom."

"Well. Anyhow, I guess I should be thankful you only have your ears and nose pierced. But don't you think it might be easier to . . . fit in here if you take that thing out?"

Fitting in had never been my *modus vivendi*.

And whether she knew it or not, Mom hadn't exactly fit in back in Boulder. Too high maintenance for a hippie, not rich enough for a socialite, and not liberal enough for an academic. Perhaps she'd fit in better here in Texas, for better or for worse.

I fiddled with the SCAN button, quick to pass over the hick tunes, Jesus music, and Republican talk shows. Finally, I found something that teetered on tolerable: an older song by The Used.

The gasoline man rapped on the side of the car as he replaced the nozzle in the pump. Mom waved her Am Ex out the window. "The hole will grow back and you'll never know it was pierced," she continued brightly, turning the music down until it was barely even audible.

"Thank you, Mrs. Browne," the man said, beads of sweat shimmering on his red face. He looked at her the way men look at attractive women. Like he'd forgotten how to blink.

I waited for Mom to correct him ("It's *Ms.*, not Mrs.") but she never did. She smiled, snatched her receipt, and pressed the gas pedal. "Pleasant Acres isn't exactly Boulder. And now that you're going to a Baptist school, the dress code is much stricter and—you read the handbook, didn't you?"

"We're not Baptist."

She sighed. "Like I said, I researched your academic options, and Calvary High is the one I felt was best for you."

"Did you ever entertain the notion that staying in Boulder would be best for me?" I muttered, picking at the raisin-colored polish on my thumbnail.

"Of course I did." Steering one-handed, she rubbed her temple with the other. "I didn't want to pluck you out of school right before your sophomore year—"

"*However*," I said in my best Professor Emily Browne voice, "the opportunity to teach at a small, up-and-coming liberal arts college and to be a big fish in a microscopic pond was all too enticing." I rubbed my hands together sinisterly.

Mom had traded in her professorship at the University of Colorado for one at Kinsley College and had dragged me to the podunk town of Pleasant Acres, Texas. It boasted white-picket-fenced neighborhoods, oil derricks at almost every corner, freakishly huge pecan trees, and a permanent notch in the Bible Belt. *Yee-haw.*

"Despite what you think, it's not all about me," Mom said without a hint of humor. "Everything I do, every choice I make, is about *us*. The cost of living is so much less here, and that means we can save more money for your college education. Besides, Pleasant Acres isn't so bad. You have to admit, the people are extremely friendly. Our neighbors in Boulder never brought us homemade casseroles and muffins."

I'd flaked almost all the polish off my nails. They looked worse than before I'd painted them, I realized with a surge of frustration. "That's because the people back home actually gave a shit about our cholesterol levels."

Mom muttered, "Watch your language, Poppy," her programmed response any time I let a curse word slip out in her presence. A few minutes later, she said, "Honey, I know you've got the jitters for your first day at a new school. To be honest, I'm a little nervous about my first day too." Her eyes—greenish-blue, so different from my own dark ones—locked with mine.

She wore a cap-sleeved blouse and a navy blue pencil skirt—clothes she'd had for years but that somehow still managed to look fresh. She'd pulled her light brown hair into a professorial chignon, accessorized with a silver pen. As always, she looked elegant and beautiful, and I had a strong suspicion that if she'd just loosen up a little, she'd have men lined up for miles. Come to think of it, she could use some girlfriends, too. Anything so I could get a little breathing room.

Maybe I should've said something reassuring like, "Oh, come on, Mom. You're a great teacher and everybody's going to adore you." Instead, I just sat there, refusing to admit to myself that she was right: I was a nervous wreck. Nausea provoked my stomach. Maybe it was a good thing I'd skipped breakfast.

The Volvo's tires glided along Calvary Road, which meandered through trees so tall and dense that only slits of the blue sky were visible above. Mom pulled up to the stately red-brick school and braked for a mob of backpack-toting guys to clear the crosswalk. They wore polos and khakis; their hair was combed and their faces clean-shaven. They looked like they were going for job interviews. Or, on second thought, like they needed to get laid.

Mom peered at them over her sunglasses and asked, "See

any potential boyfriends, Poppy?" For one scary second, I wondered if she'd read my mind.

"Now, she wants to talk about boys," I said to the Universe, crossing my arms so I didn't have to look at my nails anymore. "I thought you wanted me off guys for a while. You know, like until I'm thirty-five." She wasn't too keen on her daughter following her down the knocked-up-teenager road.

"Now, that's not true, Poppy. I had a bad feeling about that Simon guy, that's all."

"Spence. His name is *Spence*." I couldn't say why I felt it necessary to correct her for the millionth time. Turned out, she was right about him being a freak. A messed up, macabre, stuff-of-nightmares-and-horror-flicks freak. It had just taken me four months to draw that conclusion myself, and now I'd rather just erase that phase of my life, once and for all.

"Maybe you'll meet someone here, a nice young man who treats you with respect," Mom said, coasting up to the front of the school. "You know what they say about Southern boys. . . ." She parked alongside the curb and faced me.

"That they wear too-tight Wranglers, chew tobacco, and marry their cousins?"

She cracked a smile. Maybe it was being in a new place, surrounded by strange sights, smells, sounds—but it was crazy how such a small gesture gave my spirits a much-needed boost.

Before jumping out, I checked my reflection in the visor mirror. I'd decided to wear my light blond hair down, but I came prepared with an emergency ponytail holder in case I got too hot or my hair went flat. I tucked a lock behind my left ear.

"You sure you don't want to take that thing out of your nose?" Mom asked, watching me closely as I checked my makeup. With this humidity, it was a miracle my eyeliner wasn't dripping down my cheeks.

"You really think I'll scare everybody off with a little stud in my nose?" I widened my eyes and blinked angelically.

"Let's face it, Poppy. You can use all the help you can get in the making friends department." Ah, so nice to know my own mother considered me a social apocalypse. I could say something about the pot calling the kettle black, but there was no use. "Not to mention, you'll want to get in your teachers' good graces."

Taking a deep breath, I rolled my shoulders. Then I pushed open the door and unfolded myself, straightening my top: a little crocheted sweater I'd salvaged by adding some cool metal buttons. "My teachers will adore me," I said, smirking.

"Don't forget to go by the office and get your roster," Mom called out the window. "And I'll pick you up at two forty-five."

"Okay. Thanks. *Bye.*"

"Are you sure you don't want me to come in with you?"

"Only if you hold my hand and leave a big red lipstick mark on my forehead," I muttered under my breath.

Gravel crunched under her tires as she pulled away. I marched alongside the hedge, past the flagpole, up the stairs, through the main entrance, and directly to the office. The poodle-haired lady at the desk hung up the phone with a "God bless" and knocked over a little pot of violets. As she dusted the dirt onto the carpet, she beamed at me. "Welcome. You must be Poppy Browne." She opened a file cabinet and pulled out a folder. "Here is your student ID. Turned out cute as a possum, don't you think?"

I examined the teensy photo on the laminated card. Wearing my hair in a ponytail when I'd registered had clearly been a mistake. Other than looking like a bald girl with demonic red eyes, yep, cute as a possum.

"And here's your information packet and class schedule. Looks like you're taking mainly junior- and senior-level courses. You must be a very smart young lady." Or a young lady whose mother had zero tolerance for academic mediocrity.

The lady glanced down at a note paper-clipped to the folder. "Let's see . . ." She tapped her chest several times, fumbling for the reading glasses that dangled from a beaded necklace. Once they were in place, she said, "Ah, yes. A delightful junior by the name of Bridgette Josephs volunteered to be your student hostess. She'll take you to your classes and answer any questions you might have your first few days. I'm happy to answer any questions you might have as well."

"Thanks, Mrs. Winstead," I said, picking up her name from the brass-plated sign on her desk.

"You're more than welcome, Poppy." She scrutinized me, her eyeballs appearing cartoonish behind her glasses. "Now, let's see. It seems you might have some questions about our dress code. Perhaps we forgot to give you a copy of the handbook?" She opened the file cabinet at her side and slipped out a piece of light green paper. Then she ran her bright pink fingertips down the paper, paused, and read out loud: "Young ladies are to wear dresses or skirts that come no higher than the top of the knee." She cleared her throat meaningfully while I studied my skirt. It would come to the top of the knee of someone who was four feet tall. "They may also wear slacks, dark jeans, or capri pants," she continued. "Shorts, tank tops, tube tops, off-the-shoulder shirts, and spaghetti-strap dresses are forbidden. Shoes and socks or hosiery are to be worn at all times." Leaning over the side of her desk, Mrs. Winstead checked out my black boots, and though she frowned, she said nothing. I wiggled my toes and shifted my weight, suddenly realizing my feet were unbearably hot. Maybe I'd have to switch to my black Converse, at least until it got a little cooler. She flipped the paper over, her lips flapping as she read silently. Finally, she dabbed her forehead with a Kleenex and said, "There's nothing about nose jewelry. Probably because we've never had anything like *that* come up here at Calvary High. Oh well, just be sure and follow the dress code from here on out, all righty then?"

I nodded, thinking it would be funny if an official dress code enforcer policed the hallways.

"Good girl. Oh, mercy me. Here's Bridgette Josephs," Mrs. Winstead said, a gust of relief in her voice. "She's not only your student hostess—she's one of our brightest and most involved students. I'm sure you two will be the best of friends." Her feeble chuckle made me think she wasn't so sure about the last part.

Bridgette flashed me a wide, metallic smile. "Welcome to Calvary High." Her sweet-sounding voice caught me by surprise. Despite her broad nose, over-plucked eyebrows, and fashion disaster of a floral knee-length skirt, her cheeks were rosy and her hazel eyes sparkled. Overall, I found her somewhat cute, on the verge of being pretty.

"Come on, Poppy. We don't want to miss morning service. It really gets the day started off right. Now, I know you went to a secular school back in Colorado, so you've probably never had an opportunity like this. It's kind of like a pep rally, only there're no screaming cheerleaders or mascots bouncing around. I guess you can say it's a *spiritual* pep rally."

I wasn't a big fan of the pep rallies at my old school, so maybe this wouldn't be so bad. I'd just sit back and relax. Hopefully no one would even notice me.

CHAPTER TWO

Her reddish-brown French braid—which hung clear down to her butt—swished like a horse's tail as she led me down the hall. Bridgette paused beside a cluster of girls at their lockers and announced, "We have a new student today. This is Poppy Browne. She's from Colorado," like it was the most exciting news ever.

A pair of freckle-faced twins said "Hi" in unison.

I opened my mouth to say something, but before a word eked out, Bridgette dragged me away and into a large room with a multitude of arched windows. Everything was made of dark wood: the floor, the pews, the pulpit, the high-backed chair where a man wearing a navy blue suit sat cross-legged. He tapped his toes as about twenty students sang "All Things Bright and Beautiful" and an owlish woman played an upright piano.

"I like to sit in the second pew," Bridgette said. "It's the best seat in the house." To my mortification, she started up the center aisle. The students who were already seated turned to look at us, and I felt my face flush.

I grabbed Bridgette's shoulder. "I'd rather sit in the back," I said. She took another step and made a faint whimpering sound as the girls from the hall marched around us and filed into her favorite row. "But hey, if you want to go up there, knock yourself out."

She seemed uneasy with the curveball I'd thrown her, but she joined me in scooting into the desolate back pew. I took a deep breath, the smell of wood polish making my lungs burn.

Speaking of lungs, the choir held the last note forever. Then, in perfect synchronization, they snapped their mouths closed and sat in folding chairs. "That's the general choir," Bridgette informed me in a hurried whisper. "There's also the Good News Choir, which is our show choir. We meet at six fifteen in the morning, but it's worth it 'cause we get to perform all over Texas. We even go to Six Flags. You know those girls I introduced you to in the hall? They're in it with me. The Good

News Choir, I mean. Anyway, you should think about trying out. We all auditioned the week before school started, but maybe they'll make an exception since you just barely moved here." She paused like she expected me to say something. I didn't. "When you're performing, you'll probably have to take that thing out," she said, pointing at my nose stud like I had a booger. "So, what are you, anyway?"

I squinted at her. "What *am* I?"

"Are you an alto or a soprano?"

"Oh, right. I don't sing. At least not in public, and definitely not on a stage."

"Huh." Bridgette's face fell. Apparently, I'd stumbled upon a surefire conversation stopper. She folded her hands in her lap and directed her attention to the pulpit.

The preacher straightened his ivory tie and cheered, "What a wonderful day to praise the Lord!" And with that, he launched into his sermon. It felt weird being in a church service anytime other than at Easter or Christmas or my grandparents' funeral, let alone on a Thursday morning at school.

Part of me wanted Bridgette to start babbling again. It was better than having to listen to the sermon. In my experience, preachers rambled on and on, slaughtering hundred-dollar words and tossing in a few anecdotes that sounded a bit too "happily ever after" to be true. Besides, didn't every sermon boil down to the same three things: Follow the Ten Commandments, Love Thy Neighbor, and Put Money in Thy Offering Plate?

I zoned out for pretty much the entire twenty minutes, staring at the backs of heads. The guys seemed taller here in Texas, and the girls all had their glossy, styled hair—they must've visited salons all the time. Mom went to a salon back home, but I never understood having to get an appointment two weeks out. I'd just wake up, notice my hair looked like crap, and step into my friendly neighborhood Great Clips. One of the stylists brought her golden retriever to work, and I'd hang with him till my turn came up, and sometimes after my cut as well. Funny, but so far I missed that stupid dog more than anybody else in Boulder.

After a dramatic pause (a tactic preachers used—again, in my limited experience—to awaken the daydreaming congregation), the preacher said, "Let us pray." I bowed my head like everybody else. Immediately after the all-inclusive "Amen," Bridgette whispered, "Did you pray at your old school?"

I shook my head no, but of course I prayed at my old school. Like when I made less than an A on a test and desperately needed God to whip up a flood or blizzard or other natural disaster so I wouldn't have to go home and face the wrath of Mom. I also prayed for Spence to screw up beyond salvation when his band took the stage at the Spring Fling talent show.

"I saw on Fox News that more and more public schools are allowing students to get together and pray *during the school day*. I think it's wonderful, don't you?"

"It's the answer to their prayers," I said, trying to keep a serious face.

The preacher held his Bible high in the air and everyone stood and slapped their hands over their hearts. "The pledge," Bridgette whispered, and I nodded, thankful for something familiar.

"I pledge allegiance to the Bible," everybody intoned. To the *Bible*? I snapped my mouth shut and just listened to the remainder of the chant. "God's holy word. I will make it a lamp unto my feet and a light unto my path. I will hide its word in my heart, that I might not sin against God."

Next, the students angled their bodies toward a trio of flags hanging in the corner of the room and recited: "I pledge allegiance to the Christian flag and to the Savior for whose kingdom it stands; one Savior, crucified, risen, and coming again, with life everlasting for all who believe." I figured the Christian flag was the mainly white one with the red cross in the upper left-hand corner. That left the Texas state flag with its famous lone star and, of course, the American flag.

"I pledge allegiance to the flag of the United States of America . . ." I lip-synched the words that were tattooed into every American child's brain, the monotonous rhythm nearly hypnotizing me.

"Ah, good. At least you know that one," Bridgette said. "I was beginning to worry. Ready to go? You can't be late to European history." As she ushered me out into the hall, I wondered what kind of energy drink she'd had for breakfast. "Mr. O'Donnell gets his jollies handing out yellow slips," she said, giving me a conspiratorial smile.

Mr. O'Donnell wasn't that bad. In fact, once I got past morning service, my classes that morning weren't much different from those back at Flatirons High. My first homework assignment came in period two, honors English. Mrs. Oliverson wanted us to write an essay on *Hamlet*, which, as luck would have it, I'd read in the eighth grade. Bridgette was also in that class and toward the end, she turned around and said, "How about we meet at the library tonight to work on our essays? Say, seven o'clock?"

"Okay," I agreed. It wasn't like I had a full social calendar, and after unpacking more boxes this afternoon, I'd be all for getting out of the house. Plus, Mom couldn't argue about me going to the library to do homework. It might even earn me some brownie points, which I could definitely use.

"Cool. If you want, I can program my number into your cell phone," she said, and I gave her my phone. "You know, in case you need me."

Bridgette walked me to my physics class and then headed off to her third period class, her braid swishing in rhythm with her hips. The teacher, Mrs. Clemmons, immediately picked me out as the newbie, and once everybody else had filed in, she asked me to introduce myself. Reluctantly, I stood. "Hi, I'm Poppy Browne," I blurted.

"We can't hear over here, sugar," a guy called from the far wall. Like most guys at Calvary High, he sported a polo-style shirt and khakis. However, his unkempt hair and piercing green eyes made him look less . . . *tame* than the others. I half expected him to pull a cigarette out from behind his ear and light up. But he just grinned and said, "Can you repeat that?"

The room fell silent, and my stomach chose that exact instant to remind me I'd skipped breakfast. I repeated my name for Mr. Smartass, and my stomach rumbled again. In fact, it growled mercilessly throughout the entire period, taking advantage of any and all snippets of silence. Whenever I heard even the slightest giggle or chuckle, I was all paranoid it was directed at my bodily noises.

For once, Bridgette wasn't waiting for me when class was dismissed, so I fetched my lunch from my locker and took myself and my unruly stomach to the cafeteria. So far, Bridgette had personally delivered me to my rooms so I wouldn't get lost, and I'd sat in the back of every class, safe and secure in my little note-taking bubble. But now, I had no clue what awaited me behind the lunchroom's double doors.

Back in Boulder, I'd always sat at the table with the kids Mom complained about, with their tats, piercings, and general contempt for everything and everyone conformist. Did that describe me? Not really. Well, there was the nose piercing, but that was new. Anyway, I considered myself more of a vagabond, and since they accepted me—well, accepted in their dispassionate, covert way—I never felt the need to embark on a quest for a different clique.

I took a deep, cleansing, encouraging breath and then pushed open the door.

Even with the fans whirring overhead, Calvary High's cafeteria felt like a freaking sauna. Pop and water bottle machines were on one side, the food line on the opposite, and a sea of long tables in between. Two ladies donning hairnets stood behind the counter chitchatting animatedly, oblivious to the students who slid their trays along the metal rail toward a bowl of green apples and speckled bananas. A chubby old man with his baseball cap turned backward sat on a folding chair by a little cash register, grinning as he accepted meal tickets.

Okay, so nothing out of the norm there. Substandard, mass-produced food being served to hungry students. *Now to find somewhere to sit . . .*

Where the hell was Bridgette?

I scanned the room, trying my hardest not to appear as anxious as I felt, but the overly helpful girl with the insanely long hair was nowhere to be seen. I promptly switched to Plan B, searching for someone—*any*one—who seemed nice or looked familiar from one of my morning classes. However, with every second that passed, empty seats got more and more scarce. My heartbeat intensified and my armpits felt sticky. I froze, listening to my pounding heart, wishing a trapdoor would open beneath me and I'd be back at Flatirons.

A girl with a big black bow protruding from the side of her head gave me the faintest glimmer of a smile. What's more, the seat right next to her was wide open. I steeled myself and marched toward her. Before I had a chance to ask if I could sit there, though, another girl plopped down and said, "I totally miss the days when they served mac 'n' cheese like twice a week. I think I'll have my daddy write a note to the board." Then she looked at me and clapped her hand over her chest like I'd startled her. "Oh, my! You weren't going to sit here, were you?"

I shook my head, feeling totally awkward. "Nope."

"Oh, good." She turned back to Bow Head. "Anyhoo, have

you heard that Miss Babcock is finally engaged? But she said she won't marry the guy till he gets baptized."

Stepping away from the table, I turned my head side to side, blinking and breathing, blinking and breathing. Something had taken over me—something foreign and desperate and beyond my control. It was as if my legs had a mind of their own. I ran out of the cafeteria to seek refuge in the bathroom.

Just a few minutes, I told myself. I'd stay there just long enough to recoup and recover my composure and then I'd march right back into that cafeteria and sit wherever I damn well pleased.

Unfortunately, I didn't have the bathroom to myself. A classically beautiful girl with wavy, honey-colored hair struck poses at the mirror. I thought it was a bit weird that she didn't stop once she realized she had an audience.

"Does it look better like this . . . ," she asked in a soft Southern drawl, undoing the upper button on her top, ". . . or like this?" She rebuttoned it and twirled a half-turn. A small diamond cross dangled from her gold necklace.

I glanced around for anyone else she might be talking to, but it was just the two of us. "I like it unbuttoned," I said. "Makes a nicer neckline."

"But it doesn't look . . . *slutty*, does it?" she asked, unbuttoning it again.

"Oh, I'm sorry. I didn't realize that was the look you were going for. In that case, you need to take the shirt *off*."

Her big blue eyes widened in surprise. Or was it delight? She lifted her chin and nodded at her reflection. Then, turning to look directly at me for the first time, she said, "I don't believe we've met. I'm Mary Jane Portman." She offered her hand—accessorized with a French manicure and an assortment of silver rings—to shake mine.

Her introduction struck me as oddly formal, but I went with it and shook her hand. Maybe she'd just completed finishing school or something. Who the hell knew what bizarre things Southern debutante types did with their free time? "Poppy Browne."

Mary Jane's smile didn't falter when she said, "Love your nose piercing, Poppy. *Très chic*." Then she tossed her hair, said, "See ya around," and walked out, greeting a pair of younger girls as they came in and commandeered the mirror.

I busied myself with the process of washing my hands, the chilly water cooling me down. As the girls blotted their lipstick, they stole glances at me in the mirror. I dried my hands and tossed the balled-up paper towel into the wastebasket. Only I missed and had to scoop it off the floor. By the time I stood again, the girls had left. I took a deep breath, inhaling the aroma of Ajax and other not-so-savory bathroomy smells.

I stood there for quite some time, listening to the erratic drip of a faucet, the low hum of a recently flushed toilet, and the thunderous growling of my stomach. I toyed with the idea of eating my lunch on the bathroom counter, but what if somebody came in? I could always dine in the privacy of a stall, but the very thought grossed me out. Who knew what kind of diseases I might get?

Leaning toward the mirror, I searched my dark brown eyes. What the hell was my problem? I didn't want to be *that girl*, the one who spent her lunchtime in the girls' bathroom. What next? Curling into a fetal position on the floor, my hair drenched with drool? I gave my head a couple of shakes, and before I had the chance to talk myself out of it, I made a beeline for the cafeteria.

CHAPTER THREE

I'd barely stepped through the doors when a guy holding a tray came up behind me and whistled. "Lookie what we've got here. The new girl." On second glance, I recognized him from my physics class—the guy who'd asked me to repeat my name.

"My name is Poppy, remember? Or is that too much information to squeeze into that pea-size brain of yours?"

His leer sizzled right through my skin. "A feisty blonde, mmm-hmm. Looks like God answered my prayers after all."

"You'd better pray for a better line, because yours officially flopped, shithead." I walked away, fishing a granola bar out of my lunch pack.

He jogged after me. "Now that's not nice," he said, frowning.

I stopped and faced him, and thankfully he was able to stop before colliding into me. "Sorry. I meant to say, 'my dear shithead.' Better?" I tilted my head.

"Much." Something about his carefree laugh made me wonder if perhaps I'd been too harsh on the guy. But before I had the chance to worry about it, I realized we had a very attentive audience. Everybody's eyeballs bugged out of their sockets and the entire cafeteria had gone silent. With great effort, I refrained from biting my lower lip. I forced myself to hold my head high and keep walking away from him. However, had the earth opened up and swallowed me right then, I wouldn't have complained one bit.

"Poppy." I turned in the direction of the soft Southern drawl and smiled when I spotted Mary Jane Portman, the girl from the bathroom. "Where are you going?" She sat at the table by the big window, nestled among preppy-chic girls almost as pretty as she. Meticulously highlighted hair, ultrawhite teeth, and dangly earrings glistened in the celestial sunlight. Not a pimple or crooked nose among them. Mary Jane's manicured fingernails flicked in the air, waving me over. "It's a lot easier to eat if you're sitting down," she said.

I regarded the granola bar in my fist. What had happened

to the other half of it? Revitalizing my smile, I dropped it into my insulated lunch pack.

"Sit down and stay a while." Mary Jane inclined her head toward the seat next to her, which happened to be occupied by a superskinny girl with a sassy short hairdo. Mary Jane raised her chin in a quick, almost undetectable twitch, and the girl slid down to make room, causing a chain reaction down the entire bench. "I'm dying to know, did you really call David a *shithead*?" she asked, whispering the last word.

Little by little, people went back to whatever they were doing before. Except for at this table, where all the girls studied me with unabashed curiosity.

I took a deep breath. The cafeteria smelled like garlic, perfume, and a hint of bleach. Not exactly appetizing aromas, but decidedly an improvement over the bathroom. "I guess I did. Though with a little more time, I'm sure I could've come up with something better."

"I've never heard anyone put him in his place like that," Mary Jane said. "No one dares cross David. I swear they think they'll be struck by lightning."

"He thinks he's God's gift to women," the girl across from me added with an eye roll. "Too bad all those good looks come with such a bad attitude. Right, y'all?" She was a striking black girl with a strong, athletic body. Her full, sleek hair with maroon streaks swooped halfway down her back, and her sporty, light blue dress hugged her curves. Where Mary Jane resembled a Ralph Lauren model, she'd look great in a magazine ad for Nike. Her gaze landed on something behind me and her right eyebrow shot up dramatically. I shifted to see what had caught her attention.

In silence, we watched as Bridgette Josephs navigated the tables with her loaded-to-capacity tray. She took every step deliberately, like she feared she was going to fall. Or like somebody might trip her.

"I can't believe that heifer's actually coming over here," the superskinny girl whispered. "Maybe this would be a good time to tell her that if she wants to fit into that skirt she's wearing, she's got to lay off the tater tots."

Another girl said, "And while you're at it, tell her she should ship that skirt off to a polygamy sect in Utah." Everyone at the table laughed.

I shifted in my seat. A fresh layer of sweat coated my skin, and I couldn't tell whether it was because of the window or 'cause I knew I probably should say something to stick up for Bridgette. She had, after all, dedicated her entire morning to showing me around.

"Now, girls, play nice," Mary Jane said, and I was grateful that someone came to Bridgette's defense. Mary Jane inclined her head, honey-colored curls tumbling around her shoulder. She fingered the dainty cross charm on her necklace, and I noticed her friends wore similar necklaces. "Remember, the Lord loves each and every one of us."

A pious energy reigned over the table, and for a moment, I feared someone would stand, thrust her arms into the air, and shout, "Amen!" Instead, Mary Jane smiled sweetly—almost innocently—as Bridgette arrived at the table.

"Hi, Bridgette," the girls intoned.

"Um, yeah, hi. So, Poppy. Want to come over there with me?" Her usually musical voice sounded strained. She bobbed her head in the direction of a table in the corner. "There are some more people I want to introduce you to."

I leaned out a little to get a better view of the table. The girls who'd been at their lockers that morning—the ones Bridgette said sang in the choir (not just the regular choir, but the Good News Choir)—sat straight up, grins emerging on their faces as if choreographed. A few boys sat at the table, too, the types whose mothers combed their hair every morning. Then I spotted something I'd never seen before in a school lunchroom: A guy at the far end of their table read a Bible while he sipped his milk. Though I knew I should have an open mind, especially being the new girl, I couldn't see myself in that scene in a million years.

Before I had a chance to respond, Mary Jane took my hand in hers. "We'd love it if you stayed right here, Poppy. We're having so much fun getting acquainted." Then she raised her big blue eyes to Bridgette. "Maybe tomorrow?"

Just a few minutes ago, I was hiding out in the bathroom because no one wanted me, and now I felt like the rope in a game of tug-of-war. It was almost comical. "How about you sit here, Bridgette?" I suggested. "There's plenty of room."

"Actually," said Mary Jane, releasing my hand to pick up her fork, "that spot's reserved for Andrew. You understand." She stabbed a cherry tomato and popped it into her mouth. The spot opposite Mary Jane had room enough for two people, maybe even three; yet obviously no one wanted Bridgette sitting there, including Bridgette herself.

"I'll sit with you tomorrow," I said, repeating Mary Jane's suggestion.

Bridgette's nostrils flared. "Yeah, well, I guess that's okay. Oh, I almost forgot. I picked up one of these for you in the school store just now." She handed me a purple rubber bracelet with *WWJD?* stamped on it. "It stands for 'What Would Jesus Do?' Okay, I'll see you later, Poppy."

Bridgette started walking away. I felt relieved to have all that weirdness over with, when suddenly Mary Jane called out, "By the way Bridgette, love your skirt. It's *très chic*."

Bridgette peered down at her skirt like she'd spaced which one she had on. "Er, thanks. My granny made it."

"It shows," said Nike Model Chick in a way that could have easily been mistaken for a sincere compliment. The girls smiled at Bridgette as she lumbered away and then they cracked up. Why were they being so mean? I thought Bridgette's skirt was horrendous too, but they didn't have to make fun of her for wearing it.

"What was with praising that pitiful skirt, Mary Jane?" the skinny girl asked.

My thoughts exactly.

"What?" Mary Jane frowned. "I was just trying to be nice. It's what Christians do, you know. Y'all should try it sometime." Somehow, what she'd said made sense. What was the harm if Bridgette believed it to be a genuine compliment?

"Yeah, well *lying* isn't exactly advocated in the Bible," Nike Model muttered under her breath. "And you'd know that if you ever took the time to *read* it." A couple of the girls made *Ooh* noises. Apparently, that had been a low blow.

"Sweetie, you've got too much time on your hands. You need to get yourself a boyfriend," Mary Jane said, beaming as her tablemates giggled. "Oh, no. They're at it again." She aimed her fork at Bridgette's table.

One of the guys snapped his fingers and nodded his head

while a quartet of girls hummed in what sounded like an impromptu miniconcert. Oh my God. It was *Baptist School Musical*, live and unplugged. And this was a normal, everyday occurrence? If I had sat with Bridgette, I probably wouldn't have been able to keep a straight face.

Instead of joining in, Bridgette rested her head in her hand and stared off into space. Or was she staring at Mary Jane?

The skinny girl peeled the top off her cherry fat-free yogurt and said, "You never want to sit at *that* table, Poppy. You're lucky we were here to save you." If sitting at Bridgette's table required me to have some kind of musical gift, these girls were actually saving everybody with ears.

"I'm Whitney, by the way," Nike Model said. "And this is Ellen." She swished her wrist to present the superskinny chick. "You'll have to forgive Mary Jane for neglecting to introduce us. It's hard being friends with someone so boorish, but *some*-body's gotta do it. Besides, she's the only one of us who already has her driver's license." Whitney flashed a teasing grin at Mary Jane, and I could tell these two were tight.

Mary Jane said, "Yeah? Well, we're all just friends with Whitney 'cause she's got a *fab*ulous swimming pool. And parents who don't care how much we're over there."

The gorgeous blonde's smile was so lighthearted, so inviting; I found myself automatically smiling back. All that smiling was annoyingly infectious. My cheek muscles ached. I felt I might be getting sucked into their shiny-happy-people world a little too easily. Like I should step back and observe for a while—figure things out—before committing to a genuine smile.

I swallowed a swig from my water bottle and studied the girls around me. Clearly I'd found myself sitting with the proverbial popular crowd, the ones everybody else despised yet wanted to be. What did *they* care if I sat somewhere else? I arranged my sandwich, pear, and half of a granola bar in front of me. "So I'm curious. Why did you guys feel compelled to *save* me," I asked, "from sitting elsewhere?"

The girls looked at me like I'd just confessed to being an atheist. "Is there something wrong with giving the new girl a leg up on the social ladder?" asked Whitney.

Mary Jane glowered at her and then turned her big blue eyes on me. "You looked like you needed someone to sit with, that's all. Besides, I happen to like you, and I know my friends are going to like you too."

To be honest, I wasn't quite sure what I thought of Mary Jane. She seemed like someone who, if she ever had the misfortune of getting in a car wreck, would care more about how her hair looked (especially if a news cameraman showed up) than the fact she was all bloody and broken and her fancy car was totaled. Then again, I didn't see her as someone who'd be sitting in her totaled car all hopeless and wanting to die, which, I was sorry to say, described many of the chicks I hung out with at my old school.

Two guys set their trays on the table across from us. Mary Jane reached out her hand and the taller one—whom I recognized as one of the guys in the crosswalk this morning—kissed it. I tried to listen as Mary Jane gave me a quick bio on her boyfriend, Andrew, but his friend riveted me instead.

His dark hair curled at his collar. The color of his skin fell somewhere between suntanned and light brown—a big turn-on for pasty-white me—and he had warm caramel-colored eyes. In a fitted polo/T-shirt combo and jeans, he looked casually stylish—like he'd just thrown on whatever hung in his closet and it happened to work. Once again, I was glad I'd sat at this table.

He must've noticed me ogling him, because he grinned and said, "Hey. I'm Gabe Valdez. So, word is you called the preacher's son a shithead."

My mouth stuffed with ham-and-Swiss on rye, I nodded mutely as mortification seeped in. That David guy was the preacher's son? Why hadn't anyone mentioned that little morsel of information? Oh, shit. Maybe I *would* be struck by lightning.

"Don't worry. He'll get over it. I bet he hits on you again any minute now," Gabe said, and a few of our tablemates chuckled.

I shrugged and kept chewing, covertly scanning the lunchroom for the preacher's son. He was stooped over a table between ours and Bridgette's, and when he noticed me, he waved his cell phone in the air. A second later a *beep-beep* came from inside my backpack. Sure enough, David somehow had gotten my cell number and texted me: *Will you be my French tutor?*

I don't take French, I replied, against my better judgment.

Me neither.

"Who's that you're texting?" Gabe asked. "Your boyfriend?"

I shoved my phone back into its designated pocket. "I don't have a boyfriend."

"Well, I'm sure lots of boys round here will be thanking their lucky stars," Mary Jane said, and I shifted in my seat under the heat of eyes and smiles and nods.

Thankfully, the spotlight shifted soon afterward, and I just sat back and listened. Ellen and a couple other chicks seemed to be practicing their German on one another. Everybody else fired off news, gossip, and G-rated jokes. Gradually, something admirable shone through their superficial popular-kid facades. They seemed happy to be alive, eager to be out and about. Not worried about whether or not they'd get good enough grades on their report cards or if they'd get into a good enough college.

I had a hunch they didn't stuff earbuds in their ears and hide out in their dark bedrooms picking and prodding at their ever changing emotions. And though my gut told me to run and take cover, I was intrigued just enough to stick it through, at least until lunch ended.

"Hey, y'all. I have a great idea. Let's go swimming after school," Mary Jane said.

"Shoot." Whitney frowned. "They're fixin' to put in a new filtration system, so we can't. Besides, I think the garden club is meeting at our house tonight. Oh, Poppy," she said, facing me. "You should tell your mother about the garden club. It's kind of a big deal here in Pleasant Acres."

"Okay." I could mention it all I wanted, but Mom wouldn't join. She'd say it was a waste of time.

Mary Jane tapped her fingernails on the table. "How about shopping, then? You in, Poppy?"

"I'd love to go," I said, more than a little shocked at myself. But maybe I *did* want to hang out with these girls. Or at least give it a shot. But then my memory clicked in. "Shit, I can't. I have to help my mom unpack some more boxes and then write an essay for Mrs. Oliverson's class." Besides, Bridgette might be upset if I didn't meet her in the library to work on the essay, like we'd planned.

Mary Jane jutted out her bottom lip, instantly switching

from beautiful to adorable. "Oh well," she said with a subtle toss of her hair. "Maybe next time?"

"Sure, okay," I said, telling myself not to get my hopes up. She probably only invited me because I happened to be sitting next to her. She had to see that we had absolutely nothing in common.

CHAPTER FOUR

"What a day. My meeting with the dean turned into a five-act play, complete with lengthy intermissions whenever her son called." Mom shook her head, clearly annoyed. "You didn't have to wait long, did you?"

"An hour isn't that long when you consider the average American woman lives seventy whole years," I said, slinging my backpack into the backseat and clicking on my seat belt.

"Good." I looked out the window, strumming my fingers on my knee to break up the silence. Finally, Mom pulled up the driveway. I hopped out of the Volvo and slammed the door. "So tell me, how did your first day of school go?" Mom asked, following me in the house.

"The kids are actually pretty cool. Maybe I won't have to slit my wrists after all."

She patted my hand and then laid hers on top of mine. "I'm glad you're making friends. Now tell me, how were your *classes*?"

Ah, yes. For Mom, education came right after water, food, and shelter and before, well, everything else. An education meant we wouldn't have to depend on a man to make ends meet. In Mom's book, depending on a man equated with licking dog poop off a mildewed sneaker.

"My classes were fine," I said.

"Your teachers?"

"Fine."

"Did you get quite a bit of homework?"

"Not too much." I raided the fridge for a Dr Pepper and cracked it open.

"You know I expect you to make excellent grades at Calvary. Your last report card was inexcusable." She pressed her lips together.

"Just because I made a few B's here and th—"

"And a D." She stopped sifting through the mail and looked at me. I took a huge, frustrated gulp of my pop. Then I slung my backpack over my shoulder and practically ran to my room. After turning on some music, I dumped the contents of my backpack onto the bed. But try as I might, I couldn't stop thinking about Mom and how she felt the need to keep bringing up my grades. I stormed back to the kitchen, where I found Mom reading the newspaper.

I took a quick breath and she looked up expectantly. "That D was in *volleyball*, Mom. I had to do an overhead serve and make it land in a plastic crate for hell's sake. Can *you* do that?"

"That little D you don't seem to care about counts toward your cumulative GPA, the same as your other grades. You're too smart to make anything less than a 4.0, Poppy. I'm just saying . . ."

"Interesting, because I could've sworn you were saying I'm a huge disappointment or any other variation of the same theme." I crossed my arms and inclined my head.

"That's not fair, Poppy," Mom said, folding the newspaper in thirds. "It's my job as your parent to encourage you to reach your full potential. You're unbelievably smart and I have no doubt that if you apply yourself here at Calvary, you'll get your pick of universities and careers and—"

I always wondered whether I really was brilliant like she insisted, or if she suffered from delusions of progeny grandeur. But I really wasn't in the mood to take another of her IQ-type tests. "Have you ever stopped planning every detail of my life long enough to ask what *I* want?"

"Fine, I'll bite. What *do* you want, Poppy?"

The doorbell rang, and instead of waiting for my answer, Mom made a beeline for the door. I veered off to the living room and peeped through the curtains, figuring it was another neighbor bearing a casserole. A cream-colored convertible VW Bug was parked in the driveway. Diagonally.

When Mom swung open the front door, I was surprised to see Mary Jane and Whitney on my front porch. Their beautiful faces instantly lit up. Somehow, the duo looked even more chic in this *après*-school light. "Hi! Is Poppy here?" Mary Jane asked in her sweet Southern drawl.

Mom blinked a couple of times and then smiled. "Yes, she is. Come in." I didn't blame Mom for being stunned. They were a far cry from the crowd I hung with back home.

"You must be Mrs. Browne," Whitney said. "I'm Whitney Nickels and this is Mary Jane Portman."

"Nice to meet you. And please call me Emily. Now, did you say Nickels . . . ?" Mom looked at Whitney thoughtfully. "Is your mom taking classes at Kinsley by chance?"

"That's right. She suddenly got the crazy notion to finish her college degree." Whitney leaned over to sniff the lilacs on the hall tree. Yesterday, I picked them off the bush in the backyard and arranged them in a mason jar. I doubted Mom even noticed them until then.

Mom said, "I have the utmost respect for your mother. This morning in my class, she mentioned she couldn't do it without your help."

Whitney shrugged. "It's no biggie. I just tend to my little sisters when she has studying to do."

"Well, I sure was glad to hear she had a daughter Poppy's age. We were going to arrange for you two to meet each other, but it seems you've saved us the trouble. So, have you started thinking about college yet?"

I rolled my eyes so Whitney and Mary Jane could see I was in no way responsible for Mom's totally lame (yet regrettably predictable) behavior. "Can't you wait till the third date to ask that question?" I muttered under my breath.

Without missing a beat, Mom launched into the Cliffs Notes version of the lecture I'd been hearing since I hit puberty. And yes, she somehow found a way to segue from "You've reached that special time in a girl's life when she needs to start using deodorant" to "You've reached that special time in a girl's life when everything she does or doesn't do impacts her future college application—and hence her entire future."

"I know you think it might be a little premature," Mom said, "but it's getting more difficult to get into a good one.

In fact, today I signed Poppy up for an SAT prep course at Kinsley. Maybe you two can join her. As of this morning, there are seven places left in the class." The girls nodded politely, which seemingly ignited Mom's hostess manners. "Can I get you girls a drink? I have some freshly brewed iced tea."

"No, thank you," Mary Jane said. "We're just wondering if we can kidnap Poppy for a couple of hours and take her to the mall. Would that be okay with you?"

Then, as if Whitney was somehow fluent in Mom's language, she tagged on a: "We'll have her home in plenty of time to do her homework."

I held my breath and waited for Mom to say *No, homework always comes first.* Or perhaps *No, Poppy needs to help me unload some more boxes.* And to be honest, at that point, I was only 50 percent sure I even *wanted* to go shopping with these girls. My cynical side wanted to know what they were up to. It wasn't like they were desperate for a friend. What did somebody like me have that they wanted?

Their smiles were so heartwarming, though. Was it possible they were just being nice? Could they genuinely like me, like Mary Jane had said at lunch?

And wouldn't that be *interesting*? Beauties and the Beast. The Princesses and the Pauper. A couple of Glindas and an Elphaba. Those kittens and the crow on that one YouTube video.

"Do you want me to pick you up in a couple of hours, then?" Mom asked me.

"I'll be happy to bring her home," Mary Jane assured her, lowering her oversized sunglasses from the crown of her head to her nose.

I sent a quick telegraphic message to Mom: *Please don't mention you need a new pair of panty hose and invite yourself along.*

"I guess that will be all right," she said.

"Okay, see you later," I said, still not sure I'd heard correctly. Had Mom just given me her blessing to go forth and shop? And on a school night?

Whitney said, "Cool!"

Mom had this cagey grin on her face, like she thought this was some elaborate prank, and any minute my real friends would jump out from behind the couch with video cameras, and Mary Jane and Whitney would strip off their designer duds and glossy wigs to reveal band T-shirts and stringy, ebony hair, and everybody would yell, "Ha ha. We got you, sucka!"

I had to admit, I found myself wondering if—*how*—all of this was real too. "Okay, well, see you later," I repeated, giving Mom a chance to come to her senses. But she just waved and closed the door behind us.

The three of us piled into Mary Jane's convertible. Whitney sprung the seat forward so I could fold myself into the backseat.

"We hope you don't mind us popping by without, you know, calling first," Mary Jane said as we motored to the mall.

"That's okay. How'd you guys know where I lived, anyway?" I asked.

Mary Jane twirled a strand of her blond hair. "One of the many benefits of living in a small town."

She parked so her precious little VW Bug straddled two of the closest parking slots, next to the handicap ones. Back home, that would be a blatant invitation for a good key-scratching.

Who did these girls think they were? They came to my house unannounced to pick me up for a shopping trip I'd already said no to. They bewitched my mom with their charm, fancy clothes, and good looks, and ultimately they weaseled a blessing out of her. My gut told me I should be disgusted, turned off, or, at the very least, annoyed.

Yet these small-town Southern girls intrigued me, and I wanted to know more about them.

"Come on, Poppy. What are you waiting for?" Whitney called over her shoulder as they walked toward the mall's main entrance.

I brushed aside my qualms and hurried to catch up with them.

The enormous, upscale mall stuck out like a manicured thumb in the dinky town of Pleasant Acres, Texas. Dodging the ambush of shoppers, I calculated how much cash I had on hand. Since I'd neglected to ask Mom for money and I hadn't scored a job of any kind since arriving in Texas, I felt certain it fell in the category of "not enough," and more likely "not nearly enough." I mentally equipped myself for browsing only.

Whitney and Mary Jane said hi to people they knew and some I suspected they didn't. A bouffant-haired woman maneuvering a double-wide stroller stopped in front of us and said, "Well, lookie who it is! My favorite ex-babysitters!" One of her toddlers fussed with her lacy socks while the other snoozed soundly. The lady winked at me—her lashes comically fake-looking—and said, "They grew into such beautiful young ladies. I kept calling, but they'd already have plans with their boyfriends. Do you still go with that Andrew boy, Mary Jane?" Her wide-set eyes twinkled when Mary Jane nodded. "You two are adorable. And what about you, Whitney?"

"Naw, I don't babysit much anymore. I'm always too busy tending to my own little sisters."

The lady shook her head, and I swear not a single hair flittered out of place. "Well, your mom sure had it figured out, having your sisters so many years after you. She's got herself a built-in babysitter." She paused for a moment and made a scary deep-thought face. "Oh, mercy me, where are my manners?"

She held out her hand to shake mine. "I'm Marissa Vanderbilt-Strokes."

Mary Jane said, "This is our friend Poppy Browne. She's new in town—from Colorado."

Marissa (or Mrs. Vanderbilt-Strokes or whatever) nodded. "Ah, yes. Aspen, Vail . . . what lovely country. Well, Poppy, if you're ever between boyfriends and want to make a little shopping money, my dear husband and I sure could use a date night sometime." She sighed and reached into her gaudy handbag and, like a magician reaching into his hat, produced a business card. Pointing at the line that read MARY KAY INDEPENDENT BEAUTY CONSULTANT with her crimson fingernail, she said, "And if you ever want to throw a party for your girlfriends, Poppy, I'll give you a fabulous hostess discount." She giggled. "It's what I call a win-win, and what my customers call one doozy of a deal." Thankfully, someone she deemed more important called her bling bling cell phone at that very moment, and we made a quick escape behind a kiosk peddling cartoon Bible-story DVDs.

"And now you've met our local Mary Kay dynamo," said Whitney, rolling her eyes. "Don't worry. Her bark is bigger than her bite."

"Don't you mean her hair is bigger than her entire body?" I asked. Mary Jane and Whitney laughed, and a group of guys in long, baggy shorts totally rubbernecked as we passed. It stirred up a blend of excitement and queasiness in my belly. Man, these Southern boys were pretty damn hot.

"They go to Freemont," Mary Jane said, turning my head away from them. "You know, *public* school."

I nodded as if I understood, but why did it matter which high school they went to? Unless maybe theirs was one for juvenile delinquents or something.

"And they're definitely not GOV Club material," Whitney added.

Ah well, student government types never turned me on, anyhow. They acted all nice to me during elections and then forgot I even existed the remainder of the year.

"So I know Mary Jane's with Andrew, but what about you, Whitney? Do you have a boyfriend?" She had to. I mean, anyone could see the girl had it going on.

Surprisingly, though, Whitney shook her head and said, "Not really. I mean, I've been on group dates and suffered through my share of fix-ups, but—"

"Not that there's a shortage of wannabe boyfriends. Those who admire her from a distance might believe that Whitney's entirely too persnickety," said Mary Jane. "But it's the opinion of her favorite and most illustrious friend that she's just too big of a wuss. Bless her heart."

Whitney laughed and held up her palms. "Whatever, girl.

You just try and convince yourself that's what's up so we don't talk about the real issue, which is the severe shortage of decent dudes in this town."

Mary Jane grabbed my elbow and dragged me along. "Don't listen to her, Poppy. I'm starting to believe she has it in for all humans of the three-legged variety, and someday she'll be a shriveled-up old woman rocking in a squeaky rocking chair with only her cats to keep her company." With her free hand, Mary Jane clenched her heart like it was the saddest scene imaginable. Meanwhile, Whitney made a hissing noise and flexed her fingers like claws. I couldn't help laughing at them.

As we passed the Claire's window, a pair of intricate Middle Eastern–inspired earrings called my name. I paused to get a closer look, loving what I saw: an assortment of light blue and green teardrop crystals dripping from metal loops and twists. And since my Claire's Club card had enough punched holes to get a free item, they were well within my budget.

"Hey, y'all. Looks like Bridgette Josephs has a new after-school job," Whitney said. Bridgette was in the back of the store, stocking one of the hair accessory displays. I was having such a great time with Mary Jane and Whitney, I'd forgotten about meeting Bridgette at the library in a couple of hours. I didn't really feel like doing the library thing anymore. "She used to work at Pebble Street Junction."

"Never heard of it," I said.

"It was this really cool boutique in Old Town, but I heard it went out of business. It's where my watch came from," Mary Jane said, holding up her wrist to show the flashy pink watch.

"And this dress," added Whitney. "We made quite a haul there."

"Yes indeed," said Mary Jane, turning toward the window. Bridgette crouched to straighten some barrettes on the bottom row. "Her crack is showing, bless her heart."

"I've seen more dimples on a ripe avocado," Whitney whispered, sending Mary Jane into a fit of giggles. It wasn't really funny, so I was surprised when my lips curved into a smile. Bridgette glanced up at the window for just a second. Did she see us?

"I'm going to get a pair of earrings real fast," I said.

"In *there*?" Whitney's eyebrows arched, her eyes widening.

"Yeah. Um, how about I just meet up with you?" It would be easier to get out of my little library date with Bridgette without the others in tow.

Whitney shrugged and Mary Jane said, "Sure, okay. We'll be at Hamilton's."

I wandered into the brightly lit store and took the earrings off the rack. Turning to the mirrored wall, I held one up to my ear to see how they fared. They were definitely me, and they'd look perfect with the tank top I was making.

Bridgette appeared behind me. "Hi, Poppy. Fancy meeting you here," she said to my reflection.

"Yeah. Hey, I'm glad I ran into you." I spun around to face her. She wore a rubber *WWJD?* bracelet, and I realized I didn't have mine. Had I left it on the table at lunchtime? I felt bad for losing it already, but at least now I wouldn't feel obligated to wear it. "Would you mind terribly if I took a rain check on our library date?"

Bridgette frowned. "Why?"

"Well, call me a nerd, but I already finished my *Hamlet* essay." A little white lie, but I could always write it when I got home.

"So you're not ditching me to hang with Whitney and Mary Jane?"

Totally caught off guard, I did my best to appear blasé. "I don't really know what I'm doing later," I deadpanned, "but it seems a little ridiculous to go to the library when I don't have anything to work on, don't you think? It's not like we can talk or even eat anything in a library."

"Guess so." She stared at her shiny flats. "Sorry, I just, well—"

"I'll see you at school tomorrow. And we're still on for lunch, right?" I asked.

Instead of giving me a smile like I'd hoped, she frowned

even deeper. Her hazel eyes darkened to a muddy, grayish hue. The girl looked downright scary. "Be careful."

"What do you mean?" I asked.

"They're not what they seem."

Scratching my shoulder, I looked around for a possible clue. A couple of teenyboppers and a grandmotherly lady waited at the cash register with their little plastic shopping baskets. They all appeared normal enough. "Sorry, Bridgette. I'm totally lost here."

"Mary Jane Portman and Whitney Nickels. They pretend to be good Christian girls, and everyone around here believes they are. But they're not."

I laughed. I wasn't sure why; it was just my knee-jerk reaction to Bridgette's bizarre warning. She was kidding around, right?

"So, you're saying they broke one of the Ten Commandments or something?" I asked jokingly.

Bridgette's eyes shifted side to side and she lowered her voice. "I'm just trying to help you." Her voice sounded so small and distant.

I'd sensed the tension between Mary Jane's gang and Bridgette back in the lunchroom, but now I wondered if there was something more than the everyday Popular Kids versus Choir Kids rivalry going on.

"Miss? Excuse me, we'd like some help over here," the grandma said. "We're ready to check out."

"Okay, well, looks like I'd better let you get back to work. See you tomorrow, Bridgette," I said, snagging the opportunity to escape.

I hiked across the mall and then evaded the perfume-sample ladies in Hamilton's. After a quick scan of the purses on the clearance shelves, I headed up the escalator, where I found Mary Jane and Whitney flipping through racks of designer denim.

"Hey, Poppy!" Whitney said. "Oh, those earrings *are* cute."

Shit. Sure enough, I still held the earrings. I'd been in such a hurry to get away from Bridgette, I hadn't paid for them.

Then again, I'd planned to use my Claire's Club card, so they would've been free anyhow. I'd just make a point to throw away the card, and same difference. Besides, they only cost eight bucks. No big deal.

CHAPTER FIVE

"Speaking of cute, check these out." I pulled out a pair of jeans, glimpsed the price tag—$196—and backed away slowly.

An elegant saleswoman in gold-rimmed glasses and three-inch heels click-clacked toward me. "We just got these in," she trilled, pulling out the pair I'd been admiring and holding them up for us all to see. "True Religion's flap pocket denim. And this Lonestar wash is really popular, especially with Texas girls." She handed me the jeans. "If I may be so bold, I think they'd look stunning on you."

"She's right," agreed Mary Jane. "You should totally try them on, Poppy."

I had only two pairs of jeans in my closet. Not that I didn't like jeans—it was more like they didn't like me. Something about the combination of long legs (for my five-feet-three-inches height), a short waist, and curvy hips.

"Well, all right. Can't hurt."

"Splendid," the saleswoman said. "I'll hold them for you, and as soon as a dressing room opens up, I'll let you know."

"So, did you talk to Bridgette?" Mary Jane examined a pair of boyfriend jeans for a second and then wrinkled her nose and replaced them on the rack.

"A little," I said.

Mary Jane turned to face me, playing with a strand of her wavy blond hair. "Just wondering if she . . . said anything about us?"

I swallowed and flicked through the denim. What was I supposed to say? That Bridgette was on a mission to save me from their atrociously sinful lifestyles? I didn't think so.

Besides, Mary Jane and Whitney appeared to be having a grand ol' time. If I told them everything Bridgette had said, it would only upset them. Or worse, it would explode into a full-blown Bridgette bitch fest. I didn't want that.

But I had to admit that Bridgette's warning—as ridiculous as it sounded—had sparked my curiosity. What had Mary Jane and Whitney done that Bridgette believed was so horrible?

Skip church last Sunday? Add a secular track to their iPods? I couldn't help it, I laughed out loud.

"What's so funny?" Whitney asked, slinging a jean jacket over her arm.

"Well, Bridgette said you're not what you seem," I admitted. "So now that I know you're both vampires, we can all move on." The two girls exchanged looks and then cracked up.

A dressing room opened up, and the saleswoman flagged me down. While Mary Jane and Whitney chitchatted outside the door (Whitney said something about not being allowed to read the Twilight Saga until she turned eighteen, which floored me), I took a deep breath and tugged on the True Religion jeans.

The denim looked like it was ironed and starched—yet it felt soft and supple against my skin. Like magic, the jeans tucked and molded and elongated, and I hardly recognized my own body. Best of all, they were comfy enough for everyday.

However. These babies cost almost two hundred dollars, I reminded myself. And even if I put them on my Christmas list, I could hear Mom say, "I'm happy to buy you a pair of Levi's. If you still want designer jeans when you've graduated from college and have a lucrative career, you can buy them for yourself. And a pair for me, while you're at it."

After doing a final twirl in the three-way mirror, I stripped. Then I wriggled into my $14.99 skirt and swung open the door.

"Hey! You're supposed to come out and model," Whitney said with a pout. "Didn't they fit?"

"Actually, they looked great," I said. "I love them. I just can't afford them." With that, I surrendered the jeans to the saleswoman.

"Would you like me to put these on layaway, dear?" the saleswoman asked. "It's an option not many folks are aware of."

I hesitated for a minute. "No, that's okay." The saleswoman straightened her glasses, then hung the jeans back up for someone else to take home, lucky gal.

I'd never been with people as into shopping as these girls. My friends back in Boulder might've hit up Hot Topic or one of the consignment shops on Pearl Street, but then they'd get thirsty or whatever and head to a coffee shop. Conversely, Mary Jane and Whitney scoured Hamilton's, sampling eye shadows, slipping on shoes, flicking through the bra racks. My amazement gradually spiraled into boredom, and I realized we'd been there for over two hours. All I needed was a frantic phone call from Mom, demanding to know why I wasn't already home and knee-deep in homework.

"You guys about done?" I asked.

"Oh, how funny. You read our minds. We were just fixin' to leave anyway," said Whitney.

"You're not buying anything?" I asked, dumbfounded. How could they spend so much time in one store, singing the praises of so many garments, and end up without a single shopping bag? I hadn't even planned on getting anything, and I bought some earrings. Well, *took* the earrings. Whatever.

"Shopping isn't only about *buying* things, Poppy," said Mary Jane. Oh, God. She wasn't going to launch into a cheesy "it's about bonding over a rack of designer jeans" speech, was she?

Thankfully, the perfume-sample lady interrupted. I succumbed to her and let her squirt my wrists. I sniffed, nodding as the citrus-floral scent filled my nostrils. It wasn't the unisex stuff I typically used, but I thought I could probably get used to it. When the lady offered me a sample vial, I thanked her and pocketed it.

Then, out of the corner of my eye, I saw Bridgette perched at the fountain, nibbling a pretzel. Because of the ferns, I couldn't tell for certain, but it appeared she was watching us. What, was she stalking us or something? I kept peering over my shoulder. As far as I could tell, she hadn't followed us out to the car.

I climbed in on Mary Jane's side, then sunk into the backseat of her VW and strapped myself in. Starting the engine,

Mary Jane looked at me in the rearview mirror, her brow furrowed. "You're being awfully quiet, hon. Anything wrong? Are you having non-buyer's remorse? Those jeans were way fierce, Poppy. I saw the exact same ones in *Lucky* just last week. Come to think of it, you look exactly like the model who was wearing them."

"Er, thanks." Boy, these girls could sure coat it on thick. The scene at lunchtime when Mary Jane told Bridgette her skirt was *très chic* replayed in my mind. "I think I might have seen Bridgette by the fountain, watching us," I said. "What's going on between Bridgette and you guys, anyway?"

"Nothing really," Mary Jane said. "She's just jealous of us, I think."

"Oh yeah," Whitney said without hesitation. "That girl needs to get a life. I swear, she wants to be popular, but she just doesn't have what it takes."

"Bless her heart," Mary Jane added, flicking the shiny "I Heart Jesus" charm on her rearview mirror.

What was *really* going on with Bridgette and Mary Jane and Whitney? I wondered about it as Mary Jane dropped me off. Pleasant Acres was such a small town, and everybody seemed to know everybody's business. I'd only been there a few days and already people knew my cell number and my address. Give it another day or two and they'd probably have my grandmother's alcoholism, my mom's teenage pregnancy, my D in volleyball, my ex Spence, and any other skeleton in my closet dug up, dusted off, and displayed for all to see. If somebody screwed up, their reputation would be obliterated in a blink of an eye. And as far as I could tell, reputation meant a lot to the people of Pleasant Acres, Texas.

Mary Jane wasted no time driving me home. "See you tomorrow," I said, squeezing out behind Whitney.

They waved as they drove away in the convertible, their beautiful hair floating around their beautiful faces. Obviously, they were in an ugly feud with Bridgette Josephs, and though I knew it was none of my business, I was curious to find out more.

Mom was perched at her computer, reading what I presumed to be one of her student's assignments as she tapped her foot to an old Dave Matthews Band song. A stack of papers towered at her left elbow, and several classic novels, some I recognized from my own bookshelf, were piled to her right. An empty moving box and the 1940s-inspired two-toned pumps she'd worn that day cluttered the floor. Her college diplomas and a picture I'd made for her in the first grade sat on the love seat, framed and ready to hang. With crayons, I'd drawn one of my favorite daydreams: Mom and me in a field of poppies, playing with a dog. Then my teacher had helped me brush the paper with black paint. I remembered thinking it was so cool how the crayon colors emerged and seemed even brighter. Mom must've liked it for some reason too, since she'd kept it for all these years.

"What are you doing here?" I asked, pretending to be surprised. "I thought you'd be on a hot date. Or at least at a book club meeting or a Tupperware party."

Mom put her fingernail on the page to hold her spot and lifted her eyes to me. Some tendrils of her light brown hair had fallen loose from her chignon, sticking to the back of her neck and forehead. "Not in this lifetime."

"But hey, it's the only life you've got. Unless you're hoping to go to Tupperware parties in the afterlife. Oh, man. If heaven is all about Tupperware parties, I'm afraid I might have to do something incredibly sinful so I won't have to go."

"Very funny. Now go and do your homework so you won't have to rely on making a living as a comedienne." Before I made it out the door, she said, "How was shopping?"

"Fine."

She said, "Good," and then went back to grading papers.

Sometimes I felt like we were an old married couple, one of those that was always together, yet always lonely.

• • •

"Hey, Poppy," Whitney greeted me in the hall as I headed to English class. "I love your top, but did you know there's a hole right here?" She put her pointer finger on my shoulder, touching my bare skin where gray-and-white striped material should have been: a quarter-size, strategically located hole, offering everybody a peek at my black bra strap. I had no idea that pesky hole was there, and I couldn't quite figure out if I cared. Or not.

Most of my clothes came from thrift stores, and typically if there were holes, broken zippers, or missing buttons, I corrected those problems before wearing them. Nobody wants a wardrobe malfunction, especially on one's second day at a new school. But it wasn't like I had thread and a needle stashed in my backpack. "Maybe the office has a sewing kit?" I said. "Or I could always have someone staple it for me."

"Stay put," Whitney said. "I have just the thing."

She ran—not like a fast walk or even a jog, but a full-out sprint—down the hall and in no time, she returned with a sheer emerald green scarf and a safety pin. She pinned the hole together and draped the scarf around my neck and over my shoulders. Then she stepped back to admire her work and said, "Perfect."

"Wow," I said, overcome with gratitude. "Um, thank you."

She beamed. "You're totally welcome. See you later." She waved and headed off to her next class.

• • •

Mrs. Oliverson, the honors English teacher, made us read quietly all period while she graded the *Hamlet* essays we'd handed in. Any minute, she'd be reading mine. Or maybe she already had. I tried to concentrate on my book, but I kept reading the same passage over and over again, totally annoying myself. It also annoyed me that no windows graced this particular classroom, and the fuzzy strings of lint dancing in the AC vents offered the only entertainment. But even those failed to keep my attention for long.

Bridgette Josephs swiveled in her seat and peered at me over the top of her *A Tale of Two Cities*. There was an intense look in her eyes, like she was trying to send me a telepathic signal. I gave her a little wave, hoping she wouldn't go all melodramatic on me again. Even so, my mind boomeranged back to Mrs. Oliverson and her purple grading pen.

I'd started working on my essay late last night, during lulls in my IM conversation with Mary Jane and Whitney, and finished it over a bowl of Honey Bunches of Oats just a few hours ago. And though I hadn't put forth a lot of time or effort, I felt pretty good about my essay. Whether Mrs. Oliverson would like it or not, I had no clue. What I *did* know was that if she gave me anything less than an A, Mom would freak.

My mind drifted back to the last time Mom flipped out,

every word as clear and stinging as if it had happened yesterday. She held my report card like a dirty diaper, demanding to know why I'd made B's and a D. "If you would have told me you were having trouble in school, I could have found you a good tutor. But you didn't tell me, and now I have no choice but to call the school and check up on you every week. . . ."

Then I dealt a low blow, saying, "I wish I lived with my father," and she went off the deep end, calling my boyfriend a loser, as well as all my other friends. She even had the gall to ask if I were doing drugs. She went on and on, the accusations and stabs rolling off her tongue. I just sat there, shocked and speechless and trying so hard not to cry because I thought that was what she wanted—for me to break down and cry.

But then Mom burst into tears and said she was sorry and that it would be hard, but she'd like to trust me again. She said she loved me and promised that if she were ever that mad again, she'd wait and cool down before talking to me.

I never apologized for bringing my father into it, but I vowed to myself never to do it again. Ever since, I've felt extremely guilty. I knew she did her very best to give me a good life and how she made huge sacrifices every single day. I knew the whole young-single-mother gig was far from easy, and I appreciated her for it. That was why, although we rarely saw eye to eye, I did my damnedest to stay in her good graces.

Once Mrs. Oliverson started doling out essays, my heartbeat intensified and my hands went all clammy. I pretended to be enraptured with the paragraph on page forty-two, the same one I'd been staring at for a good half an hour, and then looked up with a pleasant smile as she handed me mine. "Nice work, Poppy," she whispered, and every cell in my body rejoiced when I read her note under the big purple A-plus: *Very compelling. I'm glad you're not afraid to think out of the box.* I smiled to myself, excited to show it to Mom.

As soon as Mrs. Oliverson dismissed us, I hurried out, hoping to keep a safe distance from Bridgette. She quickly caught up to me, though. The grin I gave her felt strained.

She said, "I like your earrings," and I stopped in my tracks. Oh, shit. Did she know I didn't pay for them?

CHAPTER SIX

My throat became parched and the guilt I'd felt when I first realized I'd taken the earrings—and again when I'd put them on this morning—returned with a vengeance. Maybe, hopefully, this was just Bridgette's way of making small talk, trying to make up for how weird she'd acted yesterday. "Oh, yeah?" I swallowed. "Um, thanks. How'd you do on your essay?" I tightened my grip on my A-plus paper.

"Are they new? Your earrings?" She didn't blink.

Oh my God, she had to know. Paranoia clawed at my heart. "Kind of . . . ," I hedged.

"Poppy, hold up." Mary Jane's Southern drawl penetrated

the racket made by the swarm of students. As she dragged a beaming Andrew over, I silently thanked her for the impeccably timed interruption. The smear of coral-pink lipstick just below Andrew's mouth advertised to the world their recent make-out session.

In contrast to the blurry, noisy commotion all around us, Bridgette stood silent and motionless with her fingers tucked into the belt loops of her dark brown trousers. Her face registered an odd mixture of disdain and . . . hurt? Once again, I found myself wondering what the story was between Mary Jane Portman and Bridgette Josephs.

"I'm glad I caught you . . ." Mary Jane paused to catch her breath. "Oh, that scarf looks vaguely familiar. I think I might have one like it."

"It's actually Whitney's," I said. "She loaned it to me."

"Oh, I'm sure you can just have it. We probably have fifty between us," she said.

"Fifty?" I asked. Who had *that* many scarves?

She twirled her hair. "Well, they were discounted. Deeply discounted. Oh, and lookie here: you're wearing your new earrings," she said. "Aren't they cute, honey?" Andrew glanced at my ears and gave a dutiful nod. "Now you just need to get those jeans to go with them," she said with a long-lashed wink.

"So what's up?" I asked, changing the subject. As soon as

no one was looking, I planned to remove the earrings and stuff them into the front pocket of my backpack.

"Whitney and Ellen just printed these, and they wanted me to make sure you got one." Mary Jane detached her hand from Andrew's and passed me a flyer. "It's about the GOV Club. Whitney's trying to get a scholarship—something about being a 'young African-American woman who makes a difference'—and as part of it, she decided to start a club. Anyway, you should totally join."

"Sounds fun." I stuffed the flyer in my backpack, glad to discuss something besides my earrings. "Thanks."

"You can have one too, if you'd like," Mary Jane said to Bridgette, holding out another flyer. "It's an open club."

"So I see, if *you're* in it," Bridgette muttered under her breath.

Mary Jane flinched like she'd been struck, but then quickly covered with a big, dazzling smile. "Well, you'd better hurry along to your next class, Bridgette. It would be pitiful to lose your perfect attendance award on my account."

"Yeah, well, I was just leaving. Bye, Poppy."

Although Bridgette had undoubtedly hit a nerve with Mary Jane just then, I couldn't help feeling sorry for Bridgette somehow.

Mary Jane called, "Byeeeeee," with a "Get lost, bitch" undercurrent. Then she hooked her arm through mine and dragged

Andrew and me into the mob of students plodding down the hall.

"Hi, Mary Jane!" A senior girl waved excitedly, jiggling the bracelet on her wrist. "Thanks again for the charm bracelet. I get compliments on it every single day."

Mary Jane blew her a kiss. "You're welcome, sweetie." Then she greeted a group of girls, sprinkling compliments like, "Congrats on your tennis match, Lacey," and "Bethany, that skirt is fabulous. What I wouldn't do for legs like yours!" leaving grins 'n' giggles in our wake.

Mary Jane might've held a popular girl pedigree, but she was so different from the A-listers at my old school, who wouldn't be caught dead associating with the common folk, let alone giving them gifts and singing their praises. The golden-haired beauty definitely had an effect on the other students, and being at her side lifted my spirits as well.

"Well, this is me," I said, stopping at the door of my physics class.

Andrew's arms circled Mary Jane's waist and she rested her head on his chest. "Fridays are open campus lunches, you know. So, we were thinking of going to Taco Casa," Mary Jane said. "Want to come?"

"Sounds great, but I already told Bridgette I'd eat with her in the caf," I said with a one-shouldered shrug.

Mary Jane completely froze. Then she blinked twice as her jaw slowly and steadily drooped. "You cannot be serious."

The warning "bell" sounded (it was actually the tune "Amazing Grace," which cracked me up every time it went off) and the sea of students parted around us, scurrying to get to their respective classes before the song ended.

Mary Jane spun around and lifted her chin up to Andrew for a good-bye kiss. I tried not to gag during their exchange of mushy baby-talk farewells.

"Okay, Poppy. All jokes aside, you should totally come out to lunch with us," Mary Jane said. "We have lots to talk about, like the barbecue at Pastor Hillcrest's tonight. Guess who's going to be there . . . ?"

"Um, Pastor Hillcrest?"

Her laugh rang through the hallway. "Well, yes, as a matter of fact, he *will* be there, grillin' his famous hot dogs. But so will *Gabe*. And he wanted us to be sure and let you know he'd be there." She cupped her hand to her cheek, private conversation–style, and lowered her voice to say, "I think he might have a little ol' crush on you."

I could tell my face turned beet red and I tried to hide it by looking down at my Converse. "Oh, well. I'm sure Bridgette won't mind." My gut told me she *would* mind if I ditched her yet again. But I really did want to hear more about the barbecue—my first genuine Texas barbecue—and okay, maybe there was a part of me interested in getting to know Gabe a little better.

"Do you have a sec? I need your opinion," I said, finding Mom at the kitchen counter watching the news. "Is this too . . . I don't know . . . *chichi*?" I held my wrist under her nose and she took a whiff.

"Mmm. It smells wonderful. Is it new?"

I sniffed it myself for the tenth time since being home from school. "Yeah. I got a sample at the mall."

She placed a cup of steaming water in front of me. I selected my favorite Celestial Seasonings tea from the basket and dropped it into the cup, idly dunking it with a spoon while I stared at the TV. An energetic Hispanic lady stood amongst toppled trees, destroyed furniture, and other debris, showing the world how Hurricane Phillipa had wreaked havoc on southern Texas.

"When do you think you'll get your English essay back?" Mom asked out of the blue.

"Oh, I already did." I went to fetch my backpack out of my room, and when I came back, she lowered her brow and held out her hand. She expected to be disappointed, and though that pained me, I savored the opportunity to prove her wrong. I dug out the essay and placed it dramatically in her palm.

Mom's expression softened as she scanned Mrs. Oliverson's notes. Without a word, she began reading my essay about the relationship between Hamlet and Rosencrantz and Guildenstern. I dunked the tea bag again, and it bobbed up and down, up and down while she read. The sun must have ducked behind some clouds because the kitchen went darker. Raindrops splattered against the bay window.

Eventually, she looked up at me and a smile flickered on her lips. "This is . . . *good*, Poppy. I have students in my classes who don't express their ideas nearly as eloquently as you do."

I shrugged, trying to appear casual, like it barely even mattered. Inside, I felt like I'd struck gold. It wasn't every day Mom openly praised my schoolwork. More to the point, since she set par at A-plus, it was only when I slipped beneath it that I heard any feedback at all. Pride and a rare sense of peace swelled inside of me.

"What are your plans this weekend?" she asked.

"I'm thinking of going to a barbecue at the pastor's house tonight."

"And let me guess, you want to smell good for a certain boy who's going to be there."

"Aha. Can't get much past you, Mom. Are you sure you're not a psychic?"

"I take it you're going with Whitney and Mary Jane?"

"Yeah, and I might hit the mall with them on Saturday."

"As long as you're caught up on your schoolwork. It's going to take quite a few more A's like this one to resuscitate that GPA of yours."

"I'll make sure I've got it all done." A few beats later, I said, "Mom, could I maybe have some spending money? For clothes?"

"Didn't you buy a bunch of clothes from that secondhand shop on Pearl Street right before we moved? By the way, I love what you did with that crocheted sweater—the buttons and everything."

"Thanks." Tilting the steaming cup to my lips, I took a tentative sip. "I just wanted to get some new stuff, that's all. I don't know . . . jeans . . . and maybe a pair of shoes?" Not that I needed shoes; alternating between my combat boots and Converse suited me just fine. I just said that so maybe she'd give me more money for the one thing I really did want: the True Religion jeans.

She grabbed her purse off the back of a chair and unsnapped her wallet. "I don't see a problem with that."

As I glanced at the two twenties and one ten dollar bill in my palm, my joy melted into a puddle of disappointment. It was a nice chunk of cash, but not nearly enough for the crazy-expensive jeans on my wish list. "Thanks."

"Your new friends seem really nice," she said.

"Let me get this straight. You know, so when I'm lying in bed tonight wondering if this really happened, there won't be any question in my mind."

"Okay, go on," Mom prompted.

I took a deep breath and exhaled slowly. "Are you saying you're proud of my essay and you like my fancy new friends?"

She pursed her lips pensively. "Yes, I guess I am."

"Hmm." I eyeballed Mom's cup of tea. "What's in this stuff, anyway?" Though I joked, it amazed me how much it meant to me that she was impressed, that I had her approval. At least for right then.

"Ha ha." She placed her cup on the counter and then picked up the bright pink flyer I had left there. "What's this? The GOV Club?" Her whole face lit up as she read it. "Hmm. This looks interesting. Have you joined?"

"I don't know. I guess Whitney started it up for some sort of scholarship she's applying for. Mary Jane and all of them are in it, but I don't—"

"I think you should, Poppy. It will give your college applications a boost. You know, good grades aren't enough these days." She handed me the flyer. "Oh! I just remembered. I have something for you. I'll be right back."

I glanced at the pink paper and did a double take. GOV

wasn't a shortened version of "government" like I'd presumed. It was an acronym for "Gift of Virginity."

At the heart of the GOV Club is a pledge to save the most precious gift you have for your future wife or husband. It promotes a pure, healthy, Christ-centered lifestyle. Choosing to remain a virgin until marriage isn't easy, so the GOV Club offers support, education, and inspiration to anyone who wishes to make this very important promise to God.

No freakin' way. I put down the flyer and smirked to myself. "You want me to join an abstinence-till-marriage club, Mom?"

"Sure! Why not?" she called from her office.

Well, okay, so most parents would prefer their teenage kids be virgins and not sluts—especially a parent who'd had a baby when she was a teenager and wanted her daughter not to have to struggle in the same way. No shocker there. I clicked the remote, turning off the TV.

I walked into my bathroom, turned on some music, and grabbed the metal crate I kept my polish remover, clippers, file, and polish in. Next I sat on the counter and began the process of making my fingernails look decent, the whole notion of the GOV Club weighing heavily on my mind.

First of all, if starting a school club was a requirement for a certain scholarship Whitney wanted, why had she chosen a *virginity club* of all things? Maybe it was 'cause Calvary was a religious school and even if students weren't technically virgins, they'd join so their parents, teachers, and peers would be under the illusion that they were. Would those same people treat them differently if they chose *not* to join? Would a nonmember be considered sexually active, whether or not it was true? Maybe this whole thing was just another way to build up the facade of pious perfection so many people hid behind. Or, on the other hand, it would give those who wanted to wear the proverbial white dress at their weddings a support system whenever they experienced a bout of horniness.

And what's more, what would it mean if *I* joined? Would it mean I was a fluffy white sheep in the Calvary High flock? Would it make me a good friend and supporter of Whitney Nickels and her plight to get a scholarship? Or perhaps just someone who wanted to pad her future college applications with extracurricular activities?

And would it all be worth it if it kept Mom in this joyful mood of hers?

"Oh, there you are." She poked her happy face into my bathroom and turned down my music.

I waved the fingernail file in the air. "Yep, here I am."

"Sorry. I tossed these in my office and they fell behind some boxes." She hoisted a paper bag onto the side of the tub and unloaded a variety of books, stacking them onto my bathroom counter. "Anyway, I thought you might like these." She reached into my crate, and while she shook up one of my nail polishes, I glanced at the titles: *Everything You Need to Know Before Applying to College*, *This is It: The Countdown to College*, *The Student's Survival Guide for Getting Into College*, *The Road to U.S. Colleges and Universities*, as well as several that promised higher scores on ACT, SAT, and AP tests.

Great. "Wow, Mom. Thanks," I said, unimpressed and unsurprised.

"You're welcome, honey." She set the polish she'd been shaking—a shimmery lilac I got when I was, like, twelve—next to me. "Such a pretty color."

After she left, I swapped it for my raisin polish, turned up my stereo, and painted my nails.

CHAPTER SEVEN

When the doorbell rang later that day, I stuffed the last armful of clothes into the dryer. Then I sprinted into my room to give my reflection a once-over. "It's for me," I called to Mom. "I'll be right there."

I still needed something . . . an accessory, perhaps. I sifted through my jewelry box and came up dry. Then I thought of the earrings from Claire's. I took them out of my backpack and put them on. They looked perfect. I paused a moment to see if guilt would set in—if I felt guilty all night, it wouldn't be worth it, regardless of how good they looked—but for some reason it never did. Then I blew out my candle, flung a piece of Trident into my mouth, and turned off the light.

"Don't be late," Mom said, glancing up from her computer. "And make sure you take your cell phone so I can get ahold of you. Or in case you need me to pick you up."

I waggled my cell to show it was on me and headed out the front door, where Mary Jane waited on the squeaky porch swing. Where couches bedecked front porches in Boulder neighborhoods, I quickly learned that no porch in Pleasant Acres was complete without its swing.

Mary Jane stood and poked her pretty blond head into the house to say, "Have a nice evening, Emily." Man, no wonder Mom liked these girls and their freakin' manners.

Draping my sweater—a loosely knit, light gray one that used to be Mom's—over my arm, we walked out to her car. The air smelled of laundry detergent and damp soil.

"As Andrew would say, you look 'slick as snot' tonight," Mary Jane said.

Whitney sat shotgun, filing her square-tipped nails. "You sure do," she said. "That top is way cool. Love the detail work. Where'd you get it?"

"I made it."

"You *made* it?"

"Well, I bought the tank, and then I just added some

embellishments." I'd snipped the straps, replaced them with frayed ribbons that knotted at the top of the shoulders, and stitched metal-studded viscose and coins on the front, leaving a two-inch band at the bottom. The whole process took me about a week, and like Whitney said, it turned out pretty damn cool.

"Wow," said Mary Jane. "You're good. I don't have a creative bone in my body."

"Oh, wait. I forgot your scarf, Whitney," I said. I'd draped it over the back of my chair so I'd remember it, but that tactic obviously failed.

I turned to go back inside and get it, but Whitney said, "Don't worry about it, Poppy. Just keep it. I've got entirely too many." Mary Jane gave me a "Told you so" nod.

"Thanks," I said, still shocked that anyone would own so many scarves, let alone give one away like a Tic Tac or something.

Blue sky peered through the wispy, heather gray clouds. Soggy patches stippled the lawn and puddles collected in every crack and dimple in the driveway. Birds and bugs were back in full force. As I ducked into the backseat I felt a sharp prick and squished a mosquito that just slurped his last supper from the back of my knee.

"And we're off," Mary Jane announced, reversing down the driveway.

"When's it going to start cooling off around here, anyhow?" Whitney rolled up her window and turned up the AC. Next she blotted her face with a piece of lightly powdered tissue paper she kept in a dainty silver box in her purse. "It feels like July."

"It's not so bad," said Mary Jane. "You're just anxious to wear your new denim jacket."

"Wanna see it?" Whitney bent over and, after some rustling, produced a midnight blue jacket—the one she was holding back at Hamilton's—with its tags still attached.

"It's awesome," I said, even though it looked like an ordinary jean jacket to me.

"I know. I just had to have it." She admired her new jacket a little longer and then put it down.

A rainbow of wild flowers whizzed past the window as a kitschy song rained through the speakers. The farther we cruised, the sparser, older, and smaller the houses became. Eventually we passed oil derricks and herds of longhorns in the wooded pastures. There were so many big, leafy oak and maple trees, the ponds appeared dark green instead of blue. We traveled up and down rolling hills, bumped over train tracks, and sloshed through pothole puddles.

By the time we got to Pastor Hillcrest's fifties-style ranch house, I'd chewed all the cinnamoniness out of my gum. I spit it out in the grass as the three of us headed to the backyard.

"Don't worry, Poppy," said Mary Jane. "It'll probably get boring, but we'll stay just long enough to make an appearance."

A bonfire sputtered on one side of the sizable backyard, opposite a weathered barn. Teenagers and a handful of adults joked around and gorged on hot dogs, corn chips, and neon-yellow potato salad. Some had already staked out lawn chairs or grassy patches.

"Howdy, Pastor," Whitney called. "This is our friend Poppy Browne. You're gonna love her."

The tall, slightly balding man saluted from the deck. He looked less like the man who preached the morning services every day at Calvary High and every Sunday at church, and more like just an everyday dude in his khaki shorts, "World's Greatest Dad" apron, and white tube socks. He said, "That goes without saying, if she's running round with *y'all*," as he loaded the grill with wieners.

Oh, no. Bridgette. She stood behind a table, filling a Dixie cup with lemonade. I caught her looking at me, but I pretended not to notice. In my peripheral vision, I saw her heading straight for us. She probably had some choice words for me—words I admittedly deserved for blowing her off at lunch.

I leaned out to see past Mary Jane. Bridgette hovered a mere ten feet away. This time, I couldn't pretend not to see her.

She walked right up to me—too close—and said brightly, "Hi, Poppy. Can I talk to you for a sec?"

The others looked on with apparent curiosity. "Um, okay," I said, and we walked over to the picnic table. "What's up?"

"You're not wearing the bracelet I gave you," she said, biting into a dill pickle.

"Yeah, well, it kind of clashed with what I'm wearing." Even if it weren't a lie, it sounded lame. "Listen, Bridgette, about lunch . . ." Ugh. How to say I'd rather eat ninety-nine-cent tacos with Mary Jane and the gang than my home-packed lunch with Bridgette and the Good News Choir? There was just no nice way to word it. I took a peanut from a blobby clay bowl that I guessed some child had made at school. "I want to apologize for not eating lunch with you today. I backed out on my word and that's not cool. And . . . okay, I lost the bracelet you gave me. But in all honesty, I don't think I'd wear it anyway. I'm not really one to wear something . . . like that. No offense."

I took a quick look around the yard, but I didn't see Gabe or any of his buddies. Maybe they hadn't gotten there yet. Next I glanced over at Mary Jane, Whitney, and Ellen. Several other girls had joined them in my brief absence.

"Go on," Bridgette said, gesturing to the girls. On the one hand, I wanted to get away from Bridgette. She was such a killjoy. But I didn't want her to be mad at me, either.

"I've been hanging with them 'cause I have fun with them. Not because I'm trying to hurt you or piss you off or anything like that."

She faced me, her eyes soft and pleading. When she opened her mouth to speak, I spotted a green globule wedged in her braces. "I'm just trying to help you, Poppy."

"Yeah, you said that. But what do you have against them? What terrible, unforgivable thing have they done?" I paused, giving her ample time to fill me in. But she just pressed her lips together. "Well then. I'm not in the habit of disliking a person just 'cause somebody says I should. So, thanks for your concern, but I'm fine. Really." As I left, Bridgette grabbed a paper plate off the table and scooped her spoon into the potato salad.

When I got back to the group, Mary Jane stopped talking about her sister's sorority adventures and planted her hands on her hips. "What was *that* about?"

Whitney shook her head. "Don't tell me she's ticked you went to Taco Casa with us."

"Something like that," I said, hoping to sound flippant. "But it's cool now."

"Don't let it bother you," said Ellen, brushing a piece of grass off her skinny white jeans. "Everybody knows Bridgette is supersensitive."

"And super weird." Whitney rolled her eyes.

Mary Jane said, "Bless her heart." Her dazzling smile instantly made me feel better. "Y'all ready to join the festivities or what?" She escorted Whitney, Ellen, and me to the bonfire, *Wizard of Oz*–style.

My stomach somersaulted when I spotted Gabe over in the shade of a pecan tree. He slid his hands into the front pockets of his jeans while he talked to his buddies, his vintage Texaco T-shirt haphazardly tucked in. He and a few of the other guys started heading to the fire, and I lingered, acting casual as I waited for him to catch up with me.

"Hey, Poppy. Glad you could come," Gabe said. "Can I, um, get you something to drink?"

"I'd love a drink," said a sweet-sounding voice that was definitely not mine. Guess I was too distracted by Gabe to notice Bridgette's sudden appearance to our group.

Gabe jumped a little. "Oh, uh, sure. This round is on me. What'll you have?" The question floated freely between Bridgette and me.

Bridgette's gaze drifted to me and she lifted her chin up a notch. As her lips parted to reveal a glimpse of the pickle in her metal-banded teeth, I said, "Make mine a lemonade, please. On the rocks."

"Ha! Good choice, Poppy. And what about you, Bridgette?"

Gabe looked at me even as he addressed her, and I wondered if she sensed any awkward third-wheel vibes?

"I'll have the same, I guess," she said.

Gabe took off. Though I would've rather checked out his ass as he sauntered away, I decided to give Bridgette a hand. I waited until it appeared no one was paying any attention to Bridgette and me and then pantomimed that she had something stuck in her teeth. I jabbed, pointed, and twisted, but she just stared at me like I'd fallen off my rocker. And quite unfortunately, my antics attracted an audience.

"Please tell me that wasn't some kind of Colorado mating ritual," David Hillcrest said, grinning. He was totally different from Gabe, who was almost pretty—David had a more rugged look, complete with a small scar on his left cheek and a hint of whiskers on his chin. He looked like he spent his free time under the hoods of old, beat-up cars. Each time I ran into him, whether in our physics class or just around school, I had to keep reminding myself that he was the son of a Texas preacher.

"You know David Hillcrest, don't you, Poppy?" Whitney said through tight lips.

Though Mary Jane hadn't mentioned David being there, I knew in the back of my mind that I'd see him that evening. It was, after all, his house. He wore a T-shirt with THE DEVIL SUCKS emblazoned across it, which I thought was kinda funny.

"We go way back. Right, Poppy? She even has a pet name for me," David said. "Have you mentioned it to your friends yet?"

I mumbled, "I might have; I can't remember," and plopped down next to Whitney on an enormous, flat-topped log. I hoped I didn't get splinters in my butt.

David's smile broadened. "'My dear shithead.' Has a nice ring to it, don't ya think?" he said, sitting beside me. There was plenty of room on the log, but oh no, he had to sit next to me. He scooted so close, our legs touched. "Man, you smell good," he added in a gruff whisper.

I inched away from him. "Listen, I'm really sorry—"

"Don't be," David said. "I like when a chick speaks her mind."

"Only when her mind is in the gutter, like yours," retorted Whitney with a bout of fake coughs that made her cross necklace bounce against her chest.

David failed to keep a straight face, and the jumble of expressions somehow resulted in an understated sexiness. "Well, I can't argue with that. But I was *going* to say that I might've rightly deserved what she said." A few beats later, he whispered, "That's a cool top you're wearing. Let me know if you get chilly. I can grab you a sweatshirt."

"Er, thanks . . ." *I think?*

Gabe returned and doled out the lemonades to Bridgette

and me. "Now, can somebody tell me what's wrong with this picture?" Gabe asked.

"Yeah, you didn't get one for me," David said, but Gabe ignored him.

"I'm not sitting next to the new girl. Make way, y'all." He wedged his body between David's and mine. To my surprise, David willingly surrendered his spot. I felt disappointed. Had he put up even a slight fight, it would've made for some good quality entertainment, I figured.

I listened as everybody chattered about the Dallas Cowboys, fishing holes, the new art teacher at Calvary, and the upcoming lacrosse game. Then Gabe said, "Poppy, can I ask you something?" Heads turned in our direction and all other conversations paused. The fire crackled and a cow mooed in the distance.

"Er, sure." Oh my God. Was Mary Jane right after all? Did Gabe have a crush on me? Was he going to ask for my phone number? Or ask me out, right in front of all these people? He licked his lips, and all of a sudden, my eagerness turned into uneasiness. My stomach lurched. I couldn't decide; did I want him to or not?

Gabe's lips parted and out came the question: "What time is it?"

Had I heard right?

I sensed disappointment around us. Especially from Mary Jane. Gradually, the chitchat picked up again.

"Oh." I chuckled to try and hide my shock that all he wanted from me was the stupid *time*. But at least my stomach felt better. I glanced at the clock on my cell phone. "Um, five after eight," I said, noticing that I had a new text message . . . from David?

"Really? Aw, shoot." Gabe stood and shook out his legs. "I have to pick up my sister from drill team practice."

"Okay, see you later," I said in chorus with the others, and some dude called out, "Good luck at the game tomorrow!"

"Georgia is such a cutie," Bridgette said as she followed him away from the bonfire. "I loved having her in the church musical last Easter."

David was next to me again, only there was a gap where Gabe had sat. I gave the preacher's son a weird look before opening the text message. *Wanna see how country folk get their kicks?* it read.

Let me guess, I texted back, *taking a roll in the hay?* I hit SEND and arched my brows as I watched him read it.

David's response made me grin: *Madam, I am much more than a piece of meat.*

Then he looked up at Whitney and Ellen and said, "Ladies, I have something to show Poppy. Sit tight; I'll have her back to y'all in fifteen minutes tops."

CHAPTER EIGHT

He took my arm and helped me up. Though I had no clue what I was doing, I walked with him around the house and into the garage. A pair of tabby kittens scampered out of our way. "What made you so sure I'd come with you?" I asked.

He smiled. "Wasn't sure at all, but what's life if you don't take a risk every now and then? Here, you can take Noah's." He presented me with a gray bicycle that had seen better days, and then he hopped on a red one that looked even shabbier.

"Are these safe?"

"I guess we're about to find out."

I jumped onto the bike and started pedaling, pleasantly

surprised by how fast it went. The wind blasted my face, my shoulders, the sides of my arms and legs . . . and it felt wonderful. We rode up and down a little hill and past a field with brown cows and white boxed beehives. Finally we rolled up to a railroad crossing. The train whistle tooted, warning us it was nearby. David hit his brakes and laid the bike in the ditch. I followed suit. "What are we doing, David?" I asked.

"Hold your horses, little lady." He dug a couple of coins out of his front pocket and tossed them high into the air, then caught them and spun on his heel in the dirt. "Now come on. We don't want to miss this."

I hurried to catch up with him as he eased his way through the tall, feathery grass that grew alongside the tracks. "Which one do you want?" he asked, holding his palm open to reveal two shiny pennies. I took one and he laid the other one on the top of the tracks. "Your turn."

"But won't it derail the train?" I asked.

"Naw, that's just an old wives' tale. A cow or a car might do that but not a teensy little coin."

I placed the penny next to David's and we walked a few feet away from the track to wait.

"So you do this a lot?"

"Only with pretty new girls." He winked, and for some stupid reason, heat rushed into my cheeks.

"You sure don't act like the son of a preacher."

"And how's the son of a preacher *supposed* to act?"

"I don't know . . ."

"Well, me neither. So I just act like myself." He sat on the side of the tracks and patted the space beside him. "Here, take a load off," he said, and I did. "A little birdie told me something that's made a world of difference in my life. It said—and I quote: 'Oh, lookie here. A *human*!'" He nodded once.

I waited, plucking a fistful of grass, but apparently that was the extent of his little tale. "Great story. Maybe they'll make a movie out of it."

"Don't you get it? I'm human. As in 'only human.' Sure, I can try to live up to everyone's expectations for the son of a Southern Baptist preacher. But I'd never be good enough in their eyes." He twisted his hand palm-up and gestured around us. And though his facial expression and posture indicated a casual air, I got the impression that his words were heartfelt. "So rather than spend my entire life striving to be perfect and beating myself up over every little slipup, I reckoned it made more sense for me to come up with my own expectations for myself. You know, figure out what matters to *me* and how I want to live my own life." Then he turned to face me full-on. "So do you act like the daughter of a . . . let's see, your mom's a prof, right? Hmm. Smart? Check. A subtle yet undeniable sexiness?" *Oh, God. Please don't let him notice I'm blushing—again!* "Check. Okay, so maybe you are the model daughter of a college professor. But what's your dad do?"

I shrugged, surprised David hadn't already heard my father wasn't in the Browne family portrait. "I don't really know. We don't keep in touch."

David inhaled slowly and exhaled with a huff. "Well, at least I won't have to worry about your ol' man pointing a shotgun at my groin when I come to pick you up for our first date."

First date? I wasn't sure if I should be turned off by his overconfidence or flattered. "I bet my father would be a total softy compared to my mom."

David turned to look up the tracks. "All right, here it comes!" He stood and yanked me beside him. Sure enough, a train chugged its way around a bend, getting louder and louder. A little spark flew when it reached the spot where we'd placed the pennies, but the train stayed on the tracks like David had said, pulling a vast assortment of cars past us. Some were solid orange; others boasted awesome graffiti.

A strong breeze stood our hair on end, and the loud *thump thump thump* of wheels on track revved up my heartbeat. "Kind of feels like being in the front row of a rock concert," I yelled, and David nodded. Before long, the caboose whizzed past and the train continued its journey across America.

David stepped onto the tracks and gathered the coins,

flipping them into the air. "Gotta cool 'em off a bit," he said, then he tossed one to me. "What do you think?"

I held the flatter, smoother, warmer version of the penny in my hand. "Wow."

He stuffed his hands into his pockets and smacked his lips "Well, now that I've had my fun with you, I'd better take you back to my place."

"Charming," I said, picking up his brother's bike. "No wonder people say you think you're God's gift to women."

"They say that?"

I nodded.

"Well, like I said, I can never live up to their expectations."

David jumped on his bike and started riding in circles. "Hurry up, kiddo. Last one to my house has to eat three hot dogs."

Ew, hot dogs? He was kidding, right?

I peddled like crazy, riding as fast as David's brother's bike would allow. My heartbeat accelerated along with my speed, and I struggled to keep my eyes open as the wind whipped through my hair and across my face and shoulders. Pure exhilaration spread from the top of my head to my toes. I flew.

For the most part, I stayed hot on David's trail. When the road evened out, we were handlebar to handlebar, and the possibility of winning swelled within every cell of my body.

"You must really like hot dogs," he shouted. And then, in the blink of an eye, I ingloriously ate his dust. As the boy-on-a-bike silhouette shrunk into the distance, I started laughing. I couldn't really figure out why. The thought of munching down one hot dog—let alone three—was no laughing matter. But somehow, David put me in a great mood.

When I got back to the Hillcrest's house, breathless and happy, David and Andrew were hanging out in the front yard. David nodded and pointed at me as I coasted into the garage. They appeared to be in the midst of dude talk, so I had every intention to go out back and find Mary Jane and the girls. But my ears perked up when I heard the topic of Andrew's monologue: Mary Jane. Taking longer than necessary, I stood the bike up in its place beside David's.

"Mary Jane would have a major come apart if she knew I was talking about this with anybody. It's one of her rules: 'Don't tell a soul or you'll never get any from me, ever again.'" He stated the last bit in a fake girly voice. "She has a ton of rules, man, but what can I say? It's worth it."

David asked, "What do you mean, having a girlfriend?"

"Yeah, I guess that's what I mean. My ex got off on *not* getting me off, you know? Talk about a tease. And then I got together with Mary Jane, and it rocked my world. I'm serious, dude. Suddenly, all the expensive gifts and cheesy chick flicks and . . . oh, man, all the *drama* . . . was worth it."

Was he talking about liking—maybe even loving—Mary Jane? Or was he just talking about having sex with her, or wanting to . . . ? My gut told me I needed to find out, not just to appease my curiosity, but to know for Mary Jane's sake. So I decided to see how long I could get away with eavesdropping.

"I'm not saying she's easy, 'cause I know better than to bite the hand that feeds you. Or the hand that does other fun stuff to you." Andrew chuckled and I cringed. All of a sudden, I wasn't listening in on a locker room type of conversation between two dudes I didn't know very well. I was in the computer lab back at Flatirons, the day I realized what an idiot I was for wasting so much time on Spence, a guy I only thought I knew. I clenched my fists, shoving those memories back into the dark caverns of my mind.

"But really, dude," Andrew said, "what should I do? The girls won't let it go, you know?"

"Well, from my understanding, you can still join," said David. "You're just supposed to make a fresh start. And since Mary Jane's already in it . . . Well, maybe you should just talk to her. Work it out between the two of you."

At that point, I was utterly lost. And annoyed. And ready

to stop hiding out with the bikes, tools, and a spry daddy long-legs spider. Hoping they didn't realize I'd been eavesdropping, I snuck out of the garage.

Andrew tweaked the bill of his baseball cap. "You think?"

"I think."

"Okay, maybe I'll give it a try."

"Go get 'er, tiger." David slugged Andrew's arm and then spotted me. "Oh, hey Poppy. Hungry for a hot dog?"

"You know it," I said, and he jogged to catch up with me.

"Did you hear any of that?" he whispered as we headed out back.

"Uh, any of what?"

"So you heard." He grinned knowingly, then sidled up closer to me. "I'm not really sure why, but people are always . . . opening up to me like that."

"That's good. Because I've got something very important, very *personal* to tell you right now." I relaxed my features, hoping to appear staid.

He stopped walking and faced me, and if I wasn't mistaken, eagerness lit his eyes. Oh, man, he had sexy eyes.

I cleared my throat. "I hate hot dogs."

He blinked. "You. Hate. Hot dogs."

"Like, really *really* detest them."

"I see." He took a deep breath and pressed his lips together.

"Well, I'd hate to be responsible for making you do something you didn't want to do."

"So you're letting me off scot-free?"

"No, no, kiddo. I've been training for *weeks* to beat you at that bike race." I had to laugh at that. "So you owe me, a'ight?"

"Okay, okay. Whatever. I owe you," I agreed, relieved I didn't have to consume three disgusting hot dogs and extremely interested to find out what he had in store for me.

The Portman's colonial home reminded me of the one in *Gone with the Wind*, from the gigantic oak tree and gorgeous flower beds in the yard to the sparkling chandelier I spied through a window above the red double doors. I punched the doorbell button, the sonorous chimes announcing my arrival. As soon as I heard footsteps and a dog yapping, I waved good-bye to my mom in her Volvo.

"Hi, Poppy," the older version of Mary Jane said as she whisked open the door. She wore an amethyst-colored jogging suit and her platinum blond hair in an off-centered ponytail. If not for her flashy diamond jewelry and bright lipstick, she would've succeeded in pulling off the effortless sporty look.

"That's enough, Mollie." A schnauzer sporting yellow bows on its ears yipped twice more and then stood solemnly at her owner's feet. "We've heard such nice things about you. Mary

Jane slept in this morning, so I'm afraid she's still getting ready." She gestured for me to follow her. The dog zipped past us and up the stairs, watching us with a tilted head.

Mary Jane's Brighton purse dangled from the banister and a candle infused the air with the aroma of strawberries. Photo collages covered the wall, exhibiting a lifetime of stories starring Mary Jane and her older sister, Jo Anna. Even as toddlers, they wore designer clothes and smiled with the confidence of girls who knew they were extraordinarily beautiful.

At the top of the landing, a photo caught my eye and I paused to get a better look. Mary Jane appeared to be twelve or thirteen, decked out in a fairy costume. She posed beside a beaming Bridgette Josephs, also a fairy. I did a double take, but yes, it was definitely a young Bridgette. The twosome clenched pillow cases bursting with candy. The looks on their glitter-painted faces didn't lie: Those two used to be best friends.

Mrs. Portman gave a rapid *knock knock* and then opened the door to her daughter's bedroom, a flowery, lacy, Laura Ashley barf-fest. Mary Jane swiveled on a cushy vanity stool to face us. Even makeup-free and with her long flaxen hair piled haphazardly atop of her head, she was stunning. "Oh, hey Poppy!" She waved her powder brush at me. "I was hoping it was you."

"When did you get that nightie?" Mrs. Portman asked in a prickly tone.

Mary Jane shrugged. "I've had it awhile. You like?" She stood and whirled around, the silky, polka-dotted nightgown swirling around her thighs. "It has a matching robe." She grabbed the robe off her bedpost and swung it around her shoulders.

Mrs. Portman pursed her lips while her daughter struck silly-sexy poses. "It's a little . . . short, that's all. Better not let your father see you parading around in it, young lady." Then she drew the blinds and said, "What are y'all up to today?"

Mollie the dog pranced into Mary Jane's room and dragged herself onto a satin pillow-bed by the bedside table. I stroked her soft, silver coat.

"Shopping," Mary Jane replied, getting back to her makeup.

"Ah, yes. The apple doesn't fall far from the tree," Mrs. Portman said as proudly as Mom might someday say, "Three Ivy League schools have offered my daughter full-ride scholarships." "Oh, have y'all been to Colleen's Closet yet? It's that new store out yonder in Clover Strip Mall. I haven't looked into it yet, but the ladies at the country club found some cute clothes there. And speakin' of the country club, your father and I have a golf tournament there this afternoon. It's to raise money for those poor people down South who were hit by the hurricane," Mrs. Portman added, I figured, for my benefit. "Mary Jane, why don't you meet us at the club at seven for dinner."

"Okay." She waited for her mom to leave and then said, "Sorry that barbecue last night was so lame."

"I actually had a pretty good time," I said, remembering the exhilaration I felt as the train chugged past David Hillcrest and me (since then, I'd put the penny in my jewelry box for safekeeping) and the feel of wind on my face as he kicked my ass in our little bike race.

"Isn't Gabe adorable? Y'all get along well . . ." She paused to brush mascara on her lashes, her lips forming a perfect ring shape. "Don't you think?"

"Yeah, we talked some." Kinda weird, but not a single thought of Gabe had wriggled its way into my mind since he'd left to pick up his sister last night. "You seemed to be having a great time with Andrew." I snatched the *Seventeen* magazine off the desk and flopped onto her white, pink, and red floral-printed bedspread.

Maybe I should tell her what I'd overheard her boyfriend saying to David. But then again, what exactly *had* he said? That Mary Jane had a lot of rules? So what? That his ex was a tease? Not applicable. That he didn't like chick flicks? So sue him. And he'd said something about Mary Jane being easy—er, or was it that she *wasn't* easy?

Shit. I'd hate to misinterpret him and be responsible for some kind of relationship turbulence. Besides, David advised him to talk to Mary Jane about . . . well, about whatever was bothering Andrew. So I decided to keep quiet for then, and maybe just keep an eye out for Mary Jane. And to be there for her if she needed to talk. Lord knows, if I'd had someone to talk to, maybe I wouldn't have gotten in so deep with the likes of Spence Farr.

Mary Jane puffed out her cheeks, and I detected a little extra color in them. "Yeah, well, we had a little fun, but then he started talking about football and Whitney mentioned the GOV Club and he just disappeared . . ." She shook her golden curls as if confused.

The doorbell rang, and Mollie bolted for the front door, barking ferociously. "Mom? Can you get it? I'm still not dressed," Mary Jane called. "I swear, there's never anything exciting going on in this town. I can't wait till I graduate. Jo Anna went to TCU, but I'm going somewhere far, far away. Maybe California or New York." Switching off her movie-star-dressing-room lights, she said, "Now to find something to wear."

She opened a pair of louvered doors, giving me my first glimpse of a closet so large, so organized, and so full of amazing clothes and accessories that Carrie Bradshaw would be envious. I couldn't help gasping. "Oh my God."

"It's okay," said Whitney as she walked into the room. "I'm sure I said the same thing the first time I saw it."

"Whatever." Mary Jane waved her right hand in the air dismissively. "It's nothing special."

I dropped the magazine and helped myself to a closet tour, Mollie at my heels. It had to be the size of my entire bedroom, with a little sitting area and a lighted full-length mirror. I saw cute organizer boxes that coordinated with her bedspread, shelves for sweaters and jeans, and rails with skirts and pants on one side and dresses and tops on the other—all on matching hangers. Then, the shoes: Her custom shelves showcased every color and style imaginable, from Skechers slip-ons to Manolo Blahnik wedges.

Damn. How much money did the Portmans have, anyway?

After Mary Jane slipped into her shopping outfit, I gave Mollie a good-bye pat and the three of us headed out. When I passed the Halloween photo in the hallway, I stopped and asked, "Is that Bridgette Josephs?" I knew it was; I just wanted to hear what Mary Jane had to say about it.

Mary Jane sighed. "I've told my mother to take that picture down, but she just adores those silly fairy costumes. Our cleaning lady made them from scratch."

"They *are* cool costumes . . . ," I said.

"And yes, that's Bridgette. It was a long time ago, but we used to hang out."

"Y'all were inseparable," Whitney said in a tone that bordered on teasing.

"So what happened? I'm sure she's jealous of you guys, like you said. But was there something . . . I don't know, something someone said or did? I mean, it's pretty obvious you guys aren't friends anymore."

Mary Jane hesitated. "The thing about Bridgette is, she's very protective of Andrew," she said, starting down the stairs.

"What, does she have a crush on him or something?" I asked.

"Bridgette and Andrew have known each other since their diaper days," Mary Jane explained. "Their families are always getting together for boating trips or vacations to Six Flags or whatever, and Andrew's mom makes him invite her to our parties. But anyway, to make a long story short, Bridgette doesn't think I'm good enough to be dating him." She frowned and opened the door for us.

"How could she think that?" I asked. "You two are so perfect together."

"I know, right?" agreed Whitney. "But there was this one incident . . ."

Mary Jane gasped. "You are *not* going to tell her about that."

"Okay, okay." Whitney waved her palms in the air. "All I know is, *Aunt Flow* came for a visit this morning and I'd better get some chocolate in me or I'm gonna go psycho-crazy."

I donned my sunglasses and took my spot in the back of Mary Jane's convertible. We all sat there in the garage for a few beats before Mary Jane said, "That's weird. I could've sworn I left my keys in the car."

Leaning forward, I dangled the sparkly pink star keychain in front of Mary Jane's eyes. She reached for them, but I held them just out of her reach. "Tell me about 'The Incident.'"

Whitney laughed. "Oh, she's *good*."

"Okay, okay," said Mary Jane. "I'll tell you while we drive. You do *not* want to see a Whitney psycho-crazy episode." She feigned a shiver.

I dropped the keys into Mary Jane's hands and she reversed down the driveway. Then I leaned back, making myself comfortable for story time.

CHAPTER NINE

"Last year, Bridgette Josephs' family hosted the youth group's New Year's Eve party. It was a total yawn, but that's beside the point. Anyhow, Jo Anna got some champagne for me, and Andrew and I snuck off into their garage and drank some. Right out of the bottle. Which isn't easy 'cause of the bubbles." She giggled and shook her head like she couldn't believe she had the gall to drink champagne without flutes. "I'm not sure how much we drank, but I remember feeling tingly and thinking everything was hysterical. And then Bridgette happened to come into the garage—"

"She was totally spying on you," Whitney said, a disgusted look on her face.

"Well, we can't be sure about that. But she *did* see us, and before we left that night, everyone at the party knew about it." Her blue eyes glazed over and she frowned.

"Is that why Bridgette doesn't approve of you?" I asked. "Being with Andrew, I mean."

Mary Jane tucked her blond hair behind her ear. "I think so."

"That's so lame," I said, my insides boiling. "It's not like sipping a little bubbly on New Year's is a one-way ticket to Hell." I bit my lip, wishing that had come out a little differently. The last thing I wanted to do was offend her. To Mary Jane, this was a big deal.

"Just when I think it's ancient history, someone brings it up again," said Mary Jane. "It's like no one in Pleasant Acres has ever screwed up. We're all supposed to be these perfectly behaved . . . I don't know, robots or something. Like that old movie—what's it called? Oh yeah, *The Stepford Wives*." She pulled across two parking spots and put her VW into Park.

"So now you know about 'The Incident,' and now we can get some chocolate," Whitney said, already halfway to the mall's entrance. I followed the two girls inside.

"You don't want anything, Poppy?" Mary Jane asked after she'd placed a box of chocolates on the counter at the candy shop. The white-haired, white-pinafored lady froze, her hands hovering tentatively over the cash register. I wanted to see how long she could stay like that, but I figured torturing little old ladies wasn't very cool.

"Nope, that's okay," I said.

"You're not on a diet, are you?" Whitney asked as the lady rang her up. "Man, I couldn't take it if you turned into another Ellen. I feel like such a heifer next to her."

The thought of me being on a diet was utterly ridiculous. And me, a walking Pixy Stix like Ellen? No freakin' way. But it was simpler than all that. I wanted every bit of my money to go to the jeans. If I could keep up my winning streak with Mom and maybe get a babysitting job or two, I figured in about a month, the jeans would be all mine. "Nope, I'm just not hungry."

"I've never in my life passed up chocolate. Well, I guess I'll have to eat Poppy's share, right?" Whitney whipped a ten out of her wallet. "It's on me this time," she told Mary Jane, and then proceeded to stuff her pretty face.

"I'm so glad you're fixin' to get those jeans, Poppy," Whitney said between chomps.

"Actually, I've only got fifty bucks, so I was just going to put them on layaway. You know, so they'll still be here when I have enough money."

"Well, will you at least try them on again and show us this

time?" Mary Jane asked, fingering the diamond cross on her necklace.

"Sure, if you really want me to."

As we entered Hamilton's, a man's voice boomed over the PA system: "We have a special gift with purchase available at the Lancôme makeup counter," and Whitney's eyes lit up.

"I have a great idea," she said. "Let's get Poppy a makeover."

Mary Jane did a little hop thing and clapped her hands together. "That *is* a great idea."

"What?" I said, totally caught off guard. "Thanks, but I'm just fine."

Mary Jane took my hand and led me to the makeup counter. "You have the prettiest face, Poppy. But under all that harsh makeup you're always wearing—bless your heart—it's just sometimes hard to tell. The ladies at the Lancôme counter know how to bring out your best features. It's their God-given talent."

Whitney, who'd hurried ahead, waved us over to a tall, emaciated lady with platinum blond hair smoothed back into a low ponytail. She wore what looked like a white doctor's jacket, with black hose and stilettos the exact same shade of pink as her lips. The lady put her hands on my shoulders. Looking at me like I was a stray puppy stuck in a Dumpster, she said, "Oh, dear." Then she lifted her chin resolutely and announced to my friends, "It will be my pleasure."

Mary Jane and Whitney seemed satisfied and excused themselves to peruse the store's makeup and perfume offerings while the lady invited me to sit on a cushioned barstool.

"I'm really okay," I said, once my friends were out of earshot. "I mean, I know my makeup is of the drugstore variety, but really, it suits me just fine." I didn't like people poking and prodding at me, especially people with unnaturally long, bright pink fingernails. What had I gotten myself into? Or, more accurately, what had Whitney gotten me into?

"Does it hurt?" the lady asked, pointing to the stud in my nose.

I watched my friends applying lipstick with Q-tips at the MAC counter, wishing I was over there with them. "Not anymore."

"Hmm. All right, then. Sit back and get ready to be transformed from the outside in."

The lady got a crazy gleam in her eyes, looking more like a mad scientist than a makeup artist. She swiped a cleansing pad over my entire face, creating an empty beaker for her experiment. In a frenzy of foundation, eyeliner, mascara, bronzing powder, lip liner, and lipstick, she dotted, sponged, smeared, swished, brushed, and blended until I wondered if I had any skin left on my face.

"There, that's how it's done." The lady admired her work

and then held up a mirror. I gawked at my reflection. With shiny greenish eye shadow, dark brown mascara, rosy cheeks and lips, I looked wide-awake and . . . sparkly.

I'd always assumed, through the process of elimination, that I resembled my father. But now, as I studied my face in the mirror, I couldn't help noticing that I was a younger version of my mom. It was a bizarre sensation—like I was seeing myself for the first time.

Mary Jane and Whitney came running and fussed over me like I was a bride or something. "See?" Mary Jane said. "You don't need all that black stuff smeared around your eyes. You are gorgeous."

I had to admit I looked pretty decent, but it was hard to believe it took so much *stuff* and ten whole minutes to make me look so, well, *natural*. It was like the more gunk the crazy lab-coat lady heaped onto my face, the less it looked like I had on any makeup at all.

"Thanks. It looks good. Much better," I said as I took the custom product list, application instructions, and makeup samples she handed me. However, I knew that as soon as I'd used up all the samples, I wouldn't come running back for more—not at *those* prices.

Mary Jane, Whitney, and I boarded the escalator and ascended to the designer jeans department. Luckily, the exact pair I'd tried on was on the rack. I made a beeline for the dressing room. Mary Jane and Whitney chatted away while I put them on. *Will I still love them?* I wondered. Even before I checked myself out in the mirror, I knew it was a lost cause. I was about to part with an insane amount of money for the perfect pair of jeans.

But they were more than just jeans, I noted. They symbolized the new Poppy. The Poppy who hung out with girls her mom approved of, who made straight A's, who attended a religious private school, who didn't wear black eyeliner, and who knew how to have fun.

"You're right, Poppy. Those jeans *are* amazing," said Whitney when I came out, wiggling my hips to the upbeat Carrie Underwood song raining through the overhead speakers.

"Yeah. I definitely think I'll put them on layaway," I said. "Have you seen the saleswoman?"

Though I'd been hanging out with them a lot lately, I wasn't able to decipher the look my friends exchanged. "What?" I asked.

"Can I come in the dressing room?" Mary Jane asked.

Before now, I never really had a reason to be modest; it was usually just Mom and me. But still, I found her request a little strange. The dressing room was likely the nicest I'd ever used, but it wasn't much larger than a phone booth. "Um, I guess so."

"I'm going to go look at that cute cropped jacket. I just love that ice-blue color," Whitney said, then promptly split.

"Do you trust me?" Mary Jane asked softly as she closed the door.

"Of course. What's up?"

She handed me my cargos. "Put these on."

I unbuttoned the jeans.

"No. *Over* those."

"What are you . . . ?"

She put her finger over my lips. It smelled like chocolate. She gave me one of her most gorgeous smiles. "Trust me."

I stared at her, speechless.

"You want the jeans, right? They look *great* on you. Everybody's going to think so. Especially Gabe."

"You really think so?"

"I *know* so."

"But—"

"They're really expensive, right? You said yourself that—" She yanked the price tag. "—a hundred ninety-six dollars is too much to spend on a pair of jeans." Her blue eyes widened. "So *don't.* Whitney's fixin' to run interference with the saleswoman. She's phenomenal at it; you don't have to worry one bit. And we've got your back when you go back into the mall and the alarm goes off." She clicked her nails on the white security tag on the back pocket of the jeans. "Poppy, we're your *friends*, and we'd never let you down. Have faith in us."

I sat on the little bench, unsure how much longer my knees would hold out. "You've done this before?" I asked, my voice all croaky.

She grinned. "All the time. Last Thursday, as a matter of fact. That polka-dotted nightgown and robe set? I stuffed it in my purse. It was a snap." She snapped her manicured fingers. "As you've probably already noticed, there isn't much to do around here to keep from being bored to tears. This kind of livens things up, you know?"

I concentrated on keeping my features even and unreadable. Mary Jane and Whitney went to church every Sunday. Their parents were deacons and country clubbers who gave their daughters impressive pedigrees and Hollywood looks, as well as endless allowances and support. They were the elite of Calvary High School, maybe even of the whole town. Even Mom liked these girls, and she loved that I was one of them.

How could such girls be involved in something so scandalous? So illegal? So *wrong*?

"Won't they show?" I asked, taking the pants.

"I'll help you," said Mary Jane.

I slipped the cargos over the jeans, and while I zipped them up, Mary Jane dropped to her knees and rolled up the denim.

"There." She stood and gave me a nod. Her eyes sparkled above her dazzling smile.

I glanced at myself in the mirror and remembered winter mornings in Colorado, when I layered long underwear under my pants so I wouldn't freeze my ass off while running my *Rocky Mountain News* paper route.

As if reading my mind, Mary Jane said, "No one will suspect a thing."

My hands shook . . . my whole body trembled.

Fear?

Excitement?

Maybe a little of both?

CHAPTER TEN

"Ready, Poppy?" She held out her hand.

When Mary Jane released my hand, I wondered if she noticed how sweaty it was. Not that it was the least bit hot in Hamilton's. These Texans loved their AC.

In one smooth motion, she swooped up a pair of jeans that had magically appeared between my dressing room and the one next door. "Hand me that hanger and I'll hang 'em up," she said in her Southern drawl. In contrast to the whispered tones she'd been using, it seemed as if she spoke into a megaphone. "Too bad they made your fanny look like a pancake." My mind struggled to keep up with this whirlwind of events. She winked to let me know this was all part of the plan.

I grabbed the silver hanger off the bench and passed it to her with unsteady hands. "It's okay, Poppy. You'll see," she said, reverting back to the quiet, tranquil voice.

With one last check in the mirror to make sure the jeans were fully hidden under my cargos, I took a deep, ragged breath, attempting to regulate my heartbeat. I swallowed, but it was no use. My mouth was parched, but I knew that when—*if*—I got away with this, I sure as hell wasn't stopping at the food court for a lemonade. I could only pray that I wouldn't have to speak until it was all over and I was safe in my house.

Which was a lovely thought, really. A thought I played over and over again in my mind as I followed Mary Jane out of the dressing room.

The saleswoman excused herself from the couple of college-age girls she was hovering behind, then walked toward us. Mary Jane handed her the jeans and they exchanged a few words, though I couldn't really concentrate on what they said. The noise of my cargos rubbing against the denim underneath was deafening.

The mannequins seemed to watch me knowingly, sticking up their pointy snow-white noses in disdain. Then a sharp *briiiiiing* filled the air. I froze midstep, my breath stuck in my throat. *It's just a phone*, I told myself, silencing my inner scaredy-cat. *Keep walking*.

The saleswoman floated demurely over to the cash register to answer the phone. "Oh. Hi, Harold. Yes, we do have that jacket in ice blue. Let me check the sizes. I'll be but a moment." She lowered the receiver and flashed us a rueful grin before vanishing around the corner.

When Mary Jane and I boarded the Hamilton's escalator, I felt like I'd jumped into a lake fully dressed, my waterlogged clothing so heavy I could barely keep from drowning. Mary Jane stretched out her long, thin arms and yawned. Then she whispered in a hypnotist's voice, "You do not know Whitney. Understand?" I nodded. "The alarm will go off when you leave the store. Just act like you're confused and wait for the problem to resolve itself."

I bit my lower lip, wishing I could stop the madness—wishing I could run back to the dressing room, shed the jeans, and go home. But where was Whitney, and how exactly was she involved? Would my putting the kibosh on this insane scheme put her in any danger?

"Have faith," Mary Jane said in a feather-soft voice meant for my ears alone.

I nodded again, the escalator descending steadily yet lethargically toward the main level. At the bottom, I willed my knees to support me as I plodded to the front of the store, Mary Jane at my side. Out of the corner of my eye, I spotted Whitney. She was walking away from the shoe department and, like us, was heading out into the mall. I tried to focus straight ahead, occasionally averting my gaze to Mary Jane while she delivered a nonsensical monologue. As we passed, salespeople smiled at us—a couple of teenagers enjoying an early autumn day at the mall.

Mary Jane had warned me, but the sound of the alarm still jolted my heart and sent terror zapping through my veins. We stopped and looked at each other. I knew Mary Jane was acting, pretending to wonder what had happened. All the while, she appeared innocent through and through. I could only hope that the look in my eyes passed for something similar—'cause in reality, I was screaming inside, the lifted jeans licking at my thighs like red-hot flames.

Then Mary Jane's pretty blue eyes turned on Whitney, who waved her shopping bag in the air like a white flag. A short, mustached man emerged from the shoe department and fled to Whitney, apologies flying off his tongue as he escorted Whitney back to his cash register.

I wasn't exactly sure what was going down, but when Mary Jane took my arm and steered me out into the mall, tossing her hair and giggling, I knew we'd made it.

I, Poppy Browne, had successfully lifted a pair of designer

jeans, and Mary Jane and Whitney were my accomplished accomplices.

What had gotten into me? Nitrous oxide? I couldn't stop laughing. My heart was still thumping like crazy and I was a sweaty disaster, but somehow I felt so light and . . . giddy, even. I didn't want this feeling to end.

As we sped through my neighborhood, blasting country music, Whitney and Mary Jane kept looking back at me and smiling. "Was that your first time or something?" Whitney asked.

When I was in kindergarten, I swiped one of those lollipops that look like huge diamond rings 'cause Mom wouldn't buy it for me. And what about when I ran out of Claire's with the earrings? That was shoplifting, too, wasn't it? "Sort of." Those things were so small and inexpensive, though. And these were two-hundred-dollar jeans. We got away with lifting *two-hundred-dollar jeans.* "So how'd you do it, Whitney?"

Whitney snapped the visor mirror shut and smacked her lovely plump lips. "It was a breeze. First, I grabbed a pair of similar-looking jeans off a rack and, when the saleswoman wasn't looking, tossed them into the dressing room."

"The red herring item," Mary Jane explained. "Very important, in case the saleswoman is paying any attention to what goes in and out of the dressing room."

Whitney continued. "Next, I went down to the shoe department, where my ol' buddy Harold works."

"It's no secret he's smitten with Whitney," Mary Jane said, pulling up my driveway and parking at a slant. "And Whitney can get him so flustered; he doesn't know his tiny head from his not-so-tiny rear. Bless his heart."

"Whatever, Mary Jane." Whitney punched her arm. "He just gives me extra good service because my daddy's a deacon." She looked at me and said, "Anyway, I asked Harold to call up to the designer denim department to have the saleswoman put something on hold for me—"

"It's best to keep the salespeople busy," interjected Mary Jane. "And the Saturday morning shift has fewer employees on the clock than later shifts, so there aren't as many people watching you do your thing. Of course, it also works well to hit a store when there's a big sale and too many shoppers for the salespeople to keep track of. . . . But anyway, back to you," she said, nodding at Whitney.

"I bought these off the clearance rack." Whitney tipped the lid of a shoebox, showing me the black leather sandals inside. "Fifteen bucks—what a *steal*." They both laughed. "I chatted Harold up the whole time so he'd space on deactivating the inventory control thing. And had he remembered, your tag would've made the alarm go off anyhow, and I would've had

Harold deactivate the shoes again. No one would've known the difference."

"Now all you have to do is put those babies in the freezer for an hour or two. Then pop the tag open with a nickel, and you're the proud owner of some seriously killer jeans," Mary Jane said, beaming at me.

"You guys are brilliant," I said.

"So you know what this means, Poppy?" Mary Jane cut the engine.

"What?"

"We want you to be in on our biggest secret. But you cannot tell a soul. *Ever.* Do you promise?"

Their steady and intense gazes fell on me, and I couldn't decide whether I should squirm or laugh. "I promise."

"Do you swear . . . to God?"

She said it with so much credence; I had to bite the insides of my cheeks to keep from smirking. "I swear to God."

Mary Jane let out a puff of air. "We like you, Poppy. You're really cool and smart and, well, you did a great job with those jeans."

"Which are fabulous, by the way," Whitney interjected.

Shoplifting them was no harder than taking the earrings from Claire's. A lot more exciting, though.

"This is serious business, you know. We can't risk anyone

finding out. Not our parents, not our teachers—not even Ellen. She can't keep a secret to save her life, bless her heart. So, anyway, that's why it's so important that all of our . . . *shopportunities* . . . stay between us. Just the three of us, no one else." Mary Jane paused and appeared to be gathering her next words. "It means we're in this *together*," she said, "no matter what."

Whitney leaned closer to me. "So, are you in?"

"I—"

"Take your time answering, hon," said Whitney. "We want you to be sure."

After a beat or two, I smiled and nodded. "I'm in."

"Poppy, can you come here a second?" I shed my cargos in my room, and then followed Mom's voice to the backyard. She sat cross-legged in the garden, Crocs on her feet and a sun hat on her head. Her sunscreen-coated skin glistened. "Will you pass me that spade?"

I grabbed the spade out of her gardening pail and placed it in her gloved hands.

"How was shopping?" she asked, shading her eyes as she looked up at me.

"Fine."

"You look different somehow."

"I do?"

She signaled for me to come closer, and then stood so we looked at each other eye to eye. Oh, shit. Was "shoplifter" written all over my face? Mom didn't get me, but she definitely had a gift for knowing if I was trying to hide something from her. I fought to keep steady.

"Your makeup?"

"Oh. Yeah." I exhaled in relief. "Mary Jane and Whitney forced me to get a makeover at Hamilton's, and the makeup lady gave me a few samples. . . ."

She nodded. "Yes, that's it. It looks very nice."

"Um, thanks."

"And are those the new jeans you wanted?"

I swallowed and swung my gaze over to the bag of tulip bulbs in the wheelbarrow. "I bought them with the money you gave me."

"They look really good on you. Your legs look nice and long in them."

"Yeah, I like them." And shoplifting them was such a rush. But it would be the one and only time I did anything like that.

She squatted down and poked the little shovel into the soil. "So, are you going in to work on homework now? You have two tests scheduled next week."

I should have known the pleasant little mother-daughter exchange would swing over to my academic life at some point.

Anger seeped into my body. I hated how she felt it necessary to check up on me. I silently counted *one, two, three*, letting the negative vibes ebb before turning around to face her.

"You know what, Mom? I wish you wouldn't ride me so hard about my grades."

She sighed. "I know you don't understand at your age how important a good education is, but someday you'll thank me, Poppy."

I bit the inside of my cheek and a few minutes later, I said, "I think sometimes you use education as a crutch."

"What do you mean?"

"You lean on it, hide behind it. You spend so much time learning and educating others, but you never stop to really *experience* life. When's the last time you did something social? Something purely for fun?" She dug the hole deeper and then started another. "Whitney's mom is in a garden club. Maybe you should do that," I said.

"Yes, maybe."

"See? It would be fun. Not that I have a clue what you do in a garden club . . . maybe plant daisy seeds in Dixie cups and give them to your kids on their birthdays?" My attempt at a joke fizzled under the tension.

Mom sighed. "Something like that."

"Just tell me one thing, then, before I go into my room and

study the rest of the weekend away. Are you always going to check up on me, or will there be a time when you'll trust me?"

Her sun hat cast a masklike shadow over her eyes when she looked up at me. I paused to see if she'd answer, but of course she didn't. Disappointed—no, mad—at myself for letting her get to me yet again, I turned on my heels, almost forgetting to cover the security tag on my back pocket, and went inside. I didn't want her to see me cry.

CHAPTER ELEVEN

After we prayed Monday morning, the pastor called the Good News Choir up to sing the benediction. Bridgette stood front and center on the steps, flanked by the redheaded Ulrich twins. Toward the end of the song, Bridgette stepped off from the group and performed a solo. She sang amazingly well, and her voice captivated her entire audience. While she stood up there in her black blouse and too-tight-around-the-thighs khakis, singing her heart out, I couldn't help but smile. I'd never seen this side of her before, and I had to admit it was a pleasant surprise. Once the song ended, everybody sat in silence for a few beats. I started clapping, and soon the entire auditorium filled with applause. Bridgette smiled from ear to ear, the lights reflecting off her braces.

When the clapping died down, Pastor Hillcrest returned to the microphone, and after thanking the choir, he began reading the weekly announcements. "As some of you know, our annual Sadie Hawkins dance is coming up on Saturday, September twenty-fifth. It's one of Calvary High's most popular events, and girls, it's up to you to leave no boy at home twiddlin' his thumbs that night."

Whitney said, "Excuse me," and slid out of the pew, perfectly coordinating her arrival at the podium with the preacher's invitation to the student body to make any additional announcements.

"Hi, for those of you who don't know me, I'm Whitney Nickels and I'm a junior," she said into the microphone. "Last spring, I started an organization called Gift of Virginity, or GOV for short. It's a club that helps teens stay true to themselves and their future spouses. We have a lot of fun and would love for you to come to our assembly at Peery High School next Wednesday. We'll just carpool right after school. And then we'll have another meeting here in Mr. O'Donnell's classroom on September fifteenth after school. If y'all have any questions or want more info, just stop Mary Jane Portman—wave so they see you, girl"—Mary Jane rose from the pew and waved, looking just like a homecoming queen—"or me around school and we'll be happy to fill you in. Thanks."

When Whitney finished, David Hillcrest sprinted down the aisle and took the mic. "Ah, yes, the GOV Club," he said musingly. "Everybody's doing it. Or *not* doing it, as the case may be." I couldn't help snickering, and so did quite a few others. Whitney, who was scooting back into her seat, narrowed her eyes at him. "Okay, I have an announcement too. I'm David Hillcrest, a senior, and I'm starting a paintball club. It'll be a hoot. Well, if you suck it'll be rather painful, but you'll get better and then be able to put other people in pain. Anyway, I'll have the sign-up list ready as you exit the auditorium."

"Why am I not surprised?" Whitney said under her breath, and I wiped the smile off my face.

"Paintball for Christ?" I asked, reading the slapdash sign on his little table.

"My parents told me I needed to get more involved in school and church. I thought paintball was more appealing than writing letters to missionaries or coming up with lists of video games to throw in the bonfire at the revival. So, are you a fan of paintball, Miss Browne?"

I shook my head, still stuck on the disturbing image of people dumping games into a roaring fire. "Not that I'm aware of."

"Don't knock it till you try it." He passed me a pad of paper with PAINTBALL FOR CHRIST TEAM scrawled on top in sloppy masculine handwriting. "I think you'll be really good. In fact, I'll make you a starter. First game, tonight at seven behind Liberty Park."

The name and phone number lines were completely blank. I wasn't sure what came over me—whether a part of me thought shooting paint pellets at people actually sounded fun, or I simply felt sorry for the preacher's son and his miserable failure of a project—but I picked up the pen he slid over to me.

However, it suddenly occurred to me that if I signed up for David's club, I sure as hell should sign up for Whitney's. Even if it was a public testament that I was sorta kinda a virgin. But I wouldn't go easily. Before filling in my name and contact info, I said, "Only if you promise to join the GOV Club."

"You're serious?"

I pointed the pen in the air and held his stare. He finally blinked and his shoulders slouched.

"Okay, it's a deal. But only if you're in it. Oh, and I'm not wearing a ring like the Jonas Brothers do, you hear me?" He squinted his right eye. "Hey, you look different today."

Surprised he noticed, I said, "Yeah, well, just not so much . . ." I twirled my finger by my eyes. ". . . You know, black stuff. Makeup."

He grinned. "Yeah, that's it. You have nice eyes. I don't know many blondes with such dark ones." He looked down at the table and cleared his throat.

Was the preacher's son flustered? I smiled to myself as I filled in my name and number. Then, when I finished, he snatched the sign-up sheet and held it to his chest, a goofy grin on his face. "Aw, man. All I had to do was put together a paint-ball team to get your phone number? Had I known, I wouldn't have broken into the school office."

"Poppy, what on earth are you doing?" Whitney asked. As she dragged me down the hall, I snuck a peek at David over my shoulder. I anticipated that he'd be doing something stupid, like pointing at the sign-up sheet and jumping up and down, but he just stood there, watching me with a wistful look in his green eyes. Had he really broken into the office to get my number? No one had ever gone through that much trouble—let alone done something so avant-garde—just to get my phone number. I just might've been flattered.

"Hey, Gabe," Whitney said. "What do you think of Poppy's new jeans?"

I blinked, trying to transition myself to the present. Gabe turned from his locker and gave my entire body a once-over. Then his gaze lingered on my jeans and he nodded. "They look good to me," he said.

"Uh, thanks." I shot Whitney the evil eye and walked away.

Whitney caught up with me. "What?" she asked, faking innocence.

"That was totally forced," I said. "Not to mention *lame*."

"I just wanted to draw his attention to how hot you look today. Mary Jane and I were talking and . . ."

I whirled around and planted my hands on my hips. Whitney almost ran into me. *"And?"*

"She thinks you and Gabe would be adorable together. And I agree. You should totally ask him to the Sadie Hawkins dance."

I started walking again. "I don't do dances, especially school-sponsored ones."

"But this one is different, Poppy," Whitney said, jogging to catch up. "It's girls' choice, and it's totally casual. So no rental tuxes, no limos, no corsages. You eat at a fast-food restaurant and wear matching shirts—"

"Matching shirts?"

She nodded fervidly and I sighed. "Okay, I'll think about it."

After school, I hopped in the back of Mary Jane's VW, buckling up beside Ellen. As Gabe whizzed by us in his black Toyota Celica, Andrew hung his head out the window and shouted,

"Hey, hey, hey, beautiful lay-deez." Mary Jane honked and we all laughed.

"So, Poppy, Whitney tells me you're asking Gabe to Sadie's," said Mary Jane as she pulled onto Calvary Road. Ellen squealed.

"I said I'd *think* about it," I clarified.

Whitney said, "You've had all day to get used to the idea."

"Are you guys going?" I asked.

"Mary Jane's going with Andrew," Ellen said.

"Well, I haven't exactly asked him yet," Mary Jane said as she turned into Ellen's pristine neighborhood.

"Whatever, it's not like he's going to say no," Ellen said, rolling her eyes. "So anyway, Whitney's asking this guy named Greg Styles, a track star at Kinsley."

"Whoa, a college man," I said. "You go, girl."

"He's a freshman," explained Whitney. "Our dads are both deacons at the church and they've been family friends for eons. And he has a friend named Nick I'm gonna try and get for Ellen's date."

"He'd better be cute, that's all I've gotta say." Ellen got out of the car and swung her eggplant-colored book bag—which totally coordinated with her olive green capris—over her shoulder. "Well, girls, it's been real. *Bis später*."

We all said bye and Mary Jane hit the gas. However, she

drove in the opposite direction of my house. "Where are we going?" I asked. "Is Whitney jonesing for chocolate again?"

Whitney turned around, a sparkly white smile on her face. "We want you to be at Sadie's with us. And in order for that to happen, you need a date. So we're going to help you."

"Plus," Mary Jane said, "this whole day has been a total bore, and we need to bring on a little excitement, don't you think?" She parked across two parking spots in the grocery store parking lot.

"Ah, yes. Nothing screams 'excitement' like the local Piggly Wiggly," I said, shaking my head.

We all hopped out and walked to the store, the AC flipping up our hair as we passed through the automatic doors. I took a little paper cup of animal crackers from the sample lady to ward off the after-school munchies and followed Mary Jane and Whitney to the back of the store.

". . . and then you tape the note onto the bag of Swedish Fish . . ." Mary Jane babbled on about her idea for me to ask Gabe to Sadie's. Since her sister, Jo Anna, had a successful outcome with the same "totally a-dor-a-ble" invitation three years ago, it would surely work wonders for me. Or so she insisted.

We passed an old lady with a head full of pink curlers and an Igor hump. Whitney paused to say, "Hello, Mrs. Reid. How's Pedro?"

The lady clicked her tongue and inspected a carton of eggs before adding them to the stockpile of Yoplait and All-Bran in her shopping cart. "For such a tiny animal, he has big ears and a bigger attitude. Oh, I noticed your papa passin' the crackers and grape juice last Sunday mornin'. He sure turned out to be a fine deacon. That's what I tell all the ol' girls in my knitting group, yes I do. Oh, and tell your mama hello for us. I hear she's the president of the garden club nowadays. She sure is nice for a colored woman."

I searched Whitney's face, but to my astonishment, she appeared unfazed by the old lady's racist remark. She smiled broadly and whispered to me, "And Mrs. Reid sure is nice for an old lady who pretends she didn't run over her own Chihuahua. Pedro's been dead for, like, four years." Then, very loud, she said, "See you at church, Mrs. Reid."

"Give her a break, Whitney. She's older than Methuselah," Mary Jane said. "Bless her heart."

"Well, if I'm like that when I'm old, y'all better take me out to pasture and shoot me," Whitney said.

"You got it." Mary Jane winked at me. "What are friends for?"

"Forcing each other to ask guys they barely even know to lame-ass school functions, apparently," I said.

"But of course," Whitney said. "Oh my gosh." She yanked open the cooler. "Mary Jane, remember when we used to drink these every day after school? I haven't had a Yoo-hoo in for*ever*."

Mary Jane inspected the label on the bottle of chocolate milk. "Maybe we could drink one for old time's sake, but there's no way I'm putting a Twinkie in my mouth. I might be nostalgic, but I've got a new pair of BCBG trousers to fit into."

I almost crashed into Mary Jane when she halted midway down the snack aisle. "Don't forget the Swedish Fish, Poppy. You're going to need those when you ask you-know-who to the dance." She swayed her Yoo-hoo in the direction of the candy.

"Just take it, hon," Whitney whispered, unsnapping my purse. She smiled and then turned around to pick up a box of microwave popcorn. "How about something salty to go with the Yoo-hoos, y'all?"

Mrs. Reid crept along behind us, muttering something about toothpaste. I waited. A few minutes later, she stopped to examine the chips across the aisle from me. Mary Jane and Whitney, chattering animatedly, strolled behind me and toward the front of the store.

It's just a bag of candy. No one will ever miss it. Just this one last time, and then I'll never shoplift again.

Seizing the opportunity to, well, *seize* while the lady and my friends created a diversion, I grabbed two bags of fish off the peg and dropped one into my open purse. Pretending to read something on the other bag of candy, I squeezed my purse closed with my elbow, then rehung the bag as if I'd changed my mind. My heart pounded so loudly, I actually heard it. As I made a beeline for the cash registers—*keep walking, act casual*—it felt like my purse had mysteriously filled with rocks.

"Let's see . . . ," an attractive, middle-aged lady in a Piggly Wiggly apron said, examining the conveyer belt. "Three drinks and a box of popcorn. Anything else?"

I bit my lower lip, hoping the sweaty feeling was just in my mind, and sweat wasn't actually drenching my forehead. I looked over at Mary Jane and tried to mirror her vibe: *patience, innocence, confidence.*

Mary Jane flung her honey-blond hair to the side and brought out her dazzling smile. "Nope, that's it for now."

"Well, y'all have a nice day, you hear?" the lady said as she handed Mary Jane a receipt.

We walked out of the store together, the afternoon sunshine embracing us. The candy in my purse no longer weighed me down. I felt like I could jump really high, like someone had pumped helium into my body.

Once in her VW, Mary Jane lifted her shirt and revealed a small bag of fortune cookies wedged behind her waistband.

"What are those for?" Whitney asked.

"I'm inviting Andrew to Sadie's tonight. You're gonna *die* when you hear how I'm asking him." She went on to divulge her ingenious plan, something about putting a message in the fortune cookie . . . but I couldn't concentrate.

Thinking about asking a guy to the Sadie Hawkins dance was one thing. *Asking* him was quite another. I opened my purse and stared at the little multicolored fish. On the one hand, I wasn't sure I even wanted to go. Or maybe I did want to go, but I was afraid Gabe would say no. Or maybe I did want to go, but not with Gabe. Shit. Why did it have to be so freakin' complicated?

"What's wrong, hon?" Mary Jane asked. At first, I thought her concern was directed at me, but when I looked up, she had her hand on Whitney's shoulder. "Do you have cramps?"

"No."

"I know you, and something's definitely bugging you," Mary Jane persisted.

Whitney sighed. "Nothing's wrong."

"Did you want to do the fortune cookie thing with Greg? I'm sure Jo Anna has another idea I can use for Andrew."

Whitney scratched her shoulder and gazed out the window as Mary Jane sped across the intersection. "The woman in there, the checker . . ."

"No way. That's *her*?" Mary Jane asked, clearly nonplussed.

"I'm pretty sure. Her nametag said 'Lydia,' and there can't be many women by that name in such a small town." She faced me and sat up straight. "Can you keep a secret, Poppy?"

I nodded. "Yes, of course."

"My daddy is having an affair."

I wasn't sure what to say, so of course I said something idiotic. "But your dad . . . he's a deacon, right?"

"Yeah," Whitney said, her shoulders slumped and her voice weak. "And what's worse, Mama realizes he's cheating on her. It's like she doesn't want anyone else to know, so she pretends not to notice. But I see her sniffing his shirt collars and the sad look in her eyes when he calls to say he won't be home for dinner. I know she knows. It's like a bad soap opera . . . so pitiful."

"But all of that could be circumstantial," I say, hating to see Whitney so upset. "Right?"

Her dark eyes glistened as she looked over at Mary Jane. Her beautiful best friend nodded in support. "One time, a couple of years ago, Daddy's cell phone vibrated during the twins' Tumbling Toddlers program. He excused himself. I had to use the bathroom, so I followed him out. He didn't see me. I heard everything. Her name is Lydia. They were meeting up the following night. Of course, Daddy called the next evening to say something came up at work and he wouldn't be home for dinner." Tears dripped down Whitney's cheeks. "It was horrible." Mary Jane reached into the console and handed her a Kleenex. "Thanks." She dabbed her eyes and wiped her nose. "So, anyway, that's my big secret. And everywhere I go, people tell me how wonderful and Godly he is, and I have to smile and agree with them when in reality, he's a big freakin' poseur."

"Oh, Whitney, I'm so sorry," I said. I felt so bad for her and for her mother. Hopefully her mom was hell-bent on finishing her college degree so she could kick his cheating ass to the curb.

A few minutes later, Whitney said, "Sometimes I envy you, Poppy."

"Me? Why?"

"Well, sometimes I wonder if it would be easier not to have a dad and not be required to do church stuff day in and day out. It's such a pain." She reached up to her neck and touched her gold cross charm.

Mary Jane turned to her friend. "Geez, Whitney. That was totally insensitive. She can't help that she doesn't have a father."

"Naw, it's okay," I said. "I do have a father . . . somewhere. It wasn't an immaculate conception or anything as exciting as that." I laughed. "Just two teenagers too horny for their own good, I guess."

"So where is he?" asked Mary Jane.

"I don't know. When Mom got pregnant, she decided to raise me all by herself. I guess he was cool with that, because he's never tried to contact me. At least, not that I know of."

Whitney turned around and frowned. "Does that make you sad?"

I shrugged. "Sometimes."

"Do you think you two will ever meet?" asked Whitney.

"I really don't know. It's always been just Mom and me, so . . ."

"What about her parents, your grandparents?" Mary Jane asked. "Don't they help out?"

"Yeah, they did. A little. They died when I was six, though." One snowy day, Grandma drove Grandpa home from the eye doctor and they got in a wreck. According to the reports, he died instantly. She died the following day at the hospital. They had a joint funeral at a little Catholic church by their home in the Denver suburbs, their caskets closed so we could remember them as the attractive, happy couple in the framed eleven-by-fourteen photograph propped up on the stairs amongst all the lilies and roses.

That's where I'd first heard that my grandma had been an alcoholic—at their funeral. Some ladies were talking about it by the coatracks, and when they spotted me behind a smoky-smelling trench coat, they gave me pitying looks. I always knew something was different about Grandma, like sometimes she acted downright silly and other times she just sat around all weepy-eyed.

"Way to go, Whitney," Mary Jane said. "You've upset her."

"Oh, no. I'm okay. I'm over it, all of it."

"Well, you're very brave," said Mary Jane, and I wondered if she was right.

CHAPTER TWELVE

I schlepped myself through the whole next day trying not to think about my after-school mission, but the clock worked against me. The dismissal bell sounded, and that time, I didn't feel like humming "Amazing Grace" along with it. Except for the kids with after-school club meetings or sports practices, everyone fled school grounds. I hung out in the library for an hour, trying to study for a physics exam, but my mind kept inventing scenarios for the daunting yet ridiculous task ahead of me.

The hall was a ghost town when I finally emerged from the library. As I approached Gabe's locker, my cell phone beeped. *What did he say?* Mary Jane's text message read. I swear—she was even more excited than I was.

Haven't asked him yet, I typed back. *Patience, girl!*

While asking guys to Sadie Hawkins in cutesy ways was obviously the norm here at Calvary High, I felt utterly ridiculous. And nervous as hell.

I had no clue what to expect. I'd never asked someone or been asked by someone to a school dance.

Of course, Mary Jane and Whitney offered to be my wingwomen. But I figured there'd be less pressure flying solo. Better to make a fool of myself in front of as few witnesses as possible. That was why I resolved to ask him now, while my friends were at Peery for their big GOV Club assembly. When they'd invited me along, I gracefully declined. Sitting in a gym with three counties' worth of virgins sounded even more traumatic than asking Gabe to the Sadie Hawkins dance.

Now I wasn't so sure.

As the minutes whisked around the face of the hallway clock, my grip on the bag of Swedish Fish tightened. The Swedish Fish that I stole. I suddenly felt sweaty, like when we were checking out at the grocery store yesterday afternoon.

"What did you do?"

I jumped at the sound of his voice. "David! You scared the

crap out of me," I said through clenched teeth. "And what do you mean? I didn't do anything."

"You look guilty. It's something I'm really good at. Detecting guilt. I am the son of a preacher, after all. It's in the genes."

I concentrated on keeping my expression neutral. I so didn't want to get into a conversation with David Hillcrest, not now. Lacrosse practice would let out any minute, and I needed to psych myself up for the big moment.

"We Baptists are definitely taking a toll on you," he said, rambling on.

"What do you mean?" I asked, against my better judgment.

"You said 'crap.' You've gone PG-13 on me. Oh . . ." He snapped his fingers. "I just figured it out. Why you look so guilty. You feel bad about not showing up for last night's paintball game." Shit. He was right; I'd totally spaced on it. "But don't worry about that. You see, you were the only person who showed even a glimmer of interest. So I guess I'll just have to sit back and formulate another plan."

"Maybe people just aren't ready for such an innovative idea," I said, trying not to smile. "And I thought you said you'd join the GOV Club. Shouldn't you be at the big meeting at Peery?"

"Well, I saw you standing over here without your entourage and reckoned you needed a ride. Hey"—he pointed at the bag of Swedish Fish in my hand—"I love those. Aren't you gonna share?"

"No." Looking back, I wondered why I'd been so panicked about stealing them. None of the employees at Hamilton's or the Piggly Wiggly had second-guessed any of us.

"What's the note say?" David asked, grabbing the bag of candy. I tried to get it back, but he held it just out of my reach until I gave up. After clearing his throat, he read: "Of all the fish in the sea, I want you to go to Sadie's with me." He laughed. Unsurprisingly.

My nerves freshly razzed, I snatched the bag and clutched it to my chest. The laughter stopped and he stepped backward. "Hey, I'm sorry, Poppy. It's just that it's so . . . Well, I never had you pegged for the cheesy type."

"I'm *not*."

His gaze dropped from my eyes to the note and back up again. "Of course you're not." I wanted to wipe that smug smirk off his face, but he had a point.

I tore the note off the candy and sighed. "I was going to hide a dead fish under his mattress and, if he said no, leave it there forever."

David slapped me on the back. "Now you're talkin', kiddo." Then he planted his butt in a folding chair conveniently stashed a few feet away in a little alcove where the fire extinguisher hung. "So, who's the lucky guy? Wouldn't happen to be Gabe Valdez, would it?"

"How'd you know?" Mary Jane and Whitney were the only ones who knew, and they swore to keep it in the vault.

"That's his locker you're leaning against."

"Oh, right."

"Speak of the devil . . ." David expelled a long, deflated-sounding whistle as Gabe sauntered into view.

Oh, no. This was all wrong. Andrew and a couple other dudes weren't supposed to be with Gabe, and I sure as hell hadn't planned on David Hillcrest having a front-row seat.

"Do you mind?" I whispered at David.

"What do you see in that guy?"

What was *with* him? "I'm nervous as it is, David. Please go away." I hated to beg, but if I didn't ask Gabe now, Mary Jane and Whitney would be impossible to live with till I did. And Gabe would be standing in front of me any minute now.

"Here." I tossed the bag of Swedish Fish at David. "All yours. Now leave. Please."

As he rose to his feet, David ripped open the bag and popped a school of gummy fish into his mouth. Relief rippled through my body because I'd finally gotten through to him. I whipped out my cell to text Mary Jane: *He's coming! Stand by 4 more news.*

"I hope he says no," David muttered, walking backward.

He chewed the candy slowly and, with the tip of his tongue, licked his bottom lip.

I blinked, not sure I'd heard right. "What?"

He shrugged and headed for the door. "I want to see how long it takes for Gabe to figure out something's fishy under his bed."

The closer Gabe got, the more I wanted to run after David and completely abort my mission.

"Hey, Poppy. What're you doing here?" Gabe asked.

The other guys nodded or muttered, "Hey," then resumed chattering about lacrossey stuff.

My cell phone beeped. I didn't have to look. I knew it was Mary Jane, dying for the very latest scoop. Gabe propped his lacrosse stick against the wall and twirled the combo on his locker.

"Um, Gabe? Can I ask you something?" I said, certain my cheeks were bright red.

Gabe stepped away from his buddies, giving us at least the illusion of privacy. "Yeah, sure. What's up? Do you want to know the time?"

Caught off guard, I just stood there like a dummy.

He grinned. "Remember? That's what I asked you at the barbecue Friday night. I was really going to ask if you'd like to come to my lacrosse game on Saturday, but I guess I lost my nerve. And then I realized I really did need to pick up Georgia . . ."

"Are you going to Sadie's?" I blurted.

Gabe's gaze flitted over to his buddies and then locked with mine. "Well, that depends. Are you asking me?"

I stared at my boots. They were totally scuffed. I should clean them up someday. Or maybe I should just buy a new pair. I'd worn them almost every day for what, two years? Perhaps I could figure out a way to lift a pair sometime. My thoughts trickled into that new, exciting place reserved for my shoplifting daydreams, until Gabe asked, "Are you asking me to Sadie's, Poppy?" yanking me back into the embarrassing and downright painful conversation at hand.

"Yes."

He was silent for a few beats, until I looked up. "Sorry, it's just that a lot of girls go through a whole big production. You kinda caught me by surprise." I felt my posture deflating. "But I like that you just asked outright. It's refreshing, you know? It sounds like a good time."

"So, is that a yes?" I ventured.

He grinned. "Yes."

"Come on, man," one of the lacrosse guys said, and Gabe held up a finger.

"Well, I'd better go," he said apologetically. "See ya, Poppy."

"Bye."

As the guys walked away, one asked, "What was that

about?" and Gabe answered, "She just asked me to Sadie's." I strained to hear what came next. Finally someone said, "She seems cool," and Gabe said, "Yeah." I gave myself a mental pat on the back, feeling pretty damn good about how that went.

As I wandered down the hallway, texting the good news to Mary Jane and Whitney, I heard music—symphonic instrumentals and a female singer obsessed with the word "Hallelujah." When I got closer to the art room, the music grabbed me. It was beautiful and beguiling. I wedged open the door and peeked inside. Behind the supply closet, Bridgette Josephs hunched over a long table, singing her heart out as she painted on a huge piece of paper. I froze, wondering if I could just listen unnoticed. However, she spotted me and abruptly stopped singing.

"Hey, Bridgette," I said over the accompaniment, feeling bad for having startled her. "Practicing for choir?"

She busted into an awkward little dance, positioning her body between me and her project. "Poppy. Wh-why are you here?" she asked, craning her neck to peer around me. "Are you alone?" She pointed her paintbrush at me and red Tempera splattered on the laminate tiles. Although the floor had obviously been up close and personal with countless paint drippings (and Lord knows what else), she gasped when she noticed her personal contribution.

I snatched the roll of paper towels by the CD player, which was still blasting music, and tossed it to her. Only, the roll hit the margarine tub of paint, which flew off the table. The paper towels bounced under the table like a toddler hiding from the mess he made.

"Where are Mary Jane and the rest of your posse?" she asked, her voice tinged with suspicion.

"They left. It's just me."

She crouched and reached for the towels, then ripped off a bunch. "You know they wouldn't approve of us talking like this." The statement hung in the air as she wiped up the paint, red liquid bleeding through the paper towel and onto her palms. Before going to the sink to wash her hands, she carefully folded the banner in half.

I swallowed, wishing I'd kept walking down the hall. "I don't care. I talk to whomever I want to talk to."

Bridgette sighed and then grinned. "Good for you."

"You and Mary Jane used to be close, right?" I said. "Best friends."

She nodded. "Hard to imagine, isn't it?"

"What happened?"

She cleared her throat. "Oh, I'm sure Mary Jane and Whitney have painted a real pretty picture about our past."

"They haven't said much." Just that they thought Bridgette

was jealous of them, and that she didn't think Mary Jane was good enough for Andrew (who was Bridgette's longtime family friend).

Bridgette's nostrils flared, and she seemed to be searching my eyes to see if I was telling the truth.

"Really," I said, hopefully saving her the trouble.

She turned off the CD player. "Well, all right. I guess it won't hurt anything to tell you about it." She hopped up on the counter by the sink. "We were both in church choir. I'm a soprano and she's an alto and the director liked to give us duets. We were pretty good, people said."

"I didn't know Mary Jane sings." Of course, Mary Jane sang hymns whenever we were all supposed to, and she sometimes hummed along to songs in the car or at the mall, but that was all I knew.

"When she was a freshman and I was a sophomore, we decided to try out for the school musical together. *Oklahoma!* Of course, we both wanted to be Laurey, but we expected the lead to go to an upperclassman."

"I bet you got it," I said. "Seriously, Bridgette, you have an amazing voice."

She snorted. "Maybe, but Mary Jane has an amazing face. An amazing body, amazing clothes. Amazing connections, too."

"Mary Jane got the part?"

Bridgette lifted her auburn hair off her neck for a few seconds and then dropped it again. "Mary Jane got Laurey and Andrew got Curly."

"What? You mean Andrew sings too?"

"Well, not really that well," she said with a laugh. "There aren't many guys here at Calvary who'll even audition for a musical. All the guys around here care about is sports. But I talked him into it."

Why would Andrew listen to Bridgette? I wondered. He barely even acknowledged her. She must've read my mind because she added, "He was my boyfriend."

I tried to mask my shock. Or was it disbelief? "Mary Jane mentioned you and Andrew were old family friends . . ."

"Everyone in Pleasant Acres considers themselves 'old family friends,' Poppy." Bridgette hopped down and grabbed her patchwork purse off the teacher's desk. "So she wasn't lying. She just conveniently skipped this part." She opened her wallet and showed me a strip of little photographs, the kind you get from photo booths at amusement parks and seedy tourist traps. The photos showed younger Bridgette and Andrew in a variety of poses, from side-by-side stiff, to laughing hysterically, to one of him kissing her cheek. They actually looked like they made a good couple back then—so happy.

Okay, so Mary Jane never mentioned that Andrew and

Bridgette used to be a couple. But why not? What was the big deal? If I wanted the whole story, I had to keep Bridgette talking. "So Andrew was Curly and Mary Jane was Laurey. What part did you get?"

She looked down at her black flats. "Mary Jane's understudy."

"Ooooh." That sucked.

"Yeah. Well, I tried to be a good sport about it, and I was fully prepared to get over it. That was, until opening night. It was pretty evident the kiss between Mary Jane and Andrew . . . well, let's just say neither of them are *that* good at acting." She paused a second and her jaw moved side to side, as if she were deep in a particularly disturbing memory. "The weird thing is, she acted like *nothing was wrong*. Those days before her betrayal were the days I felt the very closest to Mary Jane. Solid, you know? Like nothing could ever, ever come between us."

"Especially not a guy."

"I really liked Andrew a lot, Poppy. I think I was even in love with him."

"I can't even imagine," I said, my heart going out to her. "That had to hurt."

She laughed, but it fell flat. "Well, not nearly as much as the day Mary Jane decided that Whitney Nickels would make a better best friend." She slammed her hand on the table and then crossed her arms over her buxom chest. "I'm sure she thought it would be easier to just replace me than to try and smooth things over, you know?"

Andrew's earlier conversation with David came to mind then, and it dawned on me that the "ex" he'd spoken of—the one who "got off on not getting him off"—was, in all likelihood, Bridgette. "Maybe you're better off?" I ventured, not really sure what else to say.

She gave me a long, hard look and I read her nonverbal message loud and clear. "What do you want me to do, Bridgette? Stop being friends with them over something that happened *two years ago*? And . . . all over *a guy*?" I smiled, hoping my voice of reason gave her a much-needed wake-up call. "I mean, I know you were in love with him and I'm not denying that what she did was a horrible, bitchy thing, but . . . maybe it wasn't on purpose. Maybe it just . . . happened."

Bridgette seemed to be wrapped up in her thoughts. Then she blinked her hazel eyes a couple of times and said, "My dad got laid off around that time too. I sometimes wonder if she didn't want to be my friend anymore because my dad works at a fillin' station. She loves to shop and go to concerts and, well, after a while, I couldn't keep up. Now that she's BFFs with Whitney, it's gotten even worse. Neither of them has a job, yet those two have the biggest, most expensive wardrobes in the whole town. Even the adults talk about it." She paused. "I guess you fit in, in that respect," she said.

"Wha-what do you mean?"

"Those are True Religion jeans, right? I know those cost a couple hundred bucks."

"Yeah, well . . ." How in the world had the conversation taken such a drastic turn? I wanted to find out more about the Mary Jane–Bridgette feud, not examine Mary Jane's and Whitney's (and my) wardrobes.

"Sorry, I'm just saying. Anyhow, I can't believe their parents dole out so much money. Can you believe how spoiled those two girls are?"

"Um, I don't think their parents are funding their wardrobes."

"What do you mean?"

"Oh, nothing." Holy crap; why had I said that out loud?

"What do you mean?" she repeated.

"Nothing. I just mean that maybe their parents aren't to blame, that's all." I grinned and shrugged it off like it was no big deal.

However, Bridgette wouldn't let it go. "Then how do they afford all of it? You've seen their designer wardrobes. You've seen Mary Jane tossing out expensive gifts to people she barely even knows. How do they *get* all of that stuff?" Then, after an ominous pause, she asked, "Do they steal it?"

CHAPTER THIRTEEN

***Do they steal it?* Bridgette's words echoed in my aching** head. A sharp pain stabbed at my tummy, and I found it hard to breathe normally. *Get a grip, Poppy. She's just guessing*, I told myself. *She doesn't* know *about the shoplifting.* I gulped some oxygen and, knowing I'd trespassed into dangerous territory, steered the conversation back toward safer ground. "You don't need this." I handed her the photo strip I'd been holding all that time. "You should throw it away."

She stroked her finger over the bottom photo.

"I saw this movie once," I said, "where a girl's boyfriend hooked up with her best friend, and the girl picked up her cell and was going to call him, like a habit or something. But then she suddenly grew a backbone and deleted his number. It was very liberating. And when I broke up with my ex, I burned something of his that I'd been holding on to. Really, Bridgette. Get rid of those stupid photos. Move on."

A sliver of a smile emerged on Bridgette's face and she appeared so confident, so pretty. She tore the photo strip to shreds, her smile broadening with every rip. Then she tossed the pieces high into the air, like confetti. I was happy Bridgette had done that, and even happier she had apparently forgotten all about her shoplifting suspicions.

"What are you working on over here, anyway?" I inched closer to her top-secret project. "Is it for the Sadie Hawkins dance?" Knowing Bridgette, she headed the decorating committee. And lucky me, I'd get to experience her hard work at the dance itself.

Her hazel eyes widened. "Actually, yes."

"Need any help?"

"You want to . . . help me?"

My offer kind of caught me by surprise, too. But what the hell, I had nothing better to do at that moment. And Bridgette finally opened up to me. She let me know why she and Mary Jane didn't get along. I wanted to keep talking to her, to learn more. Oh, I still thought Bridgette was two fries short of a

Happy Meal—but maybe if I got to know her better, I'd understand where she was coming from and could maybe even help her make peace with Mary Jane and Whitney.

"Yep. I'm all yours."

Bridgette lifted the banner and handed half of it to me. "It feels good," she said, patting her heart. "I mean, I'm finally moving on. Thanks for having me get rid of those photos. And this—this very sign—is the next big step for me." Bridgette's face practically glowed. "Okay, let's get this thing hung. I'm thinking in the hallway, just above his locker." She unfolded the banner and stood back to admire it. In bright red letters, it read: HOWDY, GABE! FOR A BANNER TIME AT SADIE HAWKINS, GO WITH BRIDGETTE.

I think I might've gasped out loud.

"I know it's silly," she said, "but I wanted to do something original, something big. You know?"

"It's definitely *big*." I swallowed and configured my gaping mouth into a smile.

She paused, a worried expression on her face. "You don't like it?"

"It's, um, . . . great." Shit, shit, shit. This was so not good.

"Did I tell you Gabe drove me home Friday night after the barbecue?" she asked dreamily. "My Bronco was on the fritz and he offered. He's so sweet and we have more in common than Andrew and I ever will."

"Your truck broke down?" Not like I cared; I was just stalling so I could wrap my mind around what had transpired in the last few minutes.

"Well, not really. I just told him that." She shrugged. "Anyway, I'm really excited for him to see this tomorrow morning. And nervous, too. It'll be the first date I've gone on since Andrew, and I can't wait to see the looks on everyone's faces when they see Gabe and me together . . ." A huge smile exploded onto her flushed face. "It's going to be *perfect*."

I hadn't seen anyone that excited since the Broncos won the Super Bowl. How could I tell her that I already asked Gabe—and that he said yes?

After helping her hang the banner, I couldn't get outside into the fresh air fast enough. Dialing Mom's number on my cell phone, I almost ran smack into the back of a rickety blue pickup truck. A "Who Would Jesus Bomb?" sticker adorned the bumper, a metal bass covered the trailer hitch, and twangy country music played on the stereo. It took me a minute to recognize the cowboy in the driver's seat. I wandered up to the cab and David tipped his hat at me. Why was he there? Had he forgotten something? "Hey little lady, need a lift?" he asked.

"Yeah, I guess I do." I dropped my cell phone into my backpack and then crawled up into the cab. "You weren't waiting out here just to drive me home, were you?"

"Heck no." He turned down the music and then reached into the cup holder to produce a deck of faded cards. "I've been meaning to catch up on my solitaire, and this seemed as good a place as any."

I gave him a little courtesy laugh and he steered toward Calvary Road.

"I'm sure my reputation precedes me, but if not, I happen to be a *great* fisherman. I won the blue ribbon two years in a row at Catfish Days." He tilted his head and waggled his eyebrows. "I can go catch a fish real fast in that lake over yonder, and you can put it under Gabe's bed—"

"Thanks, but there's no need. He said yes."

"He did? Then why so glum?" He offered me the bag of Swedish Fish.

I took a couple and flung them into my mouth, thoughts of Bridgette stomping through my skull. She felt like Mary Jane stole Andrew from her. And now she was "moving on" by asking Gabe to the dance. What would she think when she found out I'd already asked him? It wasn't like I could un-ask him. How could I have known she had a crush on him?

"Oh, it's nothing," I mumbled with my mouth full.

David didn't ask me any more questions—besides how to get to my house—which I thought was cool because I didn't want to have to lie to him anymore. He dropped me off and said through the open window, "By the way, I knew all along Gabe would say yes. He might be dull as ditchwater but he ain't stupid." Then he winked at me and coasted away, leaving me in a cloud of impending doom.

And, as it happened, directly under an actual cloud: a big, dark storm cloud that was all too eager to soak me as I hauled ass across the yard. Once inside, I caught my breath and wiped the rain off my face. Then I reached into my backpack and took out my cell phone. Sliding down the wall into a somewhat comfy squatting position, I scrolled down my contact list, the lighted bar hovering over Bridgette's name.

I could call her and tell her I'd already asked Gabe to the dance. It would probably piss her off, but wouldn't it be better to piss her off now than later? Or maybe I should call Gabe and give him a head's up. Maybe he'd even consider going with Bridgette, if I insisted that it was okay with me. After all, it was a very casual affair and, from what I'd seen, Gabe didn't find Bridgette revolting or anything. Come to think of it, they looked kinda cute together.

I didn't have Gabe's number, though. I was going to a school dance with some dude I didn't even know well enough to have his phone number. Some guy I didn't find interesting enough to have asked for his number. And, obviously, vice versa.

Holy shit, I don't know what to do. And the more I thought about it, the more confused I became. Hoping a walk might help clear my mind, I grabbed my umbrella, purse, and MP3 player and headed outside.

Slogging through the rainy streets, music by Cobra Starship, Secondhand Serenade, and Social D kept me company, and I eventually found myself at the little Milk 'n' More convenience store. Whitney must've been rubbing off on me, because I suddenly craved chocolate. A Butterfinger would totally hit the spot. As an Outback wagon drove away with a full belly of gasoline, I whisked open the door. The pungent odors of hot dogs and popcorn replaced the earthy, rainy aroma I'd been enjoying. I cinched my umbrella, the excess water sprinkling the doormat. The man at the cash register gave me a cursory nod before burying his nose in the *Pleasant Acres Examiner*. Swaying my umbrella, I rounded the first aisle and browsed the rows of candies, glad to see my favorite chocolate bar.

I had the sudden, inexplicable urge to lift something.

Trying to appear casual, I glanced skyward, and when I spotted the big, round mirror in the corner of the ceiling, I felt defeated. But if the cashier wasn't looking at the mirror while I took something, he'd be none the wiser, I reasoned. And, if he wasn't keeping tabs on me, there was no reason why I couldn't get away with it. Leaning backward, I saw the cashier reading the newspaper, not paying attention to me at all. My heart thudded excitedly in my chest.

I grabbed a Butterfinger—the red herring item, as Mary Jane would call it—and as my hand lowered, I snagged a pack of gum and dropped it into the open end of the umbrella. With a *sssssk*, it slid down the nylon and landed in the tip with an almost inaudible *thud.* It was just a stupid pack of gum, nothing big or expensive. It was hardly even a challenge. Still, after I'd completed that tiny shoplifting maneuver, there was no turning back. Nowhere to go but forward. Do or die. Adrenaline surged through my veins, and my feet rocked toe to heel with energy and anticipation.

Next I waltzed up to the fifty-something man and set the candy bar on the counter. "Is that everything?" he asked without looking up. A meticulously shaped beard lined his jaw, and he wore a white T-shirt under his wrinkle-free uniform.

"Yup." *Relax, Poppy. It's a pack of gum.*

He tilted up his chin and I saw my reflection in his glasses. My light blond hair had a bit of funky wave to it since it had been wet and partially air-dried, my dark eyes appeared extra large, and my nose stud did little to interfere with the whole "innocent girl" vibe. *Good, good.* He'd never guess I had a pack of gum in my umbrella. There was nothing to worry about.

"Okeydoke. That will be eighty-nine cents."

I fished the coins out of my wallet and handed them to him. *Steady does it.*

"Want a receipt? Or a bag?" he asked, giving me a penny in change.

I shook my head and took the Butterfinger. Then I headed for the doors. *Almost out of here . . . free and clear!* My heart beat even harder behind my ribs, and a wonderful feeling of invincibility surged through my veins.

"Hey, wait just a minute."

Startled, I froze midstride and peered over my shoulder. The humidity hit me like a hammer to my knees. He gestured for me to come back. *Keep walking; don't stop*, I told myself. But if I ignored him, he'd think me rude at best and guilty of something at worst.

"What?" I asked from the doorway.

"I forgot to ask if you'd like to donate to the Hurricane Phillipa Relief Fund. It's a dollar, and you get to write your name on one of these." He held up a card shaped like a heart. Autographed hearts hung behind the counter and spilled onto the wall by the pop dispensers. *Just say "Maybe next time,"* I told myself.

"Sure, why not." While we exchanged money, the heart-shaped card, and the Sharpie, I kept asking myself why I hadn't kept walking. I would've been outside already; I could've made it out with the gum. It probably only took a minute to complete the transaction, but it felt like hours. I handed him the signed card.

He did a double take. "Poppy? So you're . . ." A languid yet genuinely happy-looking smile crept across his pale face. "You're my daughter Bridgette's new friend."

Oh, God. Great, just great. All I wanted to do was get the hell out of there, and now I was being chatted up by—of all people—Bridgette Josephs' dad.

"I thought it might be you," he said, leaning forward. "She mentioned you had a . . . nose ring. Anyhow, we've heard quite a bit about you these past few days."

The color must have drained from my face, because he quickly added, "All good, of course. All good."

A nervous laugh trickled out of my mouth. *Just wait till tomorrow*, I thought to myself. *Then you'll get an earful about how unwonderful I really am.* "Well," I said, "that's sweet of her."

"Poppy, thanks for coming in," he said. "I'm sure we'll be seeing more of you in the near future. If it's okay with your folks, maybe you can come with us to Six Flags sometime."

Before shutting my wallet, I slid another dollar across the counter. "For the relief fund." I tapped the heart-shaped card I'd signed. "Don't need another one of those, though."

I'd love to blame my philanthropic spirit for my donation—

my double donation—but as I stepped outside, I couldn't help wondering if perhaps some small part of me felt that helping hurricane victims would somehow make me feel better about myself.

The rain had tempered to a staccato sprinkle. I opened my umbrella, and the pack of gum tumbled out and plopped into a puddle on the asphalt. I tried to rescue it, but the water soaked through the packaging. I tossed the soggy mess into the first garbage can I passed. The gum was gone, as was the high I felt when I stole it.

I promised myself I wouldn't lift anything ever again.

By the time I got home, the darkest clouds had moved on and strokes of early evening sunlight rained down on me. Yet I was no closer to knowing what to do about the Bridgette and Gabe ordeal. Maybe I just needed to sleep on it. Right. I'd set my alarm a half hour earlier and get to Calvary High early enough to talk to Bridgette and give her the opportunity to take down the banner.

After finishing my homework and having a brief Butterfinger break, I hit the sack. But at eleven thirty, even after backburnering my concerns about Bridgette, I couldn't fall asleep. Jazz music permeated the walls from Mom's office, where she'd undoubtedly work into the wee hours of the night.

Sneaking into Mom's bathroom, I opened her medicine

cabinet. Thankfully, she stocked it with plenty of sleeping pills. I popped one into my mouth and swallowed it down with water straight from the faucet. Then I snuggled into my bed and tried to relax. Little by little, my muscles loosened up, but thoughts chaotically whirred around in my mind. I concentrated on bringing the happy ones to the forefront, like how my yoga teacher back at Flatirons had instructed us to do. The pride that filled me after Mom had complimented my essay, the way Mary Jane and Whitney would laugh at my jokes, how David actually had waited around to drive me home, and the rush I'd felt when sliding the gum down my umbrella.

I loved that feeling—how one minute I could be doing something as mundane as window-shopping at the mall or picking something up from a grocery or convenience store, and the next minute I was in the midst of a heart-pounding, adrenaline-pumping escapade.

I couldn't wait for the next heart-pounding, adrenaline-pumping escapade.

CHAPTER FOURTEEN

"Seriously, Mom, we've got to get going," I said, collecting her pumps.

Rubbing her temple, Mom looked up from the couch, where she'd been lounging all morning. "I'm glad you're so zealous to get to school, but I have the worst headache. I'm going to need some coffee." She lifted her feet off the ottoman and stretched her arms in the air. "I've been eager to try that little coffee shop on Second Street."

"But—"

"I'll get you one of those raspberry drinks you love."

Clearly she wasn't going to change her mind. I dropped the

shoes at her feet and hurried to her office to fetch her briefcase. Twenty minutes later, Mom's Volvo pulled up to a wannabe Starbucks. About a dozen cars sat in the dinky parking lot. I panicked. "Can't you just get a coffee at a gas station?" I asked.

"Oh, don't be silly," Mom said. "This will just take a moment. I promise you won't be late to school." As we walked into the shop, she lowered her sunglasses and quirked her left eyebrow. "Since when have you been so bent on being to school *early*?"

"It's just that I need to talk to someone. Before school starts. It's important." Oh, shit. There had to be twenty people in line, and the lone goateed guy behind the counter was more into chitchatting than concocting drinks, bagging up muffins, and sending patrons on their merry little way. When Mom finally dropped me off by the Calvary High sign, I only had fifteen minutes till morning service began.

I decided to tell Bridgette the truth—that I'd already asked Gabe and he'd accepted and I was too caught up in her empowered "out with the old and in with the new" moment to burst her bubble, blah blah blah. She might still be mad at me, but it was, I felt, the best I could do at this point. I waved good-bye to Mom and flew up the stairs and into the school, flinging greetings here and there as I sought out Bridgette Josephs.

Oh, no. Gabe was heading straight for me, straight for his

locker, straight for Bridgette's banner. I hadn't bargained on meeting up with Gabe first, but I couldn't let him get by. I jogged over to him and presented him with a huge smile, frantically juggling my thoughts. "Gabe, listen. I'm excited about going to Sadie's with you . . ."

He snaked his arm around me, and his caramel-colored eyes gleamed. "Me too." A group of girls rubbernecked as they walked by. Though I hated to admit it, there was a time I would've been drawn into the whole "Oh my God, the cutest boy at Calvary High is touching me!" mentality, but the fleeting thrill barely registered in my senses. Sure, Gabe Valdez might be pretty; but he was, I was sad to say, terminally uninteresting.

It was strange for a moment of clarity to hit me while Gabe's arm rested on my shoulder and I was under major damage-control stress. Then another strange thought hit me: David had said Gabe was "dull as ditchwater"—something we agreed about.

"But I think it would mean a lot more to Bridgette if you, um, went with her," I said.

Gabe dropped his arm to his side and squinted at me. "I'm confused. You want to go with me, don't you?"

I gave a lukewarm chuckle. "Of course. I just feel bad for Bridgette, that's all." I lowered my voice. "She finds you . . . interesting . . . you know."

"I've known Bridgette Josephs for a long time, and she always manages to bounce back. So stop worrying about her."

Shit, he was not making this easy. "Well, okay, the reason I'm—"

"Hey, Gabe! Been to your locker yet?" Andrew slapped him on his back. "Come on."

"What's the deal?" Gabe asked, shifting his gaze between his best buddy and me. As we walked to Gabe's locker, I bit my lower lip, steeling myself for the inevitable disaster that was about to unfold.

Mary Jane was frozen in the middle of the hall, one hand planted on her hip and the other reaching out, palm upward. She wore a white blouse that fluttered celestially around her shoulders and a tragic expression on her pretty face. The sides of her hair were coiled loosely into a silver barrette at the nape of her neck. She looked like a freakin' Roman goddess statue. Then her lips came to life, shattering the statuesque vibe. "Bless her heart," she said, staring above Gabe's locker.

A crowd had already gathered, and the banner was attracting the attention of more and more passersby. I realized I'd been holding my breath and inhaled deeply to replenish my oxygen. Next, I popped a piece of gum in my mouth, wishing the chomping, smacking action would magically whisk away all my nervousness.

Ellen shook her head. "Even if he hadn't already agreed to go with you, Gabe would never say yes to *Bridgette*." I doubted she realized Gabe was standing right behind her. Awkward, yes. But the fact that Bridgette herself had arrived just in time to hear made it tremendously uncomfortable.

I swallowed, and though I desperately wanted to run away, I knew I couldn't.

Bridgette tucked her reddish lips into a thin—almost invisible—line. From her spiral-curled hair to her coordinating blouse and skirt, she'd obviously taken extra care to look her best. Her posture awkward and rigid, she squeezed her hands into fists and blinked in steady rhythm, her eyes glued on Gabe. "You're going to the dance with *Poppy*?"

Gabe shifted his backpack to the opposite shoulder and grinned at Bridgette, then at me, then at Bridgette again. "I am," he said casually. "She asked me after school yesterday."

Though I wasn't looking directly at Bridgette, her negative energy all but slammed me against the wall, knocking the breath out of me.

"But I'm flattered you'd think of me, Bridgette," Gabe said. Surprisingly, he sounded genuine, and I had to give the boy props.

"You snooze, you lose," quipped Whitney, patting Bridgette on the back. "Gabe's taken. But there are *lots* of guys who still haven't been asked. Six or seven, at least. See? You just have to look on the bright side."

Bridgette made a bizarre growling noise and writhed away from Whitney.

"Looking on the bright side only gives you crow's feet," said Ellen, spinning on her kitten heels. "But to each her own, right? Well, it's time for morning service. Come on, Poppy."

I'd already been mean to Bridgette; why did everybody else feel the need to? I finally got the nerve to look Bridgette in the eye. She looked like she wanted to punch my lights out. How could I blame her? "You knew the whole time," Bridgette said, her voice surprisingly even.

My mind struggled to come up with the right words to say. "Yes. I did."

"The whole school knows you have a crush on Gabe, Bridgette. You only throw yourself at him every chance you get," said Mary Jane with a giggle. I realized this was her idea of sticking up for me, but I wished people would give Bridgette a break. Couldn't they see the girl was humiliated?

Bridgette's mouth twitched and her eyes narrowed. Two of her Good News Choir cronies sidled up to her. I felt the need to do something quick, before things got uglier. "I'm so sorry, Bridgette," I said. "I tried to get here early to talk to you, but my mom decided to try out a coffee shop and it was so crowded and the barista was a total numbskull—"

With a single militant step, Whitney closed the space between herself and Bridgette and lifted her chin. "She said she's sorry, Bridgette. Game over."

Bridgette hopped back and then reached up above Gabe's locker. She ripped the banner down in one fatal swoop, narrowly missing her choir friend's head. Without looking at me—or at anyone, really—Bridgette balled up the banner, shaking her head the whole time.

Bridgette turned to me and Gabe and said, "Well, I hope the two of you have a very *memorable* night." Next, she hurled the paper ball at us and then turned so abruptly, she knocked the books out of some poor freshman's hands. As Bridgette stomped away in the opposite direction of the auditorium, her freakishly long, curled hair streamed behind her.

"Amazing Grace" played over the speakers, and little by little, the number of spectators diminished as they headed off to morning service. Gabe passed the books he'd picked up back to the wide-eyed freshman.

For the first time all morning, I laid my eyes on David Hillcrest. He stood about ten feet behind us, his hands tucked into his pockets. Though he wore an ensemble made up of a red polo, pressed tan chinos, and shiny brown shoes, his hair stuck up on one side in the most adorable way, and he hadn't shaved.

Something about the concerned yet calm look in his green eyes made me want to run to him, to fling myself into his arms.

"So are you coming? . . . Poppy, it's time for the service. You coming?" It took me a minute to realize Gabe was talking to me.

"Naw, go ahead. I think . . . I need to talk to Bridgette," I said, nodding in the direction in which she'd stomped off.

"Okay, I'll save you a place," my Sadie Hawkins date said. Finally he left, leaving David and me alone.

"How long have you been standing there?" I asked.

"Long enough." David sidled up to me and leaned against a locker.

"Yeah, well, that went exactly as planned," I said, trying—unsuccessfully—to laugh at myself.

He nodded understandingly. "You want my advice?"

I wiped a stubborn tear off my cheek. Why the hell was I crying? It wasn't that big of a deal. Bridgette would get over it. It might take another two years, but she would. I nodded. "I figure the son of a preacher would have some freakin' good advice."

He rubbed his hands together. "Next time, don't ask anyone besides me to a school dance." He paused and then held up his pointer finger. "Or any event that is traditionally attended by couples."

My mouth fell open, and I couldn't decide whether to slug him or laugh.

"What?" he said, acting all offended. "If you'd have just asked *me*, none of this would've happened."

"Well, thanks a lot for the guilt trip. You really are a shit-head, you know that?"

He laughed. "Oh, good. There's the Poppy we all know and love."

"I've got to talk to her."

"Go for it."

I made it several feet down the hall before he said, "I bet she's in the gym. It's pretty quiet in there when morning service is going on, and she's not brazen enough to leave school grounds."

"Okay, and if she really is in the gym, I'm going to pretend it's not creepy or anything that you called it that way."

He gave me this mysterious grin and then jogged off toward the auditorium.

At the gym doors, I paused to mentally rehearse what I'd say to Bridgette. I decided to start with an apology and then go with the flow.

Bridgette turned her back on me the instant I stepped into the gym. I walked over to her and sat on the bottom row of bleachers. "I'm probably the last person you want to see," I said.

She shrugged. "Maybe not the last person, but definitely the second- or third-to-last."

"Well, that's good, I think. I really am sorry, Bridgette. I didn't realize how much you like Gabe. I don't even know him very well, and I'm sure as hell not in love with him or anything. I swear I wasn't trying to steal him from you, and I feel terrible about letting you go ahead and ask him even though I already had."

"You don't get it, do you?" When she faced me, her blood-shot eyes glistened with moisture. "Sure, coming to school this morning and finding out you already asked Gabe to the dance and didn't have the decency to share that with me wasn't exactly *fun*." She sighed and picked at the bleacher absentmindedly. "But it's not about being the laughingstock of Calvary High. It's not even about Gabe—who yes, I do, or did, like very much." Her eyes closed—her lids swiped with shimmery mint green shadow—and when they reopened, they rolled away from me. "It's about *Mary Jane*. It's not enough that God blessed her with money and style and unparalleled beauty. She takes away everything that makes me happy."

"But Mary Jane had nothing to do with it, Bridgette. She wasn't even there when I asked him."

"Whose *idea* was it for you to ask Gabe? You said yourself you don't know him very well." I hesitated and she nodded knowingly. "If I ever want something, she does everything in her power to keep me from getting it. Even you." She shook her head in apparent disbelief.

"Me? What do you mean?"

"Before you first came to Calvary, Mary Jane signed up to be a student hostess too. It's a pretty good deal—you get a credit and brownie points with the teachers, and you can be late to classes with no questions asked. But my attendance record gave me leverage, and it ticked her off when I got the position. I told her you and I were going to the library together that night—okay, so I was kind of bragging about it. But anyway, I know that's why she took you shopping that particular afternoon, right after your first day of school. She could see that we were becoming fast friends, and nothing makes her happier than to see me friendless and boyfriendless. And miserable."

"Bridgette, I get what you're saying, but—"

"I'm just so sick of it. So very sick . . ."

"I know this is a little on the eccentric side," I said, maneuvering myself until I sat beside her, "but have you ever tried *talking* to her?" It was the same advice David had for Andrew, and I thought it had a lot of merit. "Maybe she's not such an evil bitch. Perhaps it's all just a big misunderstanding, and someday soon we'll all look back and laugh about it."

"If you really think I'm going to be Mary Jane's maid of

honor someday, you're not as smart as everybody seems to think you are," Bridgette said.

Annoyed, I started to stand. I'd had enough. If Bridgette wanted to fritter away the best years of her life blaming every bout of misfortune on Mary Jane, who was I to interfere?

She grabbed my arm. "Do you know what I wish, Poppy?"

"What's that?" My legs started cramping, so I shifted—earning zero points for grace.

Bridgette's nostrils flared as she gazed over at a basketball hoop. "I wish Mary Jane Portman would get a taste of her own medicine. I wish someone would take everything away from *her*."

"Now that's not a very 'What Would Jesus Do?' attitude," I said, pointing to the purple rubber band around her wrist.

She took off the bracelet, laid it down on her seat, and stormed out of the gym. I stared down at the bracelet for a few beats, wondering if I should try and give it back to her or just leave it there on the bleacher. Well, I'd be seeing Bridgette Josephs second period, whether I wanted to or not. So I picked it up and slipped it onto my wrist for safekeeping. My day couldn't possibly get any worse.

"Here, I thought you might want this back," I said, setting Bridgette's WWJD? bracelet on her desk. She glanced up from her novel but made no move to take it. "It looks great with your shirt," I said, hoping to make her smile. Or at least stop frowning. "Well, maybe I'll just keep it, then, and when you're a famous singer, I'll sell it on eBay and live high on the hog."

Turning the page in her book, she muttered, "Suit yourself."

"Okay, class, take your seats," Mrs. Oliverson said as she walked into the classroom in a crepe polka-dotted sheath dress. I sat behind my desk and reached into my backpack for my folder. While Mrs. Oliverson prattled on about Shakespeare, I flicked through my physics notes, trying to weigh how much time I should set aside tonight to study for tomorrow's test.

"Take out your pens and clear your desks," Mrs. Oliverson said. "In light of all the essays that bore striking resemblances to the content covered in Cliffs Notes, you will be taking a pop quiz on comprehension. A sentence or two will suffice for each answer."

The room filled with groans and I about choked on my gum. I could usually gauge when teachers would hit us with pop quizzes, but this one completely sucker punched me. I took a deep breath and smiled as the guy in front of me passed me my quiz. *You can do this*, I told myself. *Remember how you aced the* Hamlet *essay?*

The first question on the sheet of paper stared up at me as I struggled to recall the details of the Shakespearean play I'd read two years ago. *Why didn't Hamlet, son of old King Hamlet, inherit the throne?* The answer totally eluded me; I couldn't even pull a halfway feasible answer out of my butt.

I read the second question: *Does Ophelia kill herself, and how did you come to that conclusion?* and then scanned the third, fourth, and fifth, but none of them gelled with my memory bank. The words blurred and blended together into thick black lines, and all hope ran out.

Before I could stop it, a tear dropped onto the quiz. I brushed it off, only to have another tear fall and smudge one of the bullshit answers I'd scrawled. As I fought to regain my composure, all I could think about was how I was about to royally fuck up. And how Mom, once she saw my failing score, would ride me even harder. And how, now that I finally had some semblance of a social life, it would be ripped away from me. I couldn't afford to do poorly on this freakin' quiz.

"Poppy? We have to pass 'em up now," the girl sitting in front of me said. With shaking hands, I watched helplessly as my pathetic answers made their way to the front of the room and onto Mrs. Oliverson's desk, like an inmate on death row.

No use worrying about it now, I told myself. I needed to find a way to forget. And just as I thought of the way, "Amazing Grace" chimed throughout the school. I stood and collected my things. It was the perfect day to hit the mall.

CHAPTER FIFTEEN

After school, Whitney and I strolled to the cream-colored convertible VW sprawled across two parking spots in the student lot. Mary Jane had beaten us and was singing along with the radio. It sounded like a Christian pop song. "I was talking to Bridgette yesterday, and she mentioned you got the lead in the school musical as a freshman. That's pretty impressive," I said. "I didn't even know you were the theater type."

Mary Jane turned down the volume. "Well, Bridgette talked me into it. It was a long time ago, back when we were friends."

"*Oklahoma!*, right? I bet you and Andrew were awesome in it." I ducked into the back and snapped into my seat belt.

"Yeah, we were okay, I guess."

"She's being modest. They were great," said Whitney.

"Not that Whitney's biased or anything," Mary Jane said laughingly. "But anyway, Bridgette was all upset that I got the lead and she didn't. She'd just sit backstage and glare at me all the time, which made it hard for me to do my best, you know? So anyway, I tried out for *The Music Man* the next year and only made the chorus. So I won't even audition this year. I've got more important things going on—"

"Like helping me with the GOV Club," Whitney said, and Mary Jane laughed.

"You guys never mentioned that Andrew and Bridgette used to be an item," I said, steering the conversation back to Bridgette.

"Really?" Mary Jane said in a way that truly seemed like she thought she had. "Well, it's true. They were. And then Andrew and I were matched up in that musical and, well, I felt really bad about it, but, well, we fell for each other." She turned onto Calvary Road and headed to the mall. "It happens all the time. Just look at Zac and Vanessa."

"Bummer for Bridgette, though," I blurted. "She really liked Andrew . . . I bet. I mean, weren't they together for quite a while before that?" I dug my lip gloss out of my purse and swiped it across my mouth, hoping my questions came across as conversational and not meddlesome.

"I tried to tell her I didn't mean for it to happen, and I begged for her forgiveness, but she was horrid!" said Mary Jane, visibly flustered. "And it killed me, because we'd been such good friends for so long."

"But no one needs a friend like *that*," said Whitney. "That girl is emotionally high maintenance."

"Thank goodness for Whitney." Mary Jane smiled over at her beautiful best friend. "They say when God closes a door, He opens a window. And this girl was waiting just the other side of that window, bless her heart."

"That's cool," I said as they exchanged cheesy little "best friend forever" promises. "I know it's been, like, two years since all that happened, but maybe you should try and talk to Bridgette about it. When I was talking to her after the whole asking Gabe to the dance ordeal, she seemed to think you wanted me to go with him so she wouldn't have the chance. And of course I told her that was ridiculous—" I paused, expecting one of them to interrupt. But Mary Jane and Whitney exchanged guilty-as-charged glances. "Bridgette was right?" I asked, dumbfounded.

"Okay, here's the deal," said Whitney. "Everybody knows Bridgette has a big ol' crush on Gabe. So when Pastor Hill-crest announced the Sadie Hawkins dance, a bunch of us teased Gabe about the likelihood of her asking him. He begged Andrew to do something so he wouldn't have to go with her."

"And Andrew came running to me, naturally," said Mary Jane. "Since Gabe had mentioned that you were cute—that part has always been true, sweetie—Whitney and I decided that you should ask him first."

"Exactly." Whitney turned around and flashed a big white smile at me.

"Oh." So Bridgette was right about Mary Jane and Whitney tricking me into asking Gabe to the dance. Only it wasn't to make Bridgette's life miserable, at least not directly. It was because Gabe didn't want to go with Bridgette, but he was too nice of a guy to tell her no without a good reason, and what better reason than to already be going with somebody, and what better somebody than the new girl?

But Mary Jane and Whitney didn't really *trick* me into asking him, since I kind of wanted to go with him, at least at first, and they couldn't have planned for me to be the one to help Bridgette hang the banner, so that part was 100 percent my fault. And now I didn't really even want to go to the dumb dance.

As confusing as it all was, two things I knew for sure. One—since I bombed my English quiz, I probably wouldn't get to go to the dance anyhow. And two—I was glad to know that Mary Jane and Whitney were not the evil bitches Bridgette believed them to be.

“Okay, girls, we’re here,” Mary Jane announced, killing the engine. “Bare Essensuals is having its big bra sale, the one it only runs twice a year. Are y’all ready to shop?”

We hopped out of the VW, and I instantly felt the worries and stress melt away. And with each SEMI-ANNUAL BRA EVENT sign we passed, my pulse raced faster and faster. I felt the whoosh of adrenaline as I looked around the store, taking in the bustling shoppers, the size-sorted bra bins, the displays of lotions, and the racks of silk, lace, and satin.

“So y’all know the plan, right?” whispered Whitney. In her pink skirt and white blouse, she blended into the trendy lingerie store’s decor like a chameleon.

Mary Jane and I nodded. Though the shopping bags were in short supply, we procured a few from the front of the store and dutifully dug into the piles of brassieres. I grabbed a turquoise-and-white satin push-up, a soft lavender lounge-around, a nude-colored everyday, a white strapless, and a lacy black demi, plus a handful of others.

Mary Jane lingered by the cash registers, sifting through the shelves of thigh-high stockings and perfumed drawer liners. She was the lookout, the distraction, the buffer—disguised as a gorgeous blue-eyed, blond-haired, God-fearing sixteen-year-old girl.

Though I probably looked like a total dork, I couldn't stop smiling at everybody I came into contact with as Whitney and I joined the dressing-room line with our bags of lingerie. A brunette with a lizard tattoo on her ankle mistook my exuberance for a request to measure me. She detangled a tape measure from her neck and fingertips and held it ominously close to my chest.

I shook my head. "I'm okay. I already know what size bra I wear. Thanks, though."

Peering into my shopping bag, she didn't back down. "Some of those are A-cups, some are C's. I'm just trying to help you figure out your real size, hon. Nothin' more pitiful than a girl wearing the wrong size brassiere."

I coughed, attempting to camouflage my laughter. Thankfully, my turn came up. "Well, just let me know if you want a different size," the lady called out.

I locked the door. As Mary Jane had predicted, discarded lingerie items littered the tiny room, the number of sloppy shoppers clearly outweighing the number of dressing-room tidy-uppers. Whitney hummed happily in the dressing room beside me, and I wondered if she would hear my pathetic attempt to harmonize. I imagined lifting the wall between us—

like an old-timey movie screen—and seeing her doing exactly what I was doing. Every movement instinctively synchronized, we connected in a way that verged on spiritual.

After I pulled my treasured thrift-shop T-shirt over my head, I checked out my reflection in the narrow, smudged mirror. My cheeks were flushed, my eyes open wide, the microstud glimmering on my nose, my bosom amply padded by the four layers of satin and lace and whatever else bras were made of—I looked beautiful. Exciting. Dangerous. Not anything like the crybaby flunking Mrs. Oliverson's pop quiz that morning.

I opened my purse and took out the darkest lipstick I owned—a color called "The Devil Wears Red." I swept it across my lips, careful to coat even the innermost corners. Then I leaned forward and kissed the mirror, right in the middle, temporarily fogging it with my breath. I could've stood there in the limelight worshipping my reflection for hours. But as was the plan, I had to keep up the harried speed of the bargain hunters.

My phone beeped, and Mary Jane's *3 minutes* message flashed onto its screen: meaning I had three minutes to make it from my dressing room to the front of the store. No problem. I handed my shopping bag—full of my random-sized red herring items—to the dressing-room attendant and acted bummed that none had worked out.

The crowd had grown since I'd been in the dressing room.

Yet the shoppers looked out of focus and seemed to be moving in slow motion, making it simple for me to locate my two friends. Whitney stood by the lotions display, rubbing her hands together. One of the glossy cashiers passed Mary Jane a Bare Essensuals signature shopping bag and thanked her for her purchase. We watched each other through the corners of our eyes, coordinating a synchronized exit. I held my breath, my heart beating like a rabbit's. No alarm went off. The mall absorbed us. We were safe.

Happy.

High.

I tried to hold on to the feeling even when I got home, knowing that by this time tomorrow, Mom would know about my pop quiz in English and all hell would break loose.

When Mrs. Oliverson passed back our pop quizzes the next day, she said, "Nice work," to the guy sitting in front of me and when she stood beside me—which she seemed to do for an entire hour—she placed the paper on my desk facedown. No "nice work" for me. Not even a measly "nice try." A knot formed in my stomach and I put off the inevitable for several excruciating minutes.

"How'd you do?" Bridgette asked. After the Sadie Hawkins disaster yesterday, I wasn't sure she'd ever speak to me again, but as Gabe predicted, she seemed to have bounced back. She flashed her A paper in my face and I gave her a thumbs-up. The knot in my stomach intensified into a cramp as I flipped over my quiz and saw a big fat C.

I told myself it was better than a D or an F, but the reality was, a C was as unacceptable in Mom's eyes as the lesser grades. Average. Seventy percent. Horrible. Unacceptable.

After that, the cramping sharpened every few minutes, and I could barely stand by the time I got to my physics class. The classroom smelled fustier than usual, and I desperately needed some fresh air. With a quivering hand, I filled in the answers to the test as best I could, skipping over the ones I didn't know. It was multiple choice, my weakest test style, but I knew deep down that I hadn't prepared enough.

Oh, I'd had every intention to study long and hard for it. When I got home from the mall, I'd gone straight to my room, stashed my stolen lingerie under my bed, and got out my physics stuff. But I kept zoning out, the "Puppies of the World" screen saver scrolling through until I'd lost count of how many times the baby Rottweiler came on. I'd IMed Whitney and Mary Jane and daydreamed about our next heist. Maybe we could take Whitney's little sisters to a store and stealthily drop merchandise into their stroller. Or perhaps we should hit the video store, take some DVDs into the bathroom and break the little sensor gizmos, and then stuff the DVDs in our purses.

I'd stayed up all night, but not because I'd been studying. Every time I started worrying about my grades, I'd try and squelch it with fantasies of shoplifting. But that's what they were: fantasies. Because I'd promised myself I wouldn't shoplift anymore.

"Okay, time's up," Mrs. Clemmons said. I quickly filled in a few more bubbles, guessing *A*, *C*, *C*, and *B* for the ones I'd skipped. "Pencils down, and pass your test to the person behind you."

The teacher sat on her desk and played with her straw-like hair while she read off the answers. Beads of sweat trickled down my forehead. If I could get the school nurse to call my mom and say I was deathly ill, would Mrs. Clemmons let me retake the test another day? Two bad grades in one day was too much. I raised my hand.

"Yes, Poppy?"

But what if the nurse wouldn't help me out, or if Mom insisted on taking me to the doctor and all he found was a bad case of nerves? "Um, sorry. I missed the last few answers. Can you repeat them?"

She quirked her lips and repeated the ones I'd missed, then read the remaining answers. When the chick who'd graded my test gave it back, I just stared at it. No matter how much I blinked, the big red B-minus wouldn't go away. Class ended but I didn't budge from my desk.

"Hey kiddo, you okay?" I looked up to see David Hillcrest, WHEN GOD MADE ME, HE WAS ONLY SHOWING OFF printed across his T-shirt and his green eyes full of concern.

"Yeah, I'm fine. Just a little tired or something." The room had cleared out, leaving just the two of us behind.

He took the pencil from my grasp. I hadn't even realized I'd smashed its entire tip, and splinters of wood and specks of lead peppered my test paper. After using the sharpener in the back of the classroom, David presented the pencil to me with its new, perfectly whittled tip. Next he lifted the pencil—and my hand—up to his lips and kissed the back of my hand. Heat rose to my face. I hoped he didn't notice how much he got to me.

"That's the customary ending to the Texan pencil sharpener ritual," he whispered.

"You seem to have it down pat," I said. And he seemed to have making me smile down pat as well.

"So was our forlorn friend hiding out in the gym yesterday?" he asked.

"What can I say? You were right."

"And everything's cool now?"

"Between Bridgette and me? Yeah, I guess so."

He sat on my desk and crossed his arms over his chest. "So are you going to tell me what's eatin' you, or do I have to get nasty?"

"Really, David, it's nothing," I said. I didn't want to admit I was some kind of grade freak.

He hopped off my desk and handed me my backpack. "Okay, how about after school we go play some paintball?"

I sighed. "I can't. Maybe another time."

"You sure are good at doggin' me."

"I'm not dogging you, David, it's just that . . ."

He raised his eyebrows, waiting for me to finish my sentence.

"Please . . . don't give up on me."

CHAPTER SIXTEEN

Mary Jane dropped me off at home after school, and I went directly into lockdown-study mode. My only hope was these grades would somehow slip under Mom's radar. But I knew they wouldn't. The woman had an uncanny ability to sniff out every "bad" grade I made. I'd just have to start preparing for next week's exam and hope she'd give me a break if I could swing an A-plus.

I tried to study with music on, my typical *modus operandi*, but even when I flipped through different playlists, the music felt like mosquitoes buzzing around my ears. And turning the music off only made the grandfather clock in the hall sound like Big Ben. I couldn't concentrate. I needed to get out of the house.

I texted Mary Jane and Whitney: *I need a break. Want to go shopping?* and anxiously awaited their responses. Whitney's answer came first: *Sorry, hon, babysitting the wonder twins and have to write an article about the GOV Club.* I waited anxiously for Mary Jane's reply but then remembered she'd mentioned going over to Andrew's house.

I looked up Andrew's number in the church directory and punched it into the phone. Andrew answered, "Hello?"

"Hey, Andrew. It's Poppy."

"Well, hello there."

"Yeah, hi. Um, can I talk to Mary Jane? That is, if she's . . . you're . . . not too busy?"

"Okay, sure. We're just . . . watching TV. Hang on, I'll get her."

I heard muffled voices and a girlish shriek before she came on. "Hey, Poppy! What's up?"

Suddenly, I felt ridiculous. Why was I bothering Mary Jane over at her boyfriend's place? Had I turned into some desperate clinger? How pathetic! "Oh, never mind," I said into the phone.

After a pause, she asked, "Are you okay, hon?"

"I'm fine. Wonderful. Perfect. Sorry to have bothered you."

"Uh . . . okay. See you tomorrow?"

"Yeah, sounds great. bye."

I hung up and then put on my Converse and jogged down Holly Lane. About five minutes later, the white-and-green bus came to a screechy halt beside me. I ascended the rubbery steps and pulled out my wallet. "Does this go to the mall?" I asked.

"Which one?"

"There's more than one?" I asked.

"Well, there's the big 'un, but then there're some small ones," said the chubby, silver-haired man. "Lots of gals been going to the Clover Strip Mall lately, over on Main and Seventh."

Clover Strip Mall—where had I heard that name before? Oh, yeah! Mrs. Portman mentioned it and said there was a new store called Colleen's Closet that would be worth checking out. Today was as good as any. "All right, to Clover Strip Mall."

The bus driver said, "Okeydoke," and took my proffered money.

The six or seven passengers barely glanced up from their handheld video games and paperbacks as I lumbered halfway down the aisle and scooted into a window seat. The overhead vents huffed and puffed regurgitated air, drying out my eyes.

Finally the bus arrived at the strip mall, and out I hopped. Colleen's Closet sold a bunch of cute stuff: Urban Outfitters–like clothes, shoes, costume jewelry, makeup, books, etc. After looking at the shoes and jewelry, I checked out the tank tops. I'd been wanting to make my friends their very own "Poppy Originals." I selected a red tank top for Whitney and a pink one for Mary Jane, and then took them up to the cashier.

On the bus ride home, it dawned on me that Colleen's Closet would be the perfect place to get matching his-and-her shirts for the Sadie Hawkins dance. In the event that I wasn't grounded for getting crappy grades, of course. Would we be able to lift six shirts—two apiece—at the same time? Just thinking about it fired me up.

As soon as I got home, I ran to my room and shut the door. I reached into my purse and pulled out a cute plastic container, one of those all-inclusive, color-coordinated kits with mascara, lip gloss, lip liner, blush, eye shadow, and eyeliner. I'd seen it in Colleen's Closet and it reminded me of the makeup the lady in Hamilton's had used on me, in the shades everybody—even Mom—apparently liked on me.

Holding the makeup kit in my lap, I closed my eyes and relived the adrenaline rush I'd felt, first as I chose the perfect moment to take it, and again as I dropped it into my purse. When I'd walked out of the store with it, my heart pounded and I felt euphoric as the oxygenated blood surged through my veins. And the high I felt from knowing I'd gotten away with it stayed with me as the bus drove me home. It felt awesome, and I couldn't wait to do it again.

I opened the homework file on my laptop. I nudged Mary Jane and Whitney on IM and typed:

> **Poppy15**: I know where we're getting our matching shirts for Sadies, ladies.
>
> **JesusRocksMyWorld**: Awesome!
>
> **NickelsW**: Let's hear it
>
> **Poppy15**: Colleen's Closet. Plenty of shirts that can work for girls or boys
>
> only 2 ppl work there
>
> no inventory control tags
>
> **JesusRocksMyWorld**: Sounds perfect. Good job, Poppy.

I thought I heard a knock. I turned down the Social D track and typed *TTYL* before saying, "Come in."

As Mom opened the door, I minimized my IM box. "Sorry I had to work so late. I'm going to pick up Chinese. What would you like?"

"Um, how about Szechuan chicken?"

"Mmm, that sounds good. So what have you been up to today?" She tucked her blouse into her pin-striped trousers where it had come loose.

"Nothing too exciting," I deadpanned, knowing any minute I'd be getting an earful for my grades.

"Oh, what's this?" She walked over to my bed and peeked into the Colleen's Closet shopping bag.

"Just a couple of tank tops I got after school. I'm going to fix 'em up for Mary Jane and Whitney."

"They'll love that. You must really like those girls." She touched the square barrette at the nape of her neck and then ran her fingers down her sleek ponytail.

"Yeah, they're cool." *Why isn't she bringing up my grades? What kind of game is she playing?*

"I'm glad you've made some good friends, but don't let your social life get in the way of your schoolwork." *Okay, here it comes.* I sucked in a breath.

"I know, I know. I'm working on a physics assignment right now," I said, in case she hadn't noticed the winding spring diagram and graph on my computer.

She hovered behind me, and I caught a whiff of the almond-scented lotion she religiously rubbed on her skin. "How did you do on your test this week?" she asked.

"You mean you don't already know?" I turned back to the computer screen, agitated. She wasn't fooling anyone.

"I decided I would stop calling the school, provided you keep me informed."

I turned to face her, searching for a sign that she was kidding. She smiled—not a teasing one, an authentic one—and shrugged.

All sorts of sarcastic responses tempted my tongue, but if she were telling the truth—and I couldn't find anything to suggest otherwise—I didn't want her to regret giving me this wiggle room. So instead of cynicism and jokes, I decided to give candor a try.

"I didn't do very well," I confessed, still stunned. I reached into my binder and handed Mom the proof. Then, biting the inside of my cheek, I braced myself for a verbal lashing and a major blow to my future social life.

After what seemed like a week, Mom set the tests down on my desk. I looked up at her, trying not to wince. Her hands were on her hips, and she looked tired. "Once you let your grades go downhill, it's hard to get them up again."

"I know."

She exhaled loudly. "Do you want me to arrange for a tutor?"

I shook my head, wanting to make a joke about "only if

he's a good kisser" or something like that, but I was still on edge. "I'll be fine. I just hit a bad spell, that's all. Maybe when I get to know my new school and new teachers a little better . . ."

"I hope you're right, Poppy." She yawned and glanced at her watch. "Well, I'll go get dinner now."

"Okay," I said.

After she left, I stared at the door for a few minutes, puzzled. Who *was* that woman? I felt like Coraline must've felt when she met the Other Mother. Only I didn't recall having crawled through a hole in the wall, and Mom didn't have buttons for eyes.

Had what I said to her last weekend in the garden actually made a difference? And why hadn't she gone ballistic when I showed her my way-beneath-par grades? Shaking my head, I tried to make sense of it. Meanwhile, a new IM message beeped at me.

sonofapreacherman: hey kiddo, R U there?

Poppy15: Hi David. What are you up to?

Poppy15: other than bugging girls who R trying 2 do homework?

sonofapreacherman: all homework and no play makes Jane a very dull girl

Poppy15: Is that in the Bible?

sonofapreacherman: U better believe it

sonofapreacherman: R U feeling OK now?

Poppy15: better, thanks

Poppy15: I'm having a hard time pegging you, David.

sonofapreacherman: I'm here 4 UR pegging pleasure.

Poppy15: Whitney was right. Your mind *is* in the gutter.

sonofapreacherman: ☹

Poppy15: I just mean I'm not sure if you should be wearing a black hat or a white hat.

sonofapreacherman: whichever matches my shoes

Poppy15: LOL

It wasn't just something I typed for the hell of it; I really did laugh out loud.

Mom called me to dinner, and I closed my IM. If I could rewind my life, maybe I would have asked David to go to Sadie's. And I would've asked him in the single cheesiest way imaginable.

Mary Jane parked at the Clover Strip Mall, her "I Heart Jesus" charm on the rearview mirror swaying a few times before coming to a stop. The sun beat down on my head the entire ride, but when I hopped out of her convertible, I felt refreshed, like standing in front of an open fridge on a sultry summer day. Or, in the case of East Texas, a sultry early autumn day worked too.

Mary Jane waltzed by and said, "Ready, girls?"

Was I ever. The clock had taken an excruciatingly long time to reach the magic time of 2:10 p.m. I seriously wondered if my teachers had powwowed in their lounge that morning and decided to have a contest for who could whip out the most boring lesson ever. If I were the judge, I'd have to get each and every one of their names engraved on the trophy.

And then, Ellen had come over to Whitney's locker and accused us of always taking off to do who knows what and making it a point to leave her behind. Which, of course, was exactly what we'd been doing, but Mary Jane said, "Sweetie, we're not leaving you behind. We just know how important it is for you to be thoroughly prepared for your upcoming trip to Germany." Ellen had signed up to be a foreign exchange student in a teensy German town. "We're just staying out of your way so we're not bad influences, that's all."

"But that's not for three more months," Ellen argued.

"It's never too early to start packing," Whitney said. "You don't want to forget anything important."

She shrugged. "Guess not."

But anyway, there we were, *finally*, and eagerness and anticipation zapped through my body like a megaoverdose of caffeine. Six shirts with my two best friends. It was the perfect ending to the shoplifting chapter of my life. That's right: This would be the last time Poppy Browne ever shoplifted. And I was beyond excited.

Mary Jane, Whitney, and I walked through the doors. *Yes, yes, yes!* This must be what football players felt like as they ran onto the field right before a pivotal game: flags waving high, instruments blaring, fans screaming at the top of their lungs, fists pumping in the air, hearts pumping in their chests.

The three of us went our separate ways in Colleen's Closet. Mary Jane engaged one shopgirl in a lively conversation about headbands with feather accents while Whitney sent the other one to the back in search of a particular ankle boot in a size eight and a half. All the while, it seemed like I was watching a movie in fast-forward—catching snippets of what the other two girls were up to while carefully, deftly, stealthily lifting a pair of shirts for Gabe and me to wear at Sadie's.

Next I hurried over to the shoe area to act all excited about the shoes Whitney was trying on. "They totally hurt my feet, though. I think they're too narrow," Whitney said with a convincing grimace. We pretended to be terribly upset that they wouldn't be the newest addition to her fall shoe collection, keeping all eyes off of Mary Jane while she did her thing. Next, Mary Jane and I worked over the salesgirls so Whitney could swipe her shirts. I felt giddier and giddier with every passing second, a surreal, exciting thrill ride.

The feeling continued buzzing through my body as we drove away, the shopgirls at Colleen's Closet oblivious to the fact that these three chatty, well-dressed teenagers had just lifted six shirts, right from under their noses.

"Gabe's gonna look gorgeous in that," Mary Jane said, slamming on the brakes at a yellow light.

There was a commotion over in the Piggly Wiggly's parking lot. Two little boys ran circles around a reddish-orange Saturn. One had a bandanna over his face and the other wore a policeman's hat and badge. The mom piled groceries into the trunk, seemingly oblivious to her sons' rowdy game.

I folded the baby-blue-and-white-striped button-downs

that I'd held up for Mary Jane and Whitney to see. "I figured he'd look good in just about any color," I said, stashing the shirts back into my purse. Admittedly, I was warming up to the whole idea of going to a dance, though I predicted the most exciting part of it—getting the shirts—had already happened.

I looked out at the Piggly Wiggly parking lot again. The mom yelled something and the little boys filed into the backseat. Thank God *I* didn't have to be inside that car right now. Actually, I couldn't think of anywhere I'd rather be than with Mary Jane and Whitney. Who would've guessed someone like me would've clicked so well with girls like them?

Whitney held up her pair of shirts: long-sleeved burgundy tees with a gray stripe across the midline.

"Oooh. Very cool." Mary Jane hit the gas pedal. "I didn't even see those."

"They were on a shelf over by the jeans," said Whitney. "Let's see yours." She held up Mary Jane's plunder: two golf-style shirts the color of Pepto-Bismol. Whitney and I cracked up.

"What?" Mary Jane asked, all offended.

"Did you get him some matching panties?" a hysterical Whitney asked.

Mary Jane yanked the shirts away from Whitney and stared at the road ahead of her. "I happen to *like* pink. And if Andrew loves me, he'll wear it."

"That's true," agreed Whitney. "At any rate, he'll be easy to find if we lose him. The six-three dude in pink." Whitney and I started laughing again.

"That was the perfect plan, Poppy," Mary Jane said in an obvious attempt to change the subject. "Almost too easy."

My pulse still elevated from the heist and my mind buzzing, I wondered what she meant. Was it so easy it wasn't any fun for her? Had they been doing it so long, they were starting to get bored? Did they feel let down, kind of like I had when I'd stolen the pack of gum at the convenience store Bridgette's dad worked at? "So do you guys want to try something a little more challenging?" I asked.

"What do you have in mind?" Whitney asked, turning to look at me. Her beautiful dark eyes were full of expectation, and even though I promised myself not to shoplift anymore, I couldn't let her down.

CHAPTER SEVENTEEN

"What if we did it, like, old-bank-robber style?" I said, my imagination ignited by the little boys back in the parking lot.

Whitney's eyebrows lifted, and I couldn't tell if she was impressed or concerned.

"Wait. Not with guns or masks . . . well, disguises would be fun. But what if you and I grab something and run for it and Mary Jane drives the getaway car? I bet that doesn't happen very often these days."

"Sounds . . . interesting," Mary Jane said, capturing my eyes in the rearview mirror.

A mischievous smile emerged on Whitney's face. "I think it sounds *awesome*."

By the time Mary Jane turned into Whitney's neighborhood, the energy in the little VW was palpable and nearly unbearable. Kind of like when the humidity is in the upper 90 percent and it really needs to rain, but the sky can't seem to squeeze out a single raindrop.

Whitney's little sisters, Keisha and Keralee, came running up to the car, all dimples, ringlets, and curious eyes. Then her mother opened the ornate front door and said, "Oh thank goodness you're home, Whitney. I'm almost late for class."

"Sorry," Whitney said, and Mary Jane said, "I'm sorry too, Mrs. Nickels. I dragged Whitney on an errand for my parents that was way farther out than I thought, and then we had to get gas and—" The lies rolled off her tongue so convincingly, I had to give her kudos.

"That's quite all right, Mary Jane. Thank you for getting her home. Now, Whitney, there's some chicken on the counter. You can heat up some green beans, and make sure the twins have milk and not soda." When she kissed Whitney's head, she noticed me for the first time. "Hello, you must be Poppy. I'm really enjoying your mother's class at KC. I'd love to chat, but I'm late."

"That's okay. Nice to meet you," I said. Then, when Mary

Jane drove me home, I said, "Whitney's mom looks just like the Millennium Princess Barbie I used to have." The Africana Studies prof at CU Boulder had given it to me when I was a little girl. In a sparkly navy-and-white ball gown with silver accents and a silver tiara in her shiny black hair, the Barbie was beautiful. However, I didn't like dolls much—and I traded it for the neighbor girl's yellow lab, Daisy. Of course, I had to give Daisy back once our moms found out, but I let her keep the Barbie.

"Yeah, she's really pretty," said Mary Jane, "and nice, too. It's so pitiful that Mr. Nickels is cheating on her like that."

"That's for sure. Do you think Whitney will ever say anything to him about it?"

"I don't know," said Mary Jane. "She might if she gets mad enough."

"Hey, do you want to come in?" I asked when she pulled up the driveway.

"Sure."

"You can park in the carport if you want. Mom won't be home for another hour or two."

Once inside, we raided the fridge for pops and string cheese, and I unearthed a bag of pretzels from the pantry. Mary Jane's cell phone rang. She smiled at the caller ID and when she said, "Hey, hon," all mushylike, I knew it was Andrew. They talked for a few minutes while I sorted the mail and leafed through Mom's new *Time* magazine.

"Crazy kids in love . . . ," I said, fluttering my fingers.

"Yeah, I guess so. I mean, I love him and all, it's just . . . complicated, I guess." Her dazzling smile faded as she slipped her phone back into her Brighton purse.

"How so?"

She picked the salt off a pretzel. "I can't believe I'm telling you this. But I feel like I can tell you anything."

"You can." I nodded.

"There's one secret I can't even tell Whitney."

"Oh, I'm sure you can," I said, a bit surprised. "Whitney's been your best friend for years."

"When I tell you what it is, you'll understand why I can't."

"Oh."

"You see, on New Year's Eve, when Andrew and I were fooling around in Bridgette's garage . . . we . . ." Her face turned a weird greenish-white color. "We went all the way. We had sex. Made love. Whatever." While scrunching a napkin in her fist, she looked up for my reaction. She frowned. "You don't look surprised," she said, clearly disappointed.

"Lots of people have sex," I said, covering for the fact I already had a hunch, thanks to Andrew's little heart-to-heart with David at the barbecue.

She slapped the side of the counter. "I know. But not *me*. I'm Mary Jane Portman."

I got it. In her eyes, she was Calvary High's Hester Prynne. "You're not a bad person, Mary Jane. If God forgives people for murdering their own kids or burning down entire villages or creating ghastly computer viruses, He'll forgive you. No problem. Don't you ever listen to Pastor Hillcrest's sermons?"

She sucked her lower lip. She looked like a twelve-year-old, and I had this weird desire to protect her, to keep her safe from harm.

"Besides, it was just that once," I said, trying to make it seem like a little slipup instead of the heinous sin she clearly believed it to be.

Tears welled in her blue eyes and she gazed at her reflection in the toaster. "We've done it . . . seven times now. Oh, wait. Eight. Yes, definitely eight."

"Okay," I said, mortified I'd made her feel even worse. "At least you're not sleeping around with every guy at Calvary."

Finally, a slight smile and a hint of a giggle. "No. Only one, thank you very much."

"Oh, thank God," I said and pantomimed wiping sweat off my forehead. "Can you imagine how terrible I'd feel if you moonlighted as the school slut?"

"Not as terrible as I'd feel." She laughed.

"True," I said, delighted that Mary Jane Portman trusted me enough to share her deepest, darkest secret. One she couldn't tell even Whitney. I wasn't sure why she was afraid to tell Whitney—except that Whitney was the president and founder of the GOV Club, and she certainly believed it was God's divine plan for everyone to remain a virgin until married.

But did Mary Jane think Whitney wouldn't be her friend anymore if she knew the truth about her? A sad and scary thought.

"Do you have a straw?" Mary Jane asked. "Stained teeth are so pitiful." I grabbed her one out of the silverware drawer. "Thanks." She tapped the straw on the counter and removed the paper.

"I know this sounds sappy, but I can totally see us getting married. Don't worry," she said, patting my hand, "I haven't already ordered 'Mr. and Mrs. Andrew Foremaster' stationery or anything. It's just that we're so in love and . . . well, one day I asked him if he wanted to become a Born Again Virgin with me, and then he said there was no need since he had every intention to marry me someday anyhow, and he acted hurt, like I didn't enjoy being with him, which is ridiculous, and I just don't know what to think anymore." She sighed and then took a swig of Dr Pepper through her straw. "So, what about you? Have you ever . . . done it, Poppy?"

I hadn't expected that question. Buying time, I pressed a

pretzel on the middle of my tongue and clicked it against my teeth. "Well, I'm . . . um, not sure?"

"Oh my gosh! I've heard of that happening. It was all over Fox News." Her blue eyes widened. "You poor thing! So was it roofies, or something else?"

"No, no. I just mean, well, it depends on your definition, I guess." I wasn't ready to talk about my sex life, especially since it would probably lead to questions about Spence.

"Oooh," Mary Jane said, the light coming on in her eyes. "I gotcha. So did you have a boyfriend back in Boulder?"

I nodded, again buying time while I figured out how much, if anything, to divulge. I'd never talked to anyone about what really happened with Spence, and just thinking about it made my stomach plummet and my palms sweat.

Although, Mary Jane had shared her secret with me, and the fact that she found me trustworthy felt so good. I took a deep breath. "His name's Spence Farr. We had a pretty rocky breakup."

Part of me wanted to stop the conversation before it went any further, but for some strange reason, the story I'd pent up inside since last spring poured out of me. "He was kind of quiet, into poetry and music and Final Fantasy." While I struggled to string my memories into a coherent story, I peeled a strand off my cheese, coiled it on my tongue, and swallowed it.

"So did y'all hang out in the same group or something?" Mary Jane prompted.

"Yeah, pretty much." I never really felt like I belonged in any one group at Flatirons High. Most of the kids in my classes were of the brainiac variety, and I was more of an independent studier. And as for the kids I sat with at lunch and sometimes hung out with on weekends—well, what with their bangs in their eyes and Skullcandy buds in their ears, I doubt they noticed (or even cared?) I was there. Except for Spence. He definitely noticed me. "Spence wrote poetry, which I thought was really cool. I had computer lab right after him, and since I always sat at the same computer he used, he'd leave me little poems on the screen."

"Oh my gosh! How romantic."

"Sure, at first. I mean, they weren't like 'Roses are red, violets are blue' poems. They were interesting and deep and . . . elusive. But then, one day about four months into our relationship, he left his notebook in the computer room. Looking back, maybe he did it on purpose. But anyway, it was a three-subject spiral notebook where he wrote his poems and drew sketches and, well, needless to say, I'd always been curious about it. So I flipped through it, and . . ." The disturbing images flashed across my mind's eye: knives of all sizes and shapes; nooses; blood; and, most alarming of all, numerous drawings of a girl who looked just like me. In some, she looked sad yet beautiful;

in others, she was completely naked and scared-looking; and in one, she was being choked by a faceless figure and she looked completely *euphoric* about it. Bile rose in my tummy and I had to pause to regain my composure. "It was just so creepy, Mary Jane. I actually vomited, and the school nurse called my mom to come pick me up." Of course, everybody just assumed I had the stomach flu or something. I never admitted to Mom that she was right about Spence all along.

"Oh, sweetie, that's *pitiful.* What a weirdo!"

"Yeah. The next time I saw him, I gave him the notebook and told him if he ever spoke to me again, I'd take the copy I made of it straight to the school counselor." Ever since Columbine, high schools—particularly those in Colorado—took things like that very seriously.

Mary Jane leaned way back on her stool. "Whoooah."

A small smile flickered on my face. "Yeah. So I broke up with him and went out and got my nose pierced to celebrate." She raised her brows questioningly. "He hated it when chicks had piercings like that. He was okay with *ears* being pierced and the occasional lower-back or ankle tattoo, but that was it."

Mary Jane laughed. "I like your nose piercing even more now."

Leaning over, I checked out the titanium microstud in my reflection in the toaster. "Me too. So anyway, I burned the copies of his sketches and poems before coming out here."

"Cool. Seriously, Poppy, your life sounds like a movie or a book or something."

I laughed. "And the moral of the story is: 'Never get together with a guy who wears more eyeliner than you do.'"

Mary Jane almost choked on her Dr Pepper. "Oh my gosh, Poppy, you're killing me. How about, 'Never get together with a guy who wears eyeliner, *period*.'"

"Yeah, yeah, okay. I can go with that."

The grandfather clock in the hallway tolled five o'clock. Mom would be home any minute now. In my backpack, a whole weekend's worth of homework taunted me. But I had more interesting things to think about. I chomped and swallowed the pretzel, then put my hand on top of Mary Jane's. "Okay, enough about guys. Let's talk about something more exciting. What store should we hit next?" I couldn't wait to put the bank robber idea into action.

The next week was, in a word, crazy. Every time I had the opportunity to lift something, I did. If I happened to be with Mary Jane and/or Whitney, we'd do it together. But if they were busy with other stuff, I had no problem flying solo. Higher and higher, until I knew I could conquer anything that stood in my way.

I put some of my earlier plans into action, and before long, my DVDs—which, to begin with included *Heathers*, *The Breakfast Club*, and *xXx*—grew into a full-fledged movie collection, full of some I loved and many I hadn't even gotten around to seeing. And for once, I had as many lotions and potions stashed in my bathroom as my mother.

Each time I lifted something, the adrenaline rush blew my mind. And when I got home, undetected by the cameras and salespeople, unnoticed by the other shoppers, and untouched by the security guards, I hid my plunder under my bed or behind the towels in my bathroom, and I sat down and I felt . . . down. And I promised myself over and over again I'd never shoplift anything ever again.

I have enough stuff. One of these times, I'll surely get caught. It isn't worth it.

But then I'd remind myself that Mary Jane and Whitney loved my bank-robber-style shoplifting idea. I predicted it would be twice—maybe even three times—the adrenaline rush as I got from the other heists. Like Christmas!

It couldn't be pulled off with just two people, though. It needed all three of us. One to drive the getaway car and two to go into the store. Mary Jane and Whitney were counting on me.

It would be the last time.

Really.

CHAPTER EIGHTEEN

A man with slicked-back black hair strutted past us and toward the cash register. A gold name tag flashed on his sports jacket. His shiny shoes squeaked on the tile floor. Was it just in my mind, or had the man eyed us suspiciously in passing? As he spoke into the phone in a hushed, professional-sounding tone, I felt him staring at us.

We'd decided to hit a midsize department store called Mumford Brothers. It was in a run-down mall in Falcon Hills, a city about forty-five minutes west of Pleasant Acres. We were pretty sure no one would recognize us out there.

Whitney wore her beret, and I cocked my baseball cap over

my eyes. We both sported lightweight baggy sweatshirts, which provided plenty of storage room.

"Let's go," I said, praying Whitney would follow. Each time I shoplifted I felt a zing of excitement mixed with nervousness, but this time, the nervousness overwhelmed me. I rubbed my sweaty palms on the front of my hoodie and turned to leave.

Whitney reached out and grabbed my shoulder. "What's wrong, hon?"

I swallowed. "I don't know. Something just doesn't feel . . . right."

Whitney giggled. "It's *not* right—and that's why it's so much fun."

The man in the suit set the phone on the counter and took off across the men's department, searching for something specific for the caller. The caller Whitney and I knew to be a beautiful blond sixteen-year-old in a convertible VW.

I sucked in a breath and dried my sweaty palms on my sweatshirt again. My heart rate accelerated like it always did when I was on the brink of swiping something. I reached out, and in one smooth, quick motion, the green-and-navy-striped Polo sweater was balled up under my sweatshirt.

Whitney winked at me, then grabbed a gray sweater, stuffed it under her sweatshirt, and took off. "Come on," she called over her shoulder. I didn't need an official invitation to get the hell outta there. However, Whitney's legs were almost twice as long as mine, and I had a difficult time keeping up.

The man in the suit dropped the tie he was holding and ran after us. "Hey! Get back here!" I heard the smacking of his shoes against the floor; he was right behind us.

I hauled ass through the store, hot on Whitney's trail as we weaved through the watches section and zipped past the luggage. A little old lady thrust her pudgy hands in the air as if we were robbing her. Then a carrottopped man in a security-guard uniform appeared from behind a mannequin and yelled, "Hold it right there!"

I slowed down, but Whitney ran even faster, heading for the exit. I dodged the security guard and rounded a display of hosiery just in time to see Whitney disappear into the parking lot.

The security guard had me by the arm. "Now I gotcha, you little thief," he said in a husky voice. I heard different voices, but I didn't turn around. My body slammed into fifth gear and I shook him off, sprinting faster than I ever thought possible. He was on my heels, yelling. Without decelerating, I threw the sweater at his face. In his fleeting blindness, I managed to escape outside. Thankfully, Mary Jane's VW idled curbside, the back door swung open.

"Get in!" they yelled, as if I needed direction. I dived into the getaway car and slammed the door as Mary Jane peeled out, leaving the cursing security guard and a breathless saleswoman behind.

None of us uttered a word as Mary Jane steered her car to the freeway entrance. My breath amplified and my chest heaving, I kept peering out the back, paranoid we were being chased. Every car resembling a cop's freaked me out, and before long, I suspected almost every car that drove fast or erratically changed lanes. After all, lots of cops drove unmarked vehicles. And I had no clue if security guards ever left the mall premises to do the whole car chase thing, but if so, there was no telling what kind of car he (or she) would drive.

Whitney was the first to speak. "Oh. My. God." She laughed robustly. "Sorry, but there's no way to express what I'm feeling without taking the good Lord's name in vain."

"Y'all took so long in there," Mary Jane said. "I seriously wondered if y'all had chickened out or something."

"No chance." Whitney shook her head side to side. "That was . . . exhilarating beyond belief."

Mary Jane's blue eyes sought out mine in the rearview mirror. I looked down at my hands and picked at my nail polish. "Poppy, are you okay? You're awfully quiet back there."

"She's probably just catching her breath," said Whitney. "Seriously, I haven't run that fast since Mrs. Reid's perverted

Chihuahua was alive." She kind of laughed, kind of shivered. "He had a thing for my ankles," she said for my benefit. (Not that I needed to know that.) A few minutes later, she said, "Great sweater, don't you think?" waving her trophy for all to see.

"Too bad you don't have a boyfriend to give it to. How about your dad?" Mary Jane said.

"Heck no. But you can give it to Andrew if you want."

"Okay, cool." Mary Jane glimpsed me in the rearview mirror. "Are you giving yours to Gabe, Poppy?"

"I didn't get one," I said. "Had to leave it behind."

"Don't worry about it, sweetie," Mary Jane said. "As long as you had fun, who cares about a stupid ol' sweater?"

Whitney shook her head while making a sound like a deflating balloon. "Dang, girl. You should've been there." Then Whitney gave Mary Jane a play-by-play, their mutual exhilaration electrifying the entire car.

I pulled up my sleeve and examined my right arm, the pressure and the redness of the security guard's grip lingering. As much as I wanted it to, the high didn't stick.

Ever since shoplifting at Mumford's, I felt like I was about to get my period. My pores sweated, my nerves bristled, my head throbbed, and my stomach wouldn't settle. With my period, a Diet Coke or a Butterfinger usually did the trick. However, the mere thought of eating or drinking anything made me feel sicker. I hadn't touched my dinner, telling Mom my school lunch hadn't settled well.

I changed out of my hoodie and jeans and into some pajama pants and a T-shirt. Then I pulled my hair into a messy bun on top of my head. I gave the mirror a cursory glance, just long enough to see that my face looked even whiter and my eyes even darker than normal.

Sitting cross-legged on my bed, I buried my head in my hands. I closed my eyes and relived running away from the security guard for the hundredth time. Only every time, the scene played out in slower motion, each detail glaringly stretched out.

The detail that stuck out the most was being all alone. Whitney had already fled outside to safety. As planned, Mary Jane sat behind the wheel of the getaway car. Neither of them saw the security guard grab my arm. They'd missed me escaping his hold with staggering strength and speed. I'd escaped with no battle wounds—except for a bruise so faint, my friends would never have noticed it unless I pointed it out. But I felt it. It hurt. I rubbed my arm, rocking back and forth, eyes still closed.

I hadn't mentioned the security guard to Mary Jane or Whitney. Maybe I'd feel better if I did? Perhaps it would give me the sense of solidarity that was missing—to prove that, even though they weren't there to witness what had happened, they were with me in spirit.

I opened my eyes and reached for the phone. I dialed the Portmans' number and Mary Jane answered right away. "Oh, Poppy, I'm so glad you called. You'll never believe this, but after I dropped you off, Whitney asked me to speak at the GOV Club meeting next week."

Unsure what reaction she was looking for, I went with the pep talk. "You'll do great. Don't worry about it."

"She gave me a lesson plan to use. It's called 'Having a Virginal Heart.' You don't think she knows, do you?"

"Doubtful. Probably just a coincidence."

She exhaled. "Well, I'm glad you'll be coming to the meetings, Poppy. And that's really cool you got David Hillcrest to join. It's hard to get guys, you know? Whitney doesn't like him much, but I don't think he's too horrid a person."

"Yeah, he's okay." I smiled, and for a split second, the terrible feeling in my gut went away.

"So what's up, Poppy? I'm sure you didn't call me to talk about the GOV Club."

"I just wanted to tell you and Whitney about . . . something that happened today. Something bad."

"I *thought* something was wrong. You were so quiet in the car. Yes, we definitely need to talk. Let's see, Whitney's at a church meeting with her family. Something about the revival. Since her dad's a deacon, and so on and so forth, he's really involved in it. But I'm coming over. So sit tight, 'kay?"

I said, "Okay," and then hung up the phone. As I waited, I hoped telling her wouldn't be a mistake.

Mary Jane arrived a lot sooner than I expected, and I was flopped out on my bed listening to Paramore instead of waiting in the living room like a good hostess. Then again, I didn't want to risk Mom seeing me like this and wanting to talk.

A silk scarf was draped loosely around Mary Jane's neck and her diamond cross charm peeked out from between the folds. She hugged me, then held me at arm's length and examined my face with soft, concerned eyes. "What's wrong, hon? Tell me." She sat down beside me.

I reached to turn down my stereo, then changed my mind. Background noise was a good thing, in case Mom happened to walk by.

"Are you afraid of getting caught?" I asked. Mary Jane had a blank look on her face, so I elaborated. "I mean, in all of your shoplifting adventures, have you ever been close to getting caught?"

"What happened, Poppy?"

"Well, I had a bit of a run-in with a security guard."

Her eyes widened and her jaw increasingly dropped as I

told her the story. "Oh my gosh, sweetie. I'm so sorry. That must've been so scary for you." She laid her hand on my knee and shook her head. "I feel horrible."

Maybe I shouldn't have told her. I didn't want her to feel bad or guilty or sorry for me. It was my idea to do it bank-robber-style. Everything we'd done up until now, we'd gotten off scot-free. "We'll just have to be more careful from now on," I said. "It wasn't that big of a deal. Don't worry about it."

Mary Jane sat straight up. "So tell me, what did it feel like?"

"What do you mean?"

"What did it feel like to have that security guard holding your arm? Not knowing whether you'd get away?"

"Well, it made me realize we're not invincible. I guess up until now, I never really thought that much about, you know . . . getting caught."

"But you *didn't* get caught, Poppy."

I felt a smile emerging, a triumphant smile. "I suddenly had this amazing strength. It was like one second I was totally freaking out, and the next second I turned into Wonder Woman or something."

Mary Jane got this wistful look in her eyes and sighed. "I love Wonder Woman."

"I was kind of joking about that part, but I have to admit it was cool to break free from that guy. I mean, he wasn't a peewee by any means. And to outrun him and another saleswoman . . . and make it out to the car . . . "

I took a second to explore these new emotions, this new way of looking at what had happened. How could I explain it to Mary Jane, though, if I couldn't explain it to myself?

I heard the tapping of Mom's shoes in the hallway and turned up the volume on my stereo.

"You know the feeling you get from, well, doing what we do?" I said, reverting to code and lowering my voice.

Mary Jane nodded eagerly.

"It's like that, only a hundred times more intense."

Her eyes all but popped out and bounced onto my bed.

Mom knocked and said, "Poppy, I'm turning in." She opened the door and poked her head into my room. "You girls have school tomorrow, so don't stay up too late."

"'Night, Mom."

Mary Jane said, "Goodnight, Emily. Don't worry. I'll be heading home in a few minutes."

Once the coast cleared, Mary Jane squeezed my hand. "You're still in, right?"

Shoplifting gave me a new lease on life. It offered a mini vacation away from my day-to-day redundancy, frustrations, and loneliness. How could I give all of that up, just because I had a little bit of a scare?

I nodded. "I'm in."

"Good." She smiled her dazzling smile. "Because the Midnight Madness sale is coming up at Hamilton's and it's *perfect.* Totally crowded, harried employees, merchandise spilling over everywhere. Whitney and I were thinking we'd go for something really expensive this time."

"Oh, yeah? Like what?"

"There's this gold bangle watch. It has a diamond on it and it's—oh my gosh!—incredible."

"Sounds cool."

Hours had passed since I'd watched Mary Jane's headlights bounce around my bedroom walls. No matter what I tried, I couldn't fall asleep. I rolled over and checked the clock. Sixteen past midnight.

I swung my legs to the side of the bed and padded down the hall to Mom's room, where a light shone beneath her door. She lay in her bed, reading a novel by lamplight. I liked seeing her like this: in her billowy nightgown, her hair flowing in waves past her shoulders, her peaches-and-cream complexion makeup-free. It was so different from her serious-career-woman look.

"Poppy? Is something wrong?" she asked.

"Just can't sleep. Seems like I haven't had a good night's sleep in forever."

"Do you want me to tuck you in, for old time's sake?"

I laughed. "Okay, sure."

"Did you see the note by the phone? A lady named Marissa Vanderbilt-Strokes called to see if you could babysit. She also said something about hosting a Mary Kay party?"

I hadn't seen it. "Thanks."

"And a boy called."

I almost gasped out loud.

"I think he said his name was . . . Gabe."

I nodded and smiled, trying not to look as disappointed as I felt.

"*And* a boy named David." She raised her eyebrows and I gave a little laugh.

"Well, I'll just talk to them at school."

In my room, Mom fluffed my pillow while I crawled under the sheets in my bed. Then she stood and walked to my niche. She seemed to be looking at the lilac bush outside my window, but her gaze was soft and glazed, and I could tell she was somewhere far away. "When you were about four years old, you couldn't sleep because you kept hearing scary noises. You were convinced a monster lived outside your window. So I lay in bed with you, and guess what?"

"You heard the scary noises too."

"That's right. So I let you sleep in my room that night, and the very next morning we went out and bought ourselves a critter trap. When I told you the trap worked, you thought for sure a hideous monster would be in it."

"But it was just a baby raccoon," I said, the image clear in my mind's eye. "It stared at me with wild beady eyes. I begged you to let it go. And you did." I smiled, and I saw that Mom was smiling too.

"I got a raise today," she said. "Not much, but definitely enough to do a little celebrating."

"That's great, Mom. So what do you have in mind?"

"Well, you seem to be into shopping lately. How about a good old-fashioned mother-daughter shopping spree? I have a staff meeting tomorrow evening, but how does Wednesday sound? I can pick you up from school and we can head to that mall you're always talking about."

"Okay, sounds fun." It wouldn't be nearly as fun as the "shopping" I'd been doing lately, though. As I shifted under my sheets, attempting to get comfy, it occurred to me that it had been ages since I'd gone shopping and not lifted something.

CHAPTER NINETEEN

"Wassup, Poppy." Andrew Foremaster set his tray down and took a seat on the table in front of me. The table tottered with the sudden onslaught of his weight. Ellen and a few others were already there, but they were speaking German. Neither Whitney nor Mary Jane had arrived for lunch yet.

"Hey," I said. It was a generic, uninspired exchange of greetings, but I couldn't help wondering what that foreign look in his pale puppy-dog eyes meant. Was Mary Jane's boyfriend leering at me?

"Gabe's real excited to be going to the dance with you next weekend."

I smiled. "Yeah, it'll be good fun." Or not.

"Do you like him?"

I recharged my smile, fervently wishing Mary Jane would get there already. "Sure, he's a nice guy, I suppose . . ."

"That's what I thought." Andrew ran his fingers through his spiky blond hair and inclined his torso toward me. "Gabe has the wild notion that you have it bad for some other dude."

Huh? Who did Gabe think I liked? Then, as if reading my thoughts, Andrew raised his cleft chin. Clearly, Andrew was under the impression that *he* was the mysterious Other Dude. Yeah, right! Gabe didn't think I was some kind of skank who'd go for her best friend's boyfriend, did he?

"Hmm, very interesting," I said, leaning back and taking a huge bite of my sandwich so I wouldn't have to talk for a while. I looked over at Ellen, but she had her nose in her German-English dictionary.

"You see, Mary Jane and me . . . well, let's just say it isn't what it used to be." I didn't exactly feel like having this conversation with Andrew. I never thought I'd actually prefer talking about the Dallas Cowboys or lacrosse or . . . I don't know, jock straps. "Nothing against her. She's real pretty and all. But it's just that—"

I spotted Bridgette walking to her table, thank God. "Oh, hi, Bridgette," I said, my mouth totally full of turkey and provolone. Bridgette stopped midstride, and her fork fell to the floor. "Here, have mine," I said, handing her the plastic fork I'd brought for my peaches.

"Thanks."

"No problem." I tapped into my small-talk reserves, trying to make her stick around, at least until Mary Jane or Whitney showed up. I knew what Andrew was getting at, and I did not want to tread on such a volatile path with my best friend's love interest.

"Bridgette, Poppy and I were having a bit of a private conversation. Would you mind runnin' along so we can finish?" Andrew said, and I groaned internally.

Bridgette's nostrils flared, and I swore I detected a gleam in her hazel eyes. "Not at all." She took a few steps, but instead of sitting at the choir kids' table, she sat at a table just behind ours.

"Let's see. Where was I?" He traced a circle on the table with his fingertip, his emerald varsity ring reflecting rays of light like a laser gun. "Oh, yeah. So I'm no two-timer or anything, but I reckon in the near future, I'll break up with Mary Jane and that'll leave you and me. Together. If you know what I mean. How would you like that?" He smiled broadly and puffed out his chest, like he expected me to jump into his arms or something. As if.

I figured Bridgette was listening in, and I wondered what was going through her mind. Surely she didn't think I'd done or said something to turn Andrew on to me. Though it was difficult, I swallowed the mouthful of sandwich I'd been chewing and took another bite.

Where the hell were Mary Jane and Whitney? Had they ditched their third period Wednesday classes for a road trip to Dallas or something?

"I should wait until after Sadie's to break it off with Mary Jane," Andrew continued, "since you'll be with my boy Gabe and I'll be with Mary Jane."

"Now, did I hear my name?" Mary Jane asked, gliding gracefully up to her boyfriend. I felt a mixture of nervousness and relief.

Andrew's face turned red and he clenched his hand into a fist. "We were just talkin' about the dance this weekend. Right, Poppy?"

I nodded, thankful I'd been stuffing my mouth with lunch. Whitney put her tray down and wiggled in next to me.

"I see." Mary Jane flashed me her movie-star smile. "And you were saying . . . ?"

"How much I love you," he said, his face still flushed.

"Aww, you're so sweet," Mary Jane said in her baby voice, and then she kissed him on his cheek. I pitied her. She had unwittingly given her heart, her virginity, and her future to a total asshole. A total asshole who made a gallant effort not to make eye contact with me the rest of the lunch period.

I tossed my garbage and wandered out of the cafeteria. Bridgette sidled up to me and said, "Mary Jane won't be happy when she finds out Andrew's already drafted a second-string girlfriend."

"He's pretty good at that maneuver, huh?" I said softly.

Bridgette stopped under the fan and her posture stiffened. Strands of her reddish hair whipped across her cheeks, yet she made no move to sweep them away. "Yes, I guess he is."

"I've got to tell Mary Jane," I said, mostly to myself.

Bridgette's jaw dropped open. "Are you crazy? She's going to hate you!"

It would break her heart, that much was true. But Mary Jane already wasted two years on Andrew, and I didn't want her to waste another minute believing he was the man of her dreams, completely and undeniably devoted to her.

Mary Jane headed right for us, her tiered skirt flapping around her tanned legs. "Excuse me," I said to Bridgette, "but Mary Jane and I need to have a little *tête-à-tête*." I grabbed Mary Jane's arm, leaving Bridgette in the dust, and led her through the school and into a semiprivate alcove by the janitor's closet.

"What's up, Poppy?"

"I have something to tell you. It's about Andrew."

She twirled her hair, a hopelessly-in-love expression on her beautiful face. "Did you see how suh-weet he was acting in the caf? Between us, I think I'm starting to win him over on the Born Again Virgin idea. I'm thinking we'll make our commitments to each other after the dance." She giggled. "Get it? Like how lots of couples actually *do it* after prom or whatever, and we'll be *not* doing it?"

She had no idea he planned to discard her like he'd done to Bridgette two years ago. As her friend, I felt duty-bound to blow the whistle on his scheme. "What if he was faking all that lovey-dovey stuff? What if he actually wants to break up with you, maybe right after the dance?"

She twirled her hair faster. "Well, that's just ridiculous. Poppy, what do you mean?"

I shrugged. "Maybe it's just this . . . feeling I have."

Her blue eyes widened and I thought I saw a glimmer of pity in them. "You're not a romantic, are you? You think all this talk about soul mates and getting married is silly."

"Okay, well, maybe I do. You're sixteen, and you have your whole life ahead of you. I just hate to see you wasting it on some loser—"

Mary Jane planted her hands on her hips. "Andrew is not a loser, Poppy. He's nothing like your weirdo ex, Spence. He's very popular. He's nice. He's good to me. Even my parents love him. Poppy, Andrew is a *good guy*."

Sighing, I shook my head. Beating around the bush had clearly failed. "Mary Jane, you need to know something about Andrew."

"What is it?"

"He's planning on dumping you . . . and replacing you . . . with someone else."

"What?" She laughed, but her eyes appeared vacant. "Who?"

"Well, that doesn't really matter, does it?" I nibbled the inside of my cheek and stared at my grungy black boots. She still watched me, unblinking. I took a deep breath. "Me."

"You're telling me my boyfriend wants to dump me, and for you?"

"Well, yeah, but—"

"So you probably want *me* to dump *him*." The bristly tone in her voice sent a shiver up my spine. I knew I had to do some serious damage control, and fast.

"Well, I think it would serve him right if you dumped him before he had the chance to dump you. But I'm not interested in Andrew, Mary Jane. I like . . . I like someone else." I wasn't ready to admit it to myself, let alone to someone else. But when Andrew said Gabe thought I "had it bad for some other dude," there was a split second when I wondered if he'd somehow picked up on the fact that I, well, "had it bad for" David. And that split second was an exciting one—one that filled me with endorphins and possibilities. Maybe having it out in the open wouldn't be such a horrible thing after all. Perhaps I should just go for it. I squeezed Mary Jane's hand and whispered, "David."

Mary Jane's expression morphed from bitter to confused to downright delighted. "You have *got* to be kidding me! Oh my goodness." She wheezed and clapped her hand to her chest, over her heart. "Well, I never saw *that* coming. For how long?"

I shrugged, suddenly embarrassed.

"Don't you know you're obligated to tell me these things, Poppy? That's what friends *do*."

"Isn't that what I'm doing?"

"Hmm. Well, I'll let it slide this time. But we have a new rule, effective immediately. We can't keep something as important as who we're crushing on a secret from each other. Okay?"

Now that she knew about David Hillcrest, she seemed to have completely forgotten about Andrew. "Okay. Now, about Andrew . . ."

She leaned against the wall. Her smile wasn't its usual dazzling self, but a certain serenity showed through. "It's just so hard. He's been such a rock in my life. Like Whitney. Like you, Poppy." She twirled her hair and giggled. "You know what? I should've known he wasn't my soul mate. I mean, way back when we started going out, he told me I reminded him of those girlie silhouettes—you know, the ones you see on the mud flaps of big rigs?"

I slapped my forehead. "Oh, man. That's gotta go in the rule book along with 'No guys who wear eyeliner.'"

"Amen, sista! Well, Poppy, thanks for letting me know. Now I know what I need to do."

"So you're okay?" I asked, suddenly scared for her.

"Well, I'm not really sure yet, to be honest. But it helps to know I've got you to help me through it."

"Damn straight," I said.

Mom picked me up after school and we drove to Pleasant Acres Mall. First stop, the Mr. Bean coffee shop to get a hot tea for her and a raspberry chiller for me. "So what's your favorite store?" she asked. "I want to get you a new outfit or two. I heard a rumor that one of these days, it's going to start feeling more like autumn around here."

"We can try Hamilton's," I choked out as I battled a major brain freeze.

I tried on about twenty things, pretending it was just a fluke that everything I liked happened to be on the sale racks. It was really nice of Mom to want to splurge on me, and there was a time I'd have let her with no qualms, but not now. Not when we were getting along so well.

And because of that, I knew I'd play this shopping trip clean. No shoplifting.

I slipped on the next outfit: a black-and-white-plaid pencil skirt with a thin belt; a silky, high-necked white tank; and a cropped gray-and-black-striped cardigan. "What do you think?" I asked, strutting my stuff in the narrow dressing-room hallway.

Mom looked up from her little lipstick mirror and grinned. "I'll never know how you manage to pull outfits like that together, Poppy. So you'll just wear your black flats with it?"

I shook my head. "Nope. I'll need some red combat boots."

She nodded. "Exactly." Though as different as night and day, we typically had a mutual respect for each other's personal styles.

I ducked back into the dressing room to change back into my clothes.

"When you get everything off, just hand it to me," Mom said, and I did. "So I haven't seen any of your schoolwork lately."

"Oh. Well, it's been a pretty uneventful week." In reality, I'd gotten my bio lab back with a B-plus grade. But I didn't want to upset Mom right before our mother-daughter shopping spree.

I heard a lady ask, "Are you ready, ma'am? I can take you over at that cash register."

When I emerged from the dressing room a few minutes later, I spotted a box pushed behind the three-way mirror, out of the way. Looked like it was full of new merchandise, stuff waiting to be set out. A brushed-aluminum-and-leather cuff caught my eye. I picked it up and admired it. It hadn't been tagged yet, so I didn't know how much it cost.

All I knew was I loved it, and holding it in my hands sparked something inside me—the same sensation I'd experienced many times before. Yes, I wanted it.

A little voice inside me said, *No, Poppy. You're with your mom. Don't even think about it.*

But it was no use. I wanted to lift it.

What about all those times you said you'd never do it again?

I had to lift it.

CHAPTER TWENTY

I made sure no one was watching. Next I opened my purse, took out some hand lotion, and rubbed it on my hands. Still rubbing my hands together, I took the cuff and dropped it, along with the lotion, into my purse. As I snapped it shut, every cell in my body danced. I felt so . . . *alive.*

I ran over to my mom, thanking her enthusiastically for my cool new clothes. She hugged me back, and the saleswoman looked on with an "aww, isn't that so sweet" expression on her face.

After Harold helped me find the perfect pair of red boots and told us about their upcoming Midnight Madness sale, we left. And, like when I'd stolen the jeans from that very store, I felt the amazing high of getting away with it.

Mom and I ate dinner at a tiny Italian restaurant with famous meatballs. Neither of us ordered anything with meatballs, though. And when we got home, Mom handed me the Hamilton's shopping bag and said, "There's a little something extra in there."

I took out a mint green box, the size used for jewelry. Inside was a sterling silver cross necklace. I loosened it from the slit in the box, and Mom fastened it around my neck.

"Do you like it? I bought it when you were in the dressing room." She took a few steps back to admire it. "I noticed all your girlfriends wear cross necklaces."

I nodded. "Yeah, they do. It's nice, Mom. Thank you." I really did like it, and I looked forward to wearing it to school.

After she left, I walked over to my bureau and checked out my reflection in the mirror. In an instant, the happy, glowing face before me melted.

I grabbed my purse off my bed and took out the leather cuff. I slipped it on and ran my fingers up and over the metal studs and along the soft black leather.

Why had I stolen it? I could've asked the saleswoman how much it cost, and if it wasn't too ridiculously priced, Mom would've bought it for me. Why had I felt the urge, the *need*, to lift it? It wasn't like I couldn't live without it. It was just a cool—yet decidedly unnecessary—accessory.

I couldn't keep from stealing something even when I was with my own mother. How could I have sunk so low?

Suddenly, the cuff felt like a shackle, heavy and imposing and restricting. I took it off—it had slipped on a lot easier than it came off—and tossed it across my room. It rolled into the darkness of my closet.

Oh, God, what is wrong *with me?* "Why can't I stop?" I whispered. I turned on my stereo, then fell to the floor, tucking my legs under me. Reaching out my arms, my face buried in the carpet, I cried.

I had to stop, once and for all. However, I wasn't strong enough to go at it alone. My shopping trip with Mom proved that. I knew I had to take drastic measures.

Then, when my tears ran dry and my stereo automatically turned off due to inactivity, I confessed to myself that I needed help. But where could I turn? I didn't want to go to jail. Every cell in my body writhed with hopelessness and shame.

I needed to admit I had a problem, to say it out loud in front of the people who mattered. I had to take control of my life, and that meant *telling* Mary Jane and Whitney I wanted out.

I'd grown to genuinely love those girls, and it terrified

me to think they might write me off as crazy. (What kind of person shoplifted every chance she got, and when she wasn't, she couldn't stop thinking about it?) Or, they might take it as a personal stab and not want to be my friend anymore. Shoplifting together had become such an integral part of our bond.

But best case scenario, they'd support me and help me overcome it. And if my stars aligned just right, perhaps I would never have to admit my problem to Mom.

I dug out the tank tops—one pink, one red—and the arsenal of adornments and tools I kept in a little tackle box. My heart weighed me down, making breathing difficult and concentrating impossible. But I forged on: sewing, ripping, cutting, and painting. Beads, sequins, shells, pieces of glass and metal, string, buttons, ribbons, thread, coins, zippers—the trinkets I'd collected over the years were born again as custom-made tops for my two best friends.

Raindrops thunked against my windowpane as I inspected my masterpieces. I hadn't even realized I'd been crying until I saw the little water marks on the material.

I folded the sequin-smattered, ribbon-stitched pink top. With its fantasylike swirled patterns and asymmetrical neckline, it screamed "Mary Jane." Knowing she'd adore it put a smile on my face.

The more exotic look of beads and fringe in geometrical patterns gave the red tank top a decidedly "Whitney" feel. I could totally see her wearing it under her beloved denim jacket. I folded it as well, then wrapped them in gold tissue paper and placed them on my dresser.

Dog tired, I lugged myself into bed. The tranquil music of late-night raindrops eventually intensified into the pounding, slapping, jarring noises of a full-blown storm. I set my jaw and flopped onto my back. Lightning struck nearby, and thunder boomed.

I couldn't sleep. Desperate, I snuck into Mom's bathroom, took her sleeping pills out of the medicine cabinet, and swallowed one.

Back in my bed, my heart pounded like I was being chased. Though my lids were closed, my eyes were wide open behind them. I tossed and turned as a jumble of recent shoplifting memories surfaced and bobbed around in my consciousness.

No one's looking. Come on! I can't keep up. Get back here! It's our secret. He's on my heels. Look casual. Can you believe it? Snap my purse closed. Three-minute warning. Open the umbrella. Run interference. A hug for Mom. You little thief! Kiss the mirror. Is that all? No one will know. Close call. Cover for them. What a rush! Shoppers everywhere. A synchronized exit. The alarms don't go off. We're victorious. We're free. Are they following us?

I sat up with a jolt. And before passing out, I realized I was trapped in my own private torture chamber.

On Thursday, I went through the motions of eating breakfast, going to school, and sitting through classes. I made eloquent small talk with Bridgette, David, and Gabe whenever I bumped into them, but for the most part, I laid low. I couldn't concentrate on anything except the conversation I had to have with my two best friends. I was scared.

"Do you really think this is a good idea?" David asked as we waited for Ellen to unlock the classroom we'd be having our GOV Club meeting in. "I mean, what if some freaks need to sacrifice a virgin or something? They could just come in and have their pick."

"It's a risk we'll just have to take, I suppose." I laughed and helped myself to the spread of refreshments by the window. I nodded at Mary Jane, Whitney, and Ellen, who congregated at the front of the classroom while David and I ducked into two desks in the very back.

Ellen stood behind the podium in her argyle sweater vest and called the meeting to order, then read an essay entitled "Why God Wants Me to Save Myself for My Wedding Night."

I had a hard time paying attention, not only because of the yawn-inducing subject matter, but because David Hillcrest kept blowing freakishly huge bubbles with his gum and poking me with his pencil. I munched on a day-old doughnut from the teacher's lounge and sipped watery Country Time while Whitney enlightened the GOV Club about famous historical people who, according to her Internet research, chose the celibate-till-married lifestyle. Like Queen Elizabeth I, Sir Isaac Newton, Andy Warhol, the Brontë sisters, Hitler, Beethoven . . . the rest went in one ear and out the other. Eventually, I completely zoned out. The meeting would end soon, bringing me closer to my moment of reckoning. Anxiety had plagued me all day, and now it had a choke hold on me.

"Poppy, do you have any ideas? *Poppy?*" Whitney asked, and I snapped to attention.

"Um, sorry." I shifted the emerald green scarf side to side on my neck. "What was that?"

"We're brainstorming ways to raise money to help spread the word about our organization to teens throughout Texas," she said, pointing behind her. So far, the words "bake sale" and "garage sale" graced the white board in Whitney's loopy handwriting.

"How about a kissing booth?"

Before I had a chance to say I was kidding, a freshman called B.J. said, "I don't think that would be appropriate."

Someone sniggered. I turned my head and saw David's

smiling face. "Hey, y'all have to admit, it's the best proposal so far," he said. I smiled back at him, and I realized just how much I appreciated our mutual sense of humor.

However, Whitney did not look pleased, and I didn't want her to be upset with me—not when I could be risking our entire friendship in short order. "How much money do we need to raise?" I asked, turning a serious leaf.

"One thousand dollars," she said.

The discussion continued. I nodded every now and then, pretending to be paying attention and actively brainstorming. At one point, Whitney was visibly frustrated and again asked my opinion. I had no clue. "Maybe we should just have the current members fork over all the money they're saving by not buying birth control. I mean, have you seen the going price for condoms?" I froze, mortified those had words escaped out of my mouth.

Slowly, Whitney's full lips curved into a smile and a rumble of laughter rippled through the room. "Not a bad idea," she said.

Afterward, Mary Jane drove Whitney and me home. Just the three of us.

"Okay, girls," said Mary Jane. "I have a brilliant idea how we can raise a thousand dollars for the GOV Club. The green scarf Poppy's wearing gave me the idea. So anyway, you know *Confessions of a Shopaholic*?"

"By heart," said Whitney.

"Rebecca Bloomwood sold her incredible wardrobe at a big auction and made a ton of money to pay off her credit card debt, right?"

"Yeah, yeah . . . ," Whitney said.

"Well, *we* can have an auction, too, and sell a bunch of our stuff."

"Stuff we lifted?" I asked.

Mary Jane nodded.

This was my golden opportunity, and I sat in the backseat trembling with fear and silently rehearsing what I needed to say. For as many times as I'd practiced in my mind, you'd think the words would just flow.

My friends chatted away about Mary Jane's idea while I grappled with the unbearable task ahead of me. Mary Jane turned onto my street far too soon.

"I have to tell you guys something. Can you come inside?" My voice sounded strained, but I couldn't help it. I liked Mary Jane and Whitney so much. I didn't want to lose them.

"Of course," Whitney said.

I darted to the kitchen and grabbed three cans of pop, three straws, and the cookie dough Mom and I bought on our last trip to the Piggly Wiggly. Strangely, my friends barely even looked at the cold, chocolate-chip mush.

Once we situated ourselves on the barstools, a surge of nausea attacked my belly and I spit my bite of dough into a napkin. I closed my eyes, blocking out the looks of concern on Mary Jane's and Whitney's faces. "This isn't easy. It might be the hardest thing I've ever done." My fingers brushed my cross charm and I opened my eyes.

Whitney took my hand. "We're your friends, and we love you."

"Um, yeah. Thanks, Whitney."

She smiled and patted my hand. "You're welcome."

"So I know you guys started shoplifting before I moved here. How long do you think you've been doing it?"

Mary Jane twirled her hair. "Gosh, I don't know . . . do you remember, Whitney?"

"Two years. Almost exactly," Whitney said, her smile having disappeared. "My first time was the same week I figured out Daddy was a lying, no-good cheater. We were coming home from church and he needed to stop and get some Tylenol at Walgreens and I stole a pair of red tights."

Mary Jane said, "You never told me that."

Whitney laughed. "It's not all that exciting."

"Can you stop?" I asked, and they just looked at me with blank expressions. "Like, if you wanted to, could you stop shoplifting?"

They exchanged a quick glance, and then Mary Jane nodded. "It's just something, you know, to break up all the monotony around here. It's not like we *need* the stuff we take. I give most of it away, you know, to people at school and at church. People who appreciate it. Why are you asking these questions, Poppy?"

The room fell silent, except for the *swoosh* of Mary Jane cracking open her Dr Pepper.

Say it quickly, Poppy, like ripping off a BAND-AID. I pressed my palms into my knees and swallowed. "I want . . . no, I *need*, to opt out. I don't want to shoplift ever again."

My friends exchanged glances, but I couldn't read whether they were angry or just confused. I braced myself, cold panic coursing through my blood.

"Why?" Mary Jane asked, her Southern drawl heavy in that single word. "Did we do something wrong?" She searched my eyes. "Is it because of the sweaters? I know that was really scary for you, but we pulled through. And I promise we'll be more careful. It won't happen again, Pop—"

"I have a problem, you guys. I tried to quit shoplifting—really, I did. I tell myself 'This is the last time,' or 'just once more,' but then I can't sleep and I can't concentrate on anything at school until I do it again. And sometimes you guys can't come, but I don't wait for you. I have to go and do it, somehow, somewhere, even if I'm alone. Even if I'm with my mom. I don't know . . . I don't know what to do." I watched a swallow fly by the window and then locked my gaze with Mary Jane's. "I think about it constantly. I swore to keep what we do a secret, and you can be sure I'll take it with me to the grave. But whenever you two have the urge to lift something . . . *please don't take this personally*, but I'm afraid you'll have to count me out."

Whitney tapped her fingernails on the countertop, her face pinched like she'd crammed a handful of wasabi peas into her mouth. "It's okay, Poppy."

There was something I needed to know before I could sleep that night. "So . . . we're still friends, right?"

"Of course," Mary Jane said, smiling warmly. She grabbed the container of cookie dough and dug in.

"For real?" I asked, and they nodded.

"Okay, hold that thought . . . ," I said and then ran to my room to fetch the tank tops I'd made them. "'Cause I don't give these to just anybody, you know." I held up the custom-made tops, and Whitney grabbed the red one without a moment's hesitation.

"Oh, Poppy." A huge smile spread across her face. "I wanted one, I really did."

"These are awesome," said Mary Jane. "*You* are awesome."

I sat back and enjoyed their reactions to the tops I'd made them, and though I was relieved we were still going to hang out, I knew things would likely change between us. I'd seen Ellen go from the Third Musketeer to just another somebody Mary Jane and Whitney said hi to in the halls and sat next to at lunch. As much as I'd miss hanging out with them as often as I had been, I reminded myself that I'd have more time to spend with other people, maybe even David.

My biology class had barely started when Mr. Kanab peered over his monitor and said, "Poppy, please come here." I walked up to his desk, racking my brain for a reason why he'd singled me out. "I just got a notice that your mother is in the office to pick you up. You're excused." He rummaged through a stack of papers and handed me last week's bio lab, with a big green A-plus on it. I'd been waiting for an A-plus to soften the blow when I showed Mom the non-A's I'd received of late, and there it was. My heart swelled with pride.

I gathered my things and headed to the school office, wondering what Mom wanted with me. Had I forgotten about a doctor's appointment? The dentist, perhaps? Nothing came to mind, but I wasn't surprised, given all the crazy shit I'd been preoccupied with.

The instant I walked into the school office, I knew something was horribly wrong. Mom stared straight at me, but it was as if she was looking through my skull at someone or something else directly behind me. Her face looked all blotchy and stone cold, her mascara smeared, like she'd been crying or rubbing her eyes.

The sign-out binder was open on Mrs. Winstead's desk, and I saw that Mom had written "personal" as the reason she was taking me out of school early.

". . . and you also have to take into account the humidity whenever you have a cake to bake . . . ," Mrs. Winstead babbled, but as soon as she realized Mom wasn't listening, she turned to me and said, "So have you asked anyone to Sadie's yet, dear? I'm sure it would make one of our boys very happy."

"Uh, yeah," I said. "I think so."

"Do you have your things, Poppy?" Mom asked, her voice so monotonous that it sounded like a robot.

I nodded, afraid that if I spoke out loud, my voice would crack. I walked with her out to her Volvo, which was parked with a front wheel on the curb. When I got in, I buckled my seat belt. "What's up?" I asked in a small voice.

"I need more time to collect my thoughts, Poppy. Just shut up for now." She sounded exhausted. I scrunched against the back of my seat, wishing I knew what the hell was going on so I could be prepared for whatever Mom was "collecting her thoughts" about.

CHAPTER TWENTY-ONE

After a long, blaringly silent drive home, Mom got out and slammed the car door. She scooped up the newspaper, then unlocked the front door with shaky hands. I followed her into the house. My nervousness and fear suddenly gave way to resentment. How dare she treat me like this. If she had something to say, *say it already*. "What have I done this time, Mom? Is this about my grades again?"

She whipped around. A section of her chignon came loose and flopped into her livid eyes. "I received a very disturbing call this afternoon." She hurled the newspaper clear across the living room. It smacked against the wall, knocking and skewing her grandmother's heirloom mirror. "Abigail Portman called to tell me my daughter is a criminal."

"What?" I felt the blood drain from my face and I fumbled for a place to sit, certain my knees would give out any second. Lowering myself onto the cream-colored sofa we never actually sat on, I tried to wrap my head around what she'd just said.

Mom sat down beside me, leaving enough space between us for another whole person, and stared out the window. "She sounded so concerned, and she asked me to let you know that she and Mary Jane were praying for you." Her pale, chafed lips quivered. "Naturally, I wanted to know what was going on, and though she wavered between telling me everything, and giving you the chance to come clean on your own accord, she eventually told me that you have a very bad habit of . . . *shoplifting*."

Mary Jane's mom ratted me out? That would mean Mary Jane ratted me out to her mom. But why would Mary Jane do that? We were best friends . . . weren't *we?*

"There was a time I would have laughed at such an accusation," she continued. "I would have told her she was delusional to think my daughter could ever do something like that. But then I went into your room." With the effort of someone who'd inexplicably gained 200 pounds in the last few minutes, she hoisted herself off the couch. My heart raced, and it took a huge amount of constraint to keep my feet from running right out the door. Though I didn't want to, I followed her into my room. "And I found these." She indicated my bed.

Suddenly dizzy, I couldn't make sense of what I saw. Were there really test papers scattered all over my bed? Some I remembered and some I didn't, but they were all bad grades—B's, C's, D's, and F's. Then I blinked a couple times and saw that it wasn't tests strewn all over my bed—it was the stuff I'd lifted. Clothes, jewelry, DVDs . . . everything. Plain as day. Proof that I was guilty of the terrible sin—the crime—Mrs. Portman accused me of.

My stomach dropped.

When had this happened? How had I lifted *that much* stuff? How had it gotten so out of control?

I'd hid all that stuff under my bed, waiting to gradually incorporate it, item by item, into my wardrobe, so Mom wouldn't notice. Or maybe I'd planned to give it away to kids at school, like Mary Jane did. But whatever the reason, the tags and packaging were mostly intact, and if I really dug deep into the depths of my mind, I might realize I never thought of any of it as *mine*. I might also find a place in my heart that was heavy with guilt.

I'd never felt such shame.

Mom turned her gaze on me, her pupils tiny specs in a sea of icy aqua. "Did you steal those things?"

I was responsible for her heartache. I'd let her down.

I felt sorry for Emily Browne, having to have me for a daughter.

The air in my room felt deflated and heavy. My entire body was crying, yet not a single tear eked out. There was nothing I could do but tell the truth. "Yes, I did."

Mom stood there like a tragic statue, seemingly letting it sink in. "I know you don't have everything your heart desires, like your friends Whitney and Mary Jane do . . ." She waved her hand over all the stuff piled on my bed. "But I've always worked hard to make sure you have everything you *need*."

"Oh, Mom. It's not about that . . ."

She stood and ran her hands down the sides of her suit. "Then tell me, Poppy. Help me understand. Tell me *why*."

A sob stuck in my throat, making my voice sound wobbly. "I don't know. I . . . shoplift something and it feels good. I feel happy. And then afterward, not so much. And I want to—no, I *have* to—steal something else." Saying it out loud made it sound so pathetic. So stupid.

"Well." Mom swallowed, apparently searching for her next words. "This is quite a predicament we're in." It seemed like hours before she said, "You are grounded, is that clear? You will not be going to your Sadie Hawkins dance Saturday night. No Internet, except to do homework. And hand over your phone."

I reached into my backpack. My fingers grazed the A-plus lab paper and twined around my cell. In the flash of time between glancing down at it and surrendering it to her, I noticed I had a new text message: *I heard Emily came to get you early. Is everything okay?* Mary Jane wanted to know if everything was okay. *Okay?* How could anything be *okay*?

"Poppy, you will return every last item to the stores you stole from. I will go with you, and it'll be up to the store managers whether they press charges or not. I don't know. I don't know." She ran her trembling hand over the things I'd lifted. "You can't keep any of this. If the stores can't take something back, we'll find a charity or something. Maybe the Hurricane Phillipa victims. I just can't believe you did this."

With that, Mom spun on her heels and stomped into the kitchen, mumbling something about "consequences." I heard the clanking of glass, followed by a shrill buzzing noise I knew was only in my head.

I thought of Mary Jane and Whitney and how much more stuff they'd lifted and how devastated their parents would be if they knew. How the entire student body of Calvary High would be floored to find out two of their elite were shoplifters. Hell, how the entire town of Pleasant Acres would be in an uproar. However, as livid as I felt, I didn't want to think about any of that.

I ducked into my bathroom and scrubbed my face—the drain slurping every last trace of light-colored, shimmery makeup down its deep dark hole. Trembling, I yanked the cross necklace off my neck and threw it on the floor.

Why did Mary Jane do this to me? And what about Whitney—was she in on it as well? Did it have anything to do with Andrew making the moves on me?

If I could go back in time knowing Mary Jane would pull this on me, I would've listened to Bridgette Josephs and stayed the hell away from her.

Then, something Bridgette had said burst into my consciousness: "The weird thing is, she acted like *nothing was wrong*. Those days before her betrayal were the days I felt the very closest to Mary Jane. Solid, you know? Like nothing could ever, ever come between us."

Well, it looked like Andrew had come between Mary Jane and me, too. Only this time, Mary Jane had something on me that she knew would ruin me.

Why?

Why?

WHY?

Midnight, and I was still wide awake. I didn't want to face Mary Jane at all, but I knew I had to, and I sure as hell didn't want to deal with all of this as a sleep-deprived zombie. Maybe

Mom's sleeping pills would help. I padded down the hall and into Mom's bathroom for a sleeping pill. Since she wasn't in her bed, I figured Mom was in her office, slaving away. But the lights were still on in the kitchen, and they drew me in like a moth.

Mom was slumped at the kitchen table, her back to me. Her left palm propped up her inert head, and her whole posture reminded me of someone on a plane who needed to sleep, yet couldn't get comfortable enough. Though she was awake, she didn't move or say anything, so I doubted she sensed my presence.

She still wore her "Professor Browne" clothes—a lavender chiffon blouse and a charcoal gray skirt—only she'd let down her hair and taken off her shoes. Once I glimpsed the bottle at her right elbow, I couldn't rip my eyes away from it. It was rectangular, with a black-and-white label slapped across its face. The bottle went up, up to her mouth, and then back down to the table with a *clunk*. Her hand trembled as it let go.

I wandered over to the table and sat across from her. Her pallor and the bluish-black shadows under her eyes made her appear old and frail and sick. She didn't look like herself at all. But the longer we sat like that, just looking at each other, the more familiar she seemed.

And then it hit me, squeezing my heart and taking the very breath out of me. She reminded me of Grandma.

"You're drinking," I said lamely. Mom used to have a glass

or two of white wine at social gatherings. But, to my knowledge, she hadn't had a drop of alcohol since Grandma died. Except for at the going-away party her CU Boulder colleagues had thrown for her before we moved.

Even then, she said she only drank 'cause people kept toasting her and she didn't want to be rude. And apparently toasting with water was bad luck. Though she claimed to be above superstition, she wanted to start our new lives in Texas with the very best luck possible. All I knew was, by the time one of them dropped her off, they must've done a hell of a lot of toasts. She couldn't walk straight and she kept laughing. She laughed, but I cried, because as I helped her into her bed, all I could think of was Grandma.

Mom shook her head slowly, like she feared the motion might cause her neck pain. "Shoplifting, Poppy?"

"I'm sorry. I know I messed up," I said. "I hate myself for it. I hate that you're mad at me. And I hate that you're drinking."

She studied the bottle of whiskey. "It's nothing, Poppy. Don't worry."

"That's what Grandma used to say."

"Fine." She clenched her hand into a fist. "Pour it out if it'll make you feel better."

After a moment's hesitation, I took the bottle and poured the amber liquid into the sink. The drain glugged it down as its sweet, biting stench infused the air. I ran the water for a few seconds, feeling so, so tired.

"Is the shoplifting . . . is it a cry for help? Are you having boy trouble? Has this move been too stressful for you?"

"No, I don't think so," I said without turning around. Actually, I kind of liked living in Pleasant Acres.

When I went back to the table, she looked up at me and pressed her lips together. "Are you addicted to it?" She raked a hand through her tangled hair and smiled a lazy, drunken smile.

"I don't know," I said. "Maybe?" Then I fumbled my way back to my room, the sleeping pill turning my world to mush.

The next morning, Mom's Volvo idled in front of Calvary High School. The flags still flapped in the breeze. The bushes were trimmed exactly the same as they had been on the first day of school. Students in ironed shirts and shiny shoes filed into the building, talking and laughing, just like every day. Nothing looked different. But everything *felt* different.

I knew I needed to confront Mary Jane, to see why in the world she found it necessary to make my life a living hell, but I wasn't ready. In the past eighteen hours, I'd hardly had time to come to grips with what had gone down, let alone to move forward.

"Mom, please don't make me go to school today."

"You're going. Now get out." Those were the first words she'd uttered to me all morning. I saw her popping Advil earlier, so I figured she had a headache—probably hung over from her little Jack Daniel's bender last night. I didn't feel all that great, either. The sleeping pill had knocked me out like it was supposed to, but I still felt groggy and shaky (though the shakiness could've been from nerves).

It killed me that Mom's and my relationship was on the rocks. We'd made so much progress the past few weeks. She'd stopped calling my school to check up on me, and I could tell she had been making an effort not to hound me about my grades quite so much. It might not be a big deal in the grand scheme of things, but it meant a lot to me. Now, however, it was worse than before we moved. Would she ever trust me again?

As I walked into the building, I tried to clear my head. But from the GOV Club poster on the bulletin board to the giggling girls who'd unwittingly accepted stolen hats, purses, and jewelry from them, reminders of my friendship with the beautiful, crazy-fun Mary Jane Portman and Whitney Nickels slapped me in the face. By the time I made it to the commons, I'd become a walking, sobbing disaster. Before anyone could see me, I sought refuge behind a big "Last Chance for Sadie Hawkins Tickets" sign.

"Who are you hiding from, little girl?" David asked in a wolfish voice.

"Just wanted a minute to myself, that's all." Mortified, I blotted my eyes on my shirt and attempted to regain my composure.

"Does that mean you don't want any company behind that sign?" He waggled his eyebrows.

I almost laughed, but I caught myself. "Okay, what the hell." I really could use a friend right about then. A *true* friend. "Come on back."

He stooped over in an obviously uncomfortable position. "So how's it going?"

"Oh, I've had better days. You know, like when a bee flew into my can of Sprite at summer camp and I didn't know and I took a sip and it stung my tongue and I went running to the nurse's office through a patch of poison oak and—"

"There's *more*?"

"Oh, yes. You see, the boy I was crushing on was at the nurse's office—with a splinter—and he got to see me in all my swollen-tongued, red-legged, tear-stained-face glory."

David quirked his mouth. "Hmm. Sounds like you need to talk to the son of a preacher, and this is your lucky day, 'cause I happen to know one. I also know a great little park just up the street with some kick-butt swings. Perfect for chitchatting. What do you say?"

"I can't ditch, David." All I needed was to get caught and have Mom be even madder at me. "I'm already grounded for who knows how long."

"Grounded?"

"Yeah, it sucks."

"It's cool if you don't wanna tell me what for," David said. "I've done things I wouldn't want you to know about. Like when I put habanero peppers in my big bro's pimento cheese sandwich and we had to rush him to the hospital." He slapped his hand over his lips and widened his eyes, acting like he couldn't believe he just said that.

"You're terrible," I said. "Thanks, David." My smile came naturally. Neither of us said anything for a few seconds. I wished I could go with him, get out of the school and into the fresh air. Plus, it would be good to sort out my feelings before I confronted Mary Jane.

"Now, back to my brilliant idea of going to the park. Let's see . . . if memory serves, once upon a time I clobbered you in a bike race. And the loser was supposed to eat three hot dogs. But you—aka the *loser*—told me you didn't like hot dogs, and I graciously allowed that terribly un-American comment to slide."

"I know, I know. I owe you. But really, David. I can't ditch. Not today."

He frowned and started rubbing his lower back. "I have an idea. Stay put, kiddo. I'll be back before you can say 'blueberry pie.'"

"Blueberry pie."

"Okay, maybe not that fast." We laughed, and already I felt a bit better.

In his absence, I spotted Gabe at the bulletin board, and after taking a deep breath, I straightened myself and sidled up to him. Might as well get this over with, I figured.

"Hey, Gabe." I touched his shoulder and he turned around. "Have a sec?"

He smiled. "Sure, what's up, Poppy?"

"I can't go to the dance with you."

His handsome face remained virtually unchanged, but he balled his hands into tight fists at his sides. "What's going on with you?" His voice sounded strained, like he couldn't quite figure out whether to be mad or concerned.

I dropped my neck back and stared at the tiled ceiling. "I'm grounded."

After a pause, he said, "Oh. I'm sorry to hear that."

He gave me an inquisitive look, but I didn't want to get into it, so I just said, "Well, yeah, it kind of sucks. Anyway, I know there're only four days to work with, but maybe you can go with someone else."

He frowned. "You wouldn't care? If I went with another girl, I mean."

I hesitated for a second, knowing full well it was a loaded question. A variation of the infamous "you're a nice person *but*," "let's just be friends," or other such let-the-poor-sucker-down-gently speeches.

But I decided the truth was the best way to go. "No. I know you want to go. I think you should go. And I think you know someone who'd be over the moon to go with you."

"Okay. Well, let me know when the ankle bracelet comes off, and maybe we can do something sometime."

"Maybe." I saw David in the distance, half jogging over to me, and I smiled. "Maybe not."

CHAPTER TWENTY-TWO

"Okay, it's all arranged," David said. "Mrs. Winstead sent messages to our teachers. We're free for a whole hour."

"How'd you get her to do that?" I asked.

He winked. "I have my secrets. Now come on."

We jumped into his pickup, and he drove to the park he'd mentioned, which was nestled between towering pecan trees. It consisted of a rusty merry-go-round; a wide, mirrored slide; a sandbox; a duck and a pink elephant to ride on; and, of course, swings with chains that shot clear into the sky. Except for the pair of gray squirrels rustling about in a pecan tree, we were all alone.

"Penny for your thoughts," David said as we headed over to the swings. He dug into his pocket and placed a penny in my palm. Only it wasn't a regular penny: It was the flattened one from the train tracks. *He kept it with him.*

I closed my fingers around the penny. "I'm not even sure where to begin. And I'm afraid you won't understand. And that you'll hate me."

"You won't believe how amazing these swings are," he said as he sat on one. Had he heard a word I'd said? "They're like magic. You just start swinging, and all of a sudden"—he snapped his fingers—"nothing's as bad as it seemed."

I slipped the penny into my pocket and lowered myself onto the swing next to him. I leaned back and started pumping my legs, gaining speed and height. For a few seconds, David and I were right next to each other, "married," as elementary school kids called it. But then I broke free and glided up into the sky. The breeze blew through my hair and into my face, and I closed my eyes as fresh air filled my lungs.

"I didn't realize I had such a fine swinger on my hands." David chuckled as he swung higher and higher.

The trees were below us, and we touched the clouds with our feet. And just when I knew I couldn't go any higher, my muscles relaxed and I surrendered myself to gravity, the peaceful rocking motion slowing steadily until I came back down to earth.

"I'm a shoplifter," I said. As I stared at my boots, my fingers slid down the chains, taking in each smooth, warm link in turn.

David reached over and lifted my chin, forcing me to look him in the eyes. Wide open green eyes fringed with dark lashes. He wasn't judging me. "That's it?"

I let out a weird snort noise and pulled back from him. "Isn't that enough? David, I'm a thief, a criminal. I'll probably end up picking up trash on the side of the highway in a neon orange vest. I might end up in jail!" He didn't say anything, and when I looked at him, his eyes were all glassy. "Did you hear me?"

He blinked a few times and smirked. "Yeah, sorry, just imagining you doing community service. You'd look hot in orange." He whistled and I rolled my eyes.

"Gee, thanks."

"Okay, in all seriousness, all of that sounds plenty bad." He laughed good-naturedly. "I just thought maybe something worse had happened."

"Well, there is losing my mother's trust . . . and losing my best friend. So I guess . . ." I felt tears welling up again and blinked to keep them from spilling out. I swayed side to side on the swing, resting my head on the chain.

"Talk to me," David said. And I did. He listened intently, nodding every now and then like he understood. He was so easy to talk to. And yeah, sometimes he'd make a reference to a Bible story, like when he compared Bridgette and Mary Jane to King Saul and David, which kind of went in one ear and out the other, but all in all, he had very good, very uplifting input.

"Well, I guess we'd better get back," David said.

"Or we can just jump in your truck, drive like crazy, and start a commune wherever we happen to be when the gas runs out."

"Awesome. You've just answered one of the questions I've been meaning to ask you."

"Oh? What's that?"

"You know, the one that goes, like, 'If we were the only two people on earth—or starting a commune, as it were—would you hook up with me?" He cleared his throat. "You know, for purely procreational purposes."

I shook my head, floored how I could be in the crux of one of the hugest tragedies of my fifteen-year-old life, and he somehow knew exactly what to do and say to cheer me up.

"No?" he asked, raising his brows.

"If we were the only two people on earth—or starting a commune, or being abducted by aliens—I'd hook up with you for purely *recreational* purposes at first . . . and maybe for procreational purposes later on, like when we're thirty."

David laughed, and as we climbed into the cab of his

pickup, I realized no matter what my future held for me, I wanted David to play a very important, very real part of it.

A mile or two down the road, David flicked on his blinker and pulled over. The truck slanted as my half sunk into a ditch full of a bunch of late-season wildflowers and a grayish lump about the size of a watermelon. "What, are you going to give that armadillo mouth-to-mouth or something?"

"Naw, poor guy's already destined for the roadkill castle in the clouds," he said, cutting the engine.

"Do you believe animals go to heaven?" I asked. I didn't know why the thought had popped into my head. Maybe 'cause fuzzy little corpses were easier to talk about than what I'd just told him at the park.

"Definitely."

"Does it say so in the Bible? I heard that if it does, it's gotta be true."

"Well, there's only one way to find out." He reached across the cab to pop open the glove compartment. I pretended not to notice that his hand dropped to my thigh, or that he didn't seem to be in any rush to remove it. He pulled out a worn black Bible, stuffing the Ford-emblematized owner's manual back in its place. He handed me the Bible. "Turn to first John, chapter one," he instructed.

I thumbed through the book, and when I hadn't found it

in a few minutes, David said, "It's at the back, between second Peter and second John."

Still no luck. He scooted closer to me, and while the Bible was spread out on my legs, he flipped the delicate pages, finding the exact page within seconds.

"Impressive," I said.

He grinned. "Bible drill champion, second grade through sixth."

"Now I'm *really* impressed," I teased.

He pointed to a verse. "First John, one eight. Read it."

"If we say we have no sin, we are deceiving ourselves, and the truth is not in us." I laid the Bible down. "That's not about animals going to heaven," I said, confused.

"I know." He jumped out of the truck, walked around to my side, and signaled for me to roll down the window. I did.

"I just wanted to let you know I'm here for you." He picked a big orange flower and handed it to me through the window. It was a poppy. "I know you're going through a rough patch, but we all make mistakes. It says so in the Bible, so it's gotta be true."

I had the wild urge to kiss him, and before I could stop myself, I leaned forward and touched my lips to his. It was a little too abrupt, but he definitely got the message and kissed me back with a sexy softness I'd never experienced before. For one glorious moment, I didn't give a damn about my upcoming confrontation with Mary Jane, my disintegrating relationship with my mother, or my shoplifting problem.

When the kiss ended, I laughed, more than a little embarrassed. David brushed a strand of my hair out of my eye, and I felt his warm breath on my cheek. Then he grinned at me like he knew I'd kiss him all along. He jogged around the hood and hoisted himself into the driver's seat. Then he started up the engine and pulled onto the road, the tires crunching on some loose gravel. A few heartbeats later, he stretched out his arm and reached for my hand.

I pulled away, just out of reach. "You sure you want to do that?" I asked.

He winced. "What do you mean?"

"They're sticky. My fingers. Sticky fingers." Each word I uttered quivered and seemed to weigh a hundred pounds. "Get it?" My attempt at making light of the situation was failing miserably.

Without taking his eye off the road, he grabbed my hand, capturing it like a frightened kitten or a grasshopper or something. He held it firmly and turned it palm-up, examining my fingers. "They don't look sticky to me." Next he held up my hand to his nose and sniffed. "Don't smell sticky . . ."

He held my hand the rest of the drive back to school. His

hand was warm and dry, and I liked touching it. We didn't say much. I felt drained, like I was on the mend from a wicked stomach flu. It was an oddly peaceful sensation, though, like maybe someday I'd be ready to take on the world. When David pulled into the student parking lot, he slowly let go of my hand.

"David?"

"Mmm?"

"Just so you know, you definitely wear the white hat," I said and hopped out.

"Poppy, Poppy!" The soft Southern drawl that used to make me happy now made the bile rise in my stomach. Then I saw she had the gall to wear the top I'd made especially for her and my blood boiled. She separated herself from the gaggle of girls who surrounded her and walked briskly over to me, her flouncy skirt swaying and her honey-colored curls bouncing behind her plumed headband. Her features registered a sense of urgency and perhaps a bit of concern, so I held my tongue and waited to hear what she had to say—praying David was right and there was a logical explanation, a simple misunderstanding, *something* to attest that Mary Jane and I still could be friends.

"I heard you backed out of going to Sadie's with Gabe. Is it true?"

Was she talking in some kind of code, or was that really

what she was so determined to talk about? I decided to play along.

"I'm grounded. I had no choice."

"Seriously? Oh, Poppy. I thought for a minute you'd figured out a way to go with David or something. But grounded? How pitiful! What did you do? It's not your grades, is it?"

I shook my head, the same head that couldn't figure out what the hell was going on. But I was sick of playing her little game. It was time to call her out on it. "I'm grounded for shoplifting. You of all people should know that."

"Shoplifting?" She held her hand up to her mouth, and her big blue eyes looked side to side, as if she couldn't believe she'd just said the dirty word out loud.

"Yes, shoplifting. Apparently your mother found it necessary to call my mom and let her know you two were praying for me to stop."

Her hand slowly lowered to reveal her wide-open mouth. Just then, one of the Ulrich twins walked by and called, "Hey, Mary Jane. Cool about your mom winning that golf tournament." Mary Jane gave her a limp wave but never took her eyes off of me. "I have no clue what you're talking about, Poppy. How . . . ? How did my mom find out?"

"You tell me," I snapped. I put my hands on my hips and waited.

Mary Jane lifted her eyes to the ceiling. "You're mad at me. I can tell. But I swear, Poppy," she said, looking at me now, "I never told my mother. Why in the world would I do that?"

"I don't know," I said bitterly yet honestly. "That's what I've been trying to figure out. Maybe someone got suspicious, and you pointed your manicured finger at me. Maybe I don't fit into your perfect little life anymore? Maybe it's because of Andrew."

"Andrew? What's *he* got to do with it?" she asked, her face getting paler every second. She swallowed, and I heard the faint *gulp*. "Are you trying to pick a fight with me so you don't feel guilty when you go for Andrew? Is that what this is all about?"

I rolled my eyes. "This is about the fact that your mom called and"—I made the quotes sign with my fingers—"'spilled the beans' and now I'm in deep shit. And I'm not really sure why I'm the only one in deep shit, because I thought we were all in this together, Mary Jane."

"Poppy, I feel terrible your mom found out, but I don't—"

"You really had me going." I clenched my hands into fists, digging my nails into my damp palms. "I thought we were friends. But you're nothing but a two-faced bitch." Though I truly thought I meant it, I couldn't come to look Mary Jane in the eye after I'd said those words.

The tune of "Amazing Grace" filled the hallway. Lockers

slammed and kids scattered this way and that. Neither Mary Jane nor I budged, not even when Whitney came over to show us an article in the local paper about the GOV Club.

"I have to go," I said, the hymn nearing its end. "I can't be late."

"Okay, you can just take it and read it whenever you get the chance," Whitney said, completely oblivious to the tension between her two best friends. I grabbed the newspaper and hurried off to my second-period class, more upset and confused than ever.

"I heard you're not going to Sadie's anymore," Bridgette whispered as I got out my paper and pen. Normally I'd freak over having my personal life exposed at Calvary High Gossip Central, but I was still struggling to comprehend why Mary Jane acted like she didn't have anything to do with her mother's call. Or didn't even know about it, for that matter.

"That's a bummer if it's true," said Bridgette. "You never can believe anything that goes on around here, though. Not without hearing it from the horse's mouth."

I nodded distractedly. "It's true. So if you want to ask him again, he's up for grabs." What the hell. I figured if Gabe really didn't want to go with Bridgette, he could man up and tell her no. And then Bridgette could start the arduous process of getting over it.

"I saw you and Mary Jane talking in the hall just now. Y'all looked like you were in a fight or something."

"I don't know, maybe," I said, copying the teacher's notes as she scribbled them on the whiteboard.

"Well, I hope not. Fighting with your best friend is the worst. I'll be praying for you."

Remembering something I still needed to do, I pulled my purse out of my backpack, and then took the Claire's Club card out of my wallet. "Take this," I said, giving it to Bridgette. "Give it to your boss or whatever. It's for the earrings."

She twirled the card in her fingers and flared her nostrils. A little while later, Bridgette raised her hand to ask a question. Maybe I was just hypersensitive to somebody else's good mood, since I felt so sad and hopeless, but as her melodic voice filled my ears, I could tell something had lifted Bridgette's spirits. A cheerful energy radiated from Bridgette, and despite the fact that she sat in the confines of her desk, I sensed a rare spring in her step.

I closed my eyes and recaptured the memory of swinging beside David—high above the pecan trees, gliding through the air, my feet in the clouds—and tried to wipe away my despicable shoplifting problem, like Mrs. Oliverson erasing the whiteboard.

CHAPTER TWENTY-THREE

"We'd like to speak with the store manager, please," Mom said to the lady at the makeup counter at Hamilton's.

I felt exhausted from a long, turbulent day at school, and now my shame and fear merged into an emotional muddle. Though it was difficult to admit, I agreed with Mom that I should do this; it was only right. But returning something under completely legit circumstances—like something that didn't fit or work or whatever—was tough enough for me. I couldn't even begin to imagine the humiliation of admitting my crime to the stores I'd stolen from. And then being at the managers' mercy as to whether they had me arrested . . . ? I couldn't bear to think about it.

The miasma of designer fragrances got the better of me, and I coughed.

The lady looked at Mom and then at me, and I wondered if she remembered putting shimmery makeup on my face the day I became a shoplifter. Had it really been only a month ago?

In my mind's eye, I saw Whitney and Mary Jane playing with the makeup samples, laughing at each other. Then, when the makeup lady had finished with me, their sweet, approving smiles. I'd felt so pretty that day. Now I'd never felt uglier. My hands went all sweaty as I realized this was the first time I'd gone to the mall without shoplifting something—anything—for quite a while. I coughed some more.

"Just a moment. I'll see if she's available." A moment later, the lady hung up the phone and said, "If you'll just go up the escalator and take a right, her office is beside the gift-wrapping booth."

Since stepping foot into the department store, Mom hadn't given me a cursory glance, let alone spoken to me. I would've sworn she didn't even know I was there. However, once we stood outside the door with MALLORIE LIVINGSTON, MANAGER on the nameplate, she squeezed my hand. A small gesture that told me she still loved me.

Mom rapped on the door twice. I wasn't sure if her inhale or mine was deeper.

"Come in," a woman's smooth baritone voice called.

A dead ringer for Queen Latifah—only younger and with short, curly hair—peered at us over her funky reading glasses and inclined her head toward two small armchairs in front of her desk. "Please, ladies, have a seat." Before resting her elbows on the desk, she moved a 32-ounce Coke cup to the side. Pink lipstick coated the top of the straw. I wondered if she always drank out of a straw to keep her teeth from being stained by cola or tea. Like Mary Jane and Whitney.

I caught a whiff of pizza and noticed a personal-sized pizza box in the tiny wastebasket. Usually, I adored the smell of pizza, but it didn't play well with the butterflies in my stomach.

"So what can I do for y'all?" Mallorie asked.

Mom leaned back and crossed her legs, her foot flexed in what appeared to be a very awkward position.

I set the shopping bag on the Oriental rug and sat down, feeling like the Tin Man before his WD-40 spa treatment in the Land of Oz. I swallowed, unable to generate enough saliva to speak without croaking. "My name is Poppy Browne. I came here today . . . I shoplifted from your store, and I'm here to bring everything back. I wore some of it, and I will work like crazy to make enough money to pay back every penny I owe." I gnawed on my lower lip for a second or two, then added, "Plus, of course, any punishment you feel is appropriate."

I lifted the shopping bag onto her desk, its weight straining my muscles. Mallorie's brown eyes grew even bigger as she peered into it. She smacked her lips and blinked. I sunk into my chair, expecting the worst. For some reason, though, I wasn't afraid. Whatever happened happened. I'd live through it and go on many more years, though my life would be decidedly different.

Finally, Mallorie spoke. "Poppy, how old are you?"

"Fifteen."

She nodded contemplatively and pulled out a few of the things in the bag. "Old enough to know better . . ." She examined the True Religion jeans, then refolded them and lay them on her desk. "I have to admit, I've never had a shoplifter turn herself in."

I scratched my ear and said, "Yeah, kinda defeats the purpose." Mom shot me a death glare. "Er, I'm just kidding. I make jokes when I'm nervous. What I meant to say was, I'm very sorry I stole these things, and I feel horrible, and I want to make things right." I gave Mom a little smile. "I'll do whatever it takes."

It seemed like forever before she addressed us again. "There's a lot to be said for a young person who takes responsibility for her actions, I hand you that. And I have a feeling that you won't ever shoplift again. With that in mind, you are banned from Hamilton's for an entire year. Also, you will pay

Hamilton's the cost of the merchandise that can't be sold. I will have to do some figuring, but I estimate the total to be around five hundred dollars. The items that cannot be sold, whether they've been damaged or washed, will be donated to the local women's shelter."

I nodded along with each of her commandments, and when she seemingly finished, I asked, "So you're not pressing charges?"

Mallorie folded her hands on the desk. "Don't make me regret my decision, Poppy." I sucked in a breath and gave her a big smile.

"That went surprisingly well," Mom said once we were back in her car. "I wouldn't expect every store manager to be that easy on you."

A dark cloud still hovered over my head, but I got the feeling that a ray of sunshine was trying to gain enough strength to break through. Then Mom said, "Now we'd better hurry home. I have some research to do."

Something gnawed at me, something beyond the accountability of raising hundreds of dollars and the possibility of another store manager pressing charges. I couldn't get Mary Jane out of my head. She had a point: Why would she tell her mom about my shoplifting? It was too risky; it surely would come back to bite her in the ass. It made no sense. But if she didn't tell her mother I was shoplifting, who did?

While Mom spread the Indian food on the kitchen table, infusing the house with scents of curry and steamed rice, I helped myself to a cold Dr Pepper and unloaded my backpack. I briefly glanced at the newspaper article about the GOV Club Whitney had given me on Tuesday.

"That's Mary Jane's mother, isn't it?" Mom pointed at the newspaper with her chicken-loaded fork. Sure enough, a color photo of Abigail Portman in a preppy golf outfit holding a huge, shiny gold cup graced the front page of the *Pleasant Acres Examiner* sports section. "Looks like she won the Magnolia Cup Open," Mom said.

I couldn't bear to look at Mrs. Portman's sunny, gorgeous face without despising her for calling my mom. Why couldn't she have kept her mouth shut? Or at least talked to me about it first?

But Mom was reading the stupid golf article, so while I waited patiently for her to finish, I scanned the first few lines.

"Mom? What time did Mrs. Portman call you on Monday? You know, when she called to tell you I shoplifted."

Mom shrugged and wiped her lips with a paper napkin. "I don't recall. Why?"

"Think hard, Mom. I need to know."

"Let's see. I came home for lunch at noon, so it would've been around one, I guess."

Which would've been in the *middle of the golf tournament.*

Mom picked up the phone and scrolled through the caller ID. "Hmm. I don't see the Portmans' home number on here that day."

I shook my head over and over again, trying to splice it all together. I snatched the phone from her. The only phone number it could've been was one that appeared to be a cell number.

"Can I see my cell?"

She took a bite of curry, swallowed, and then took a couple sips of her tea. "I'm afraid not."

"I'm not going to call anyone. I just need to see something real quick. Please?"

"I'm going to heat this one up in the microwave," she said, indicating the bowl of chicken curry we were supposed to be sharing but that I hadn't sampled yet. And while she was up, she fetched her purse and laid my phone in front of me.

"Thanks, Mom." I powered it on. A picture message—one from David—waited for me. Excitedly, I opened it, hoping Mom wouldn't notice. It was a snapshot of a poppy. I couldn't tell what it was on; but on second glance, it looked like a swing. Yes, definitely a swing. So cheesy yet sweet. It meant the world to me that he was thinking of me. Next I noticed an old text message that Mary Jane had sent. Quickly, I clicked on it. *Mom's having a soiree at our house Sat. night at 7 and wanted me to tell you your mom must come. Oh, and remember the Midnight Madness sale! Yay!*

Ah, yes, Hamilton's biggest sale of the year, promising crowds and chaos and the perfect opportunity to lift the gold-and-diamond watch Mary Jane had her heart set on. Would they still go for it, after all that had happened?

The microwave beeped. "What are you doing?" Mom asked.

I deleted the message. "Um, nothing. Just getting to my contact list." I scrolled through the numbers programmed in my cell phone, my hands shaking as I highlighted the number Bridgette Josephs had given me on the first day of school. An exact match. Oh my God. I lost my balance, but luckily a barstool caught me.

It was as if all the lights in the world turned on at once, and I could finally see through all the confusion. I wasn't dog-paddling, and I wasn't drowning, either. I was swimming. Against the flow, for sure, but at least I was getting somewhere.

"Mom, Mrs. Portman's voice . . . was it *musical*?"

She sat on the barstool and set the steaming bowl of nuked chicken between us. "I guess I could describe it as such. . . . Poppy, what is going on?"

"Bridgette totally set me up, Mom. She knew that Mary Jane, Whitney, and I shoplifted."

"Wait. You're telling me Mary Jane and Whitney do it, too?" Her voice wavered with disbelief.

"Yes." I knew that in the last thirty seconds, Mom's impression of my two best friends took a drastic fall from grace into a sticky puddle of imperfection. I could only hope she would allow me to keep hanging out with them. That was, if they even wanted to hang out with me.

Mom's forehead furrowed. "Your friends got you into it? The shoplifting was peer pressure?"

"Maybe a little, at the very beginning. But, Mom, that's not the point. It's Bridgette." The lying, conniving little monster! "Mary Jane and Bridgette used to be best friends until a musical and a boy and money came between them. Bridgette hates Mary Jane for that, and she hates Whitney for being her replacement, and now me for letting her go ahead and ask Gabe to the dance when he'd already said yes to me. Bridgette hates all of us and formulated this evil plan to get me to hate them—to get us to hate each other. Which, of course, began with a call to you"—I was almost shouting by then, but I couldn't help it—"*pretending to be Abigail Portman.*"

Had Bridgette banked on me being grounded for Sadie's,

leaving Gabe up for grabs? And had she predicted I'd have a mega come-apart with Mary Jane and Whitney, subsequently betraying them and totally destroying all three of our reputations? Was *this* her big plan to give Mary Jane a taste of her own medicine, to make her suffer in the way she'd made Bridgette suffer so long ago? My head spun. I had so many questions, and I wanted to pin Bridgette down and demand to know the answers. *How dare she toy with my life*—our *lives—like this!*

And what about Mary Jane? An avalanche of emotions blindsided me: pure joy, followed by relief that Mary Jane had told the truth—she had no idea her mom called because her mom *hadn't* called. All that rage I'd felt toward her—totally unwarranted since Mary Jane hadn't ratted me out after all. And the anguish on her beautiful face when I'd called her a bitch. Remembering those things made me feel sick. Nausea set in—so intense, I could hardly see straight. Then, it felt as if the sky was falling and there was no escape.

I grabbed Mom's hands, my entire body trembling. Forcing myself to speak slowly and clearly, I said, "Mom, I know I'm grounded, but can I please use my phone? I need to talk to Mary Jane. And then to Bridgette, to tell her just how unimpressed I am with her evil scheme."

"You can talk to them at school."

"I know, but it's important. It can't wait that long. I've got to let her know what Bridgette did and that we'd been deceived and that I'm sorry I ever doubted her."

She blinked several times. "You know, Poppy, I'm not condoning what Bridgette did, but I have to admit I'm glad she did. Otherwise, I might have never found out about your shoplifting problem. Now, please eat your dinner before it gets cold again."

She had a point, though it was unpleasant to my ears. Maybe being out in the open about my problem wasn't such a terrible thing after all. Perhaps Mom knowing about it was my best ammunition to stop shoplifting once and for all. Regardless, it killed me that I'd called the best friend I'd ever had a two-faced bitch.

Thunder crashed and rattled the whole house. It was crazy how quickly storms rolled in around there.

"Mom, I called Mary Jane a bitch. I'm pretty sure other people heard, too. I was awful. I really want to apologize to her. I know you think Mary Jane and Whitney are terrible people because they shoplift, but they're the best friends I've ever had, and—"

"I don't think they're terrible people."

"You don't?"

"I just want what's best for you, Poppy."

"I know. You always say that."

I sunk onto the barstool, trying not to look as disappointed as I felt. No one said anything for quite a while, and as I picked at the goopy rice, I watched the rain out the window.

Mom took a few bites of her dinner and then stared down at her plate. "Maybe I should step back from time to time and let you have a say in what's best for you."

"You mean it?" I asked, astonished.

"I do." She sighed as she handed me the phone. "All right. Hardened criminals are given one phone call, so I might as well extend that formality to you. One phone call."

"Cool, thanks, Mom." I pondered for a few minutes whose number to dial. Which mattered most—giving Bridgette a piece of my mind or giving Mary Jane a much-needed explanation?

I dialed Mary Jane's cell number, grateful to Mom for giving me the opportunity, yet nervous to actually speak with my friend. Her voice-mail message came on, and I felt disappointed. Not that I was surprised. She probably saw it was my number and decided not to answer. I couldn't really blame her. I left a message anyway: "Hi, Mary Jane. I'm kinda wondering what you're doing. And I'm kinda thinking some of what you're doing is hating me. And I kinda feel bad about that. No, I mean, I *do* feel bad about that. Really bad. I'm not really allowed to use the phone when I'm grounded. Mom just made an exception 'cause she gets how important it is that I talk to you. So I guess I'll just have to talk to you at school. Okay, bye." I knew it sounded like I was shit-faced or something, but I didn't feel like rerecording it, especially with Mom right there, so I just hung up and handed over the phone.

"That went well," Mom said.

"Liar." I smiled for the first time in a while and then took a bite of chicken. "Oh, I almost forgot. Mary Jane's mom invited you to a party she's having this weekend." I jotted the details down on a sticky note. On one level, I knew it was a waste of ink and paper. I'd been trying to get Mom to do something social since we'd moved with no success. But then again, I didn't want to give up. "It'll probably be really fun, and you can meet your own fancy friends. You should go." I passed her the sticky note.

"Hmm. Maybe I will." She folded the note in half and smoothed it out.

After slinking back to my room, I powered on my computer and halfheartedly worked on my European History homework. About thirty minutes later, I thought I heard Mom's voice so I turned down my stereo and wandered into her room. She'd lit her green tea candles and lowered the lights, creating an atmosphere that was at once revitalizing and peaceful.

Mom was sprawled across her chaise lounge in her terry cloth robe. "Thanks for the invitation, Abigail," she said into the phone. "Yes, I look forward to getting to know you, too.

And I'd like to bring one of my famous apple pies if that's okay." She chuckled at whatever Mary Jane's mom said. "Sounds good. Okay. Good-bye." Leaning backward, she dropped the phone into its charger and then stretched out her arms. She looked borderline happy, borderline panic-stricken.

"It's going to be fun, you'll see," I said in an upbeat tone. I thought about saying, "I'm proud of you," but that sounded odd coming from her daughter. Hopefully she'd make some friends and shake up her work-study-sleep routine. "I'll help you find something cool to wear," I offered.

"You don't have to do that . . ."

"It's not like I have anything better to do. I'm grounded, remember?" I perched on the edge of her chair and then wiggled up to her. "Are you going to tell Mary Jane's and Whitney's parents about shoplifting?" Surely she'd see them at the party Saturday night, and I wanted to warn my friends.

"Do you think I should?"

"I honestly don't know."

"Well, hopefully they'll tell their parents of their own accord, and I won't have to worry about it."

"Okay." It was out of my hands, and for that, I was glad.

CHAPTER TWENTY-FOUR

When I hurried to my closet to get my shoes the next morning, something hard and sharp poked into my foot. My cross necklace. I stooped to pick it up and then fastened it around my neck. The charm dangled just above my heart, feeling warm against my skin.

"Are you sure you're ready?" Mom asked once we were in transit.

"I'm really nervous," I admitted, picking at the polish on my thumbnail. "What if they're so pissed at me, they won't even listen?"

"I have a feeling they'll listen. And before you know it, you three will be best friends again."

I bit my lower lip. "I hope so."

"And if not, you can tell your therapist all about it, and he'll help you get through it."

"My therapist?"

She nodded. "That's just my way of letting you know I made you an appointment with Dr. Linkin, a highly respected psychologist who specializes in addiction."

"Oh, great." I didn't want her to know that I actually thought seeing a therapist was a pretty decent idea. With all that had been going on, I was trying to keep myself distracted. However, every so often, I found myself craving a shoplifting adventure in the worst way. I didn't want to be like this forever.

"Are you sure you don't want me to come with you for moral support?" Mom asked as she pulled up to Calvary High School.

"What? *No.*" I gave her an "are you crazy?" glare and her greenish-blue eyes twinkled.

"Just kidding."

"Good." I smiled, and my smile grew when I spotted David Hillcrest in a group of kids over by the flagpole. He threw back his head when he laughed at something, and then he slapped a really short guy on the back.

"Who's that handsome fellow?"

"Which handsome fellow?" I asked, playing dumb.

"The one walking straight for the car, waving at you."

"Oh, that one. He's a senior. Actually, he's the preacher's son." She raised her eyebrows, and I was glad she was too into him to notice my dorky blush. "Oh, but don't worry," I said. "It's not like he's all goody-two-shoes and straitlaced. He's funny and crazy and even kind of crude sometimes."

"Oh. Well. *That*'s a relief."

His T-shirt read, IF YOU CAN'T SAY SOMETHING NICE . . . and it had a simple drawing of a face with duct tape over its mouth. I laughed to myself. Though I started getting out, David loped over to Mom's side of the Volvo. She rolled down her window and beamed at him.

"You must be Ms. Browne," he said, and I could tell Mom was impressed he got the "Ms." part right. "I'm David Hillcrest. I'm sure Poppy's told you, but she's my number-one gal."

"Oh?" Mom said, and I felt the whoosh of heat as that little blush of mine intensified.

"Yup, she's the number-one gal on my future Paintball for Christ team."

"Paintball. I see." She gave me a sideways look and I shrugged.

"Well, it's mighty nice to finally meet you, Ms. Browne.

Have a nice day." David skirted the hood of the car as he walked back to the sidewalk.

"Okay, I guess I'd better get going," I said, realizing, with more than a touch of giddiness, that David was waiting for me. But before getting out, I leaned over and kissed Mom on the cheek. I couldn't remember the last time I'd done that, and it felt good.

"So, how's it going?" David asked when Mom drove off.

"Truth?"

"Always." He stopped walking and faced me, giving me his undivided attention.

I took a deep breath. "Okay, I'm not really sure how I am. Let's just say I have some explainin' to do." We walked behind the hedge, where I briefed him on the latest developments.

Though I expected him to act surprised or repulsed or something, he just shifted his backpack to the opposite shoulder and muttered, "There's always so much drama."

"And it's not going to stop any time soon, is it?" I said. "Once Mary Jane finds out what Bridgette did, she'll figure out a way to get revenge. Then Bridgette will do something horrible to get Mary Jane back. I wish I could just get everybody in one place to hash it out."

"I think that's a brilliant idea. Get Bridgette, Mary Jane, and Whitney to sit at the same table at lunch. It won't be pretty, but it just might work."

When I'd gotten out of bed that morning, I truly hadn't planned on changing the world. Sure, I wanted to straighten things out with Mary Jane and give Bridgette a verbal smack-down. And I knew I had to deal with all the inglorious consequences of my shoplifting. But what if David was right? What if I could put a stop to this ridiculous drama, once and for all?

"Okay, I'll do it," I said. "And afterward, how about we go to the park to celebrate?"

"Are you asking me on a lunch date?"

I nodded, and as we walked through the front doors of Calvary High School, David put a hand on my shoulder and gave it a little squeeze. "You're on, kiddo."

I popped by Mary Jane's locker and then Whitney's with no luck. I was about to check the bathroom when I heard Whitney's voice in the school store. Sure enough, the stylishly clad duo stood before the drink cooler, deciding which bottled coffee-ish drink to try. With all the school merchandise and snack foods it offered, the store felt uncomfortably cramped and warm. I accidentally bumped a fishbowl full of multicolored WWJD? rubber bracelets. Who would've guessed that the sweet girl who gave me a rubber bracelet on my first day at Calvary High would ultimately screw me over?

I felt the weight of Mary Jane's and Whitney's eyes, and with every passing second, my heartbeat intensified. I looked up from the fishbowl and tried for a friendly smile. *Here goes . . .* "Hi, guys," I said lamely. "I have something to tell you, and I've come here to ask—to beg—for you to hear me out."

Whitney sipped her beverage and looked over at Mary Jane. Mary Jane frowned, but I thought I detected a spark of hope in her big blue eyes. "Okay, we'll listen," she said, just above a whisper.

An Ulrich twin nearby busied herself unpacking a Costco-size box of M&M's and chocolate bars and arranging them on a shelf. When she stocked the Butterfingers, I wondered if that day at the Milk 'n' More convenience store would put me off Butterfingers forever.

"Okay." I moved a mirrored book bag to the side so I didn't have to see distorted little pieces of my face. Then, after a girl from Ellen's German class took her bag of bagel chips and left us in virtual privacy, I said, "I made a huge mistake. The thing is, Bridgette called my mom pretending to be your mom, Mary Jane." After their shocked reactions and responses, I went on to explain exactly what had happened, and to my relief, I could tell my friends followed me play-by-play. "I should've known you'd never do something like that, Mary Jane. I should've trusted you." My knees shook and exhaustion overwhelmed me.

Mary Jane spoke first. "Oh my gosh, Poppy. I don't know what to say. That is crazy! And all this time I've been feeling physically ill because I didn't want to fight with you."

"What should we do about Bridgette?" Whitney asked with a mischievous gleam in her dark eyes. "We can't let her get away with th—"

"Hey, wait a minute. How'd Bridgette know about the shoplifting?" Mary Jane asked in a low voice.

I bit my lower lip and inhaled through my nose. "I think I might have . . . let it slip. Once. A while ago. It's my fault she found out. I wasn't thinking clearly." The threat of tears made my nose sting.

"It's okay, hon," Mary Jane said, twisting the silver rings on her fingers. "I mean, it definitely sucks, but we'll get through this." I was glad to hear her say that.

The Ulrich twin cleared her throat and said, "Hey, y'all. I've gotta close up shop for mornin' service."

"Okay, we're out of here," said Whitney, and we walked down the hall.

"You know what?" I folded a piece of gum into my mouth. "I'd rather stay on campus for lunch today. Is that cool with you guys?"

"No problem," said Mary Jane, and I congratulated myself for successfully getting two of the three hostiles to the table.

Before we went through the auditorium doors, Miss Peabody, the art teacher, stopped Whitney and Mary Jane. "Ladies, no food or drink in the auditorium."

"Finish your frappés; I'll save your seats," I said.

Strolling into the auditorium alongside Ellen, I searched for David but spotted Bridgette instead. Hustling to catch her as she walked up the center aisle, I called, "Hey, Bridgette, hold up." She whipped around, and I had to swerve to keep from running into a wall of her auburn hair. I was tempted to say (in a booming Godlike voice), "I know what you did," but instead, I said, "Just wondered if you wanted to eat lunch with me today." Hopefully Bridgette thought I hated Mary Jane, in which case, my invitation wouldn't strike her as fishy.

Her hazel eyes widened and she gave me a big metallic smile. "Okay. Sure!" Then, as if chastising herself for being insensitive, she blinked and arranged her features into a much more sympathetic expression. "So it's true you and Mary Jane aren't friends anymore?" she asked.

"It's not like it used to be, that's for sure," I said vaguely, giving her a sad little frown.

She put her hand on my shoulder. "Oh, Poppy. I know it's hard. But with God's help, you'll get through it."

"Thanks."

"You're welcome. That's what friends are for, right?"

I nodded, but I had to bite my inner cheek to keep from laughing.

"So, anyway, I'd sit with you right now but I'm performing."

Yes, you are, I thought to myself.

Bridgette tromped up to the stage with the rest of the Good News Choir, and I sat back and enjoyed some good gospel music while I made eyes at David across the pew.

Slowly but steadily, Calvary High student bodies infiltrated the cafeteria. Mary Jane, Whitney, and I leaned across our usual table, lowering our voices so passersby wouldn't overhear the sensitive subject matter.

Mary Jane twirled a strand of her shiny flat-ironed hair. "Oh my gosh, y'all. I'm so scared to tell my parents. Poppy, was it just awful?"

"Pretty much." I sympathized with Mary Jane and Whitney. Hopefully their parents wouldn't go ballistic, but I had a strong suspicion their lives were about to change even more drastically than mine. Of course, my foreseeable future looked pretty damn dismal. "Let's see. I'm grounded for life, I have to take everything back that's returnable and hope the stores don't send me to the guillotine, I'm banned from Hamilton's, and Mom made me an appointment with a shrink who'll probably make me look at inkblots and conclude that my biggest problem is I have penis envy." But in a weird way, I almost felt closer to Mom in the wake of everything that had happened since moving to Texas. Last night, we stayed up till after eleven, lolling on Mom's chaise lounge, talking. Really talking. Clearly, we still had a lot to iron out, but the good news was that we were stuck with each other, so we had no choice but to give it our best shot.

Mary Jane nibbled a slice of cantaloupe. "Do you know what's pitiful? Even though we're in a whole heap of trouble and have bigger things to worry about, I can't stop thinking about that watch we were going to lift at the Midnight Madness sale—and how much I still want to do it."

"I know. Believe it or not, it crosses my mind too," I confessed. "You two can always do it without me, I guess."

"No way," said Mary Jane. "We're off shoplifting for good."

"Argh! I still can't believe Bridgette did that," Whitney said.

Mary Jane shook her head, her golden hair swishing around her shoulders. "It was a pretty good plan, when you really stop and think about it."

"Ours has to be even better, naturally," said Whitney, cracking her knuckles.

I'd like to say I couldn't believe my own ears—or my eyes when Mary Jane nodded in wholehearted agreement.

However, I figured they'd be hell bent on getting revenge.

"Oh, hang on," I said when I spotted Bridgette at the fruit bowl. "Bridgette!" I waved her down. Ellen and her German-speaking cronies stopped eating and gawked. I noticed quite a few other heads turned in our direction, too.

"What are you doing?" Mary Jane asked through clenched teeth, and I just smiled at her and fiddled with my cross charm.

I spotted David at the doors, and he launched into a series of pantomimes, from "hello" to "I'll be right over here" to "good luck." Just knowing he was there gave me a much-needed boost of confidence.

"I'm inviting Bridgette to sit with us," I said. People were whispering all around us, but I tried to ignore them.

"What? Is this some sort of joke?" Whitney asked.

"No, I'm dead serious," I said, hoping the crack in my voice wasn't too obvious. "It's time to bury the hatchet, don't you think?"

Balancing her tray, Bridgette approached us with an air of trepidation. "Hi, Poppy. I thought—"

"Have a seat." With a nod, I indicated the open space next to Mary Jane.

"I'd rather not . . ." Bridgette ducked her eyes, turning all shades of flustered.

"Sit," I said sternly. She sat. Mary Jane groaned and pushed her salad away from her. "I've totally lost my appetite," she said, and Whitney added, "Me too."

The three girls just sat there with sour expressions on their pretty faces. The tension mounted with each passing minute, until they appeared to be on the verge of panic attacks. Or maybe it was me who was about have one. I took a deep breath, shoving aside my "What will they think of me?" insecurities. "I'm just going to say it, so you guys might as well get comfy. Bridgette, I know you're the one who called my mom. All three of us know, and it was a terrible thing to do."

Bridgette's face went from red to lily white. She stuck her pointer finger in the air and opened her mouth to speak, but I cut her off. "It's true that Mary Jane, Whitney, and I got into something very sinful and illegal and we are ashamed of it. But it's in the past, and as much as we'd like to, we can't change it. So I wouldn't waste your lunch period talking about that. Instead, you should talk about something that you *can* change. And that's the future. Now, you three, especially you two," I said, indicating Bridgette and Mary Jane "have a very turbulent past with a bunch of unresolved issues. So I suggest you sit here until you've hashed it all out—every nitty-gritty, dirty detail."

My proposal earned a round of gawks and heavy silence. I waited for Mary Jane to tell me to go screw myself, and I was fully prepared for Whitney to sock me. At the very least, I expected Bridgette to run away and seek refuge with her choir cronies. But to my surprise, no one did any of those things.

Mary Jane started twirling her hair and eventually, she rolled her big blue eyes and said, "Fine."

My heart leapt when the labored "Okay" left Bridgette's quivering lips.

I took that as a good sign that they'd give it a go, and perhaps they wouldn't spend the next two years of their lives alternately making evil plans and having to watch their backs. Maybe they agreed that their stupid feud had gone on long enough.

Relieved, I caught David's eye and grinned. When he started coming over, I stood and picked up my lunch pack.

"Where are you going?" Mary Jane asked.

"I have a very important lunch date."

"With . . . ?" Whitney's body couldn't have been more rigid.

"Ah, here he is now."

Whitney gaped and Mary Jane said, "Really, Whitney. Where have you been?"

"Hope y'all don't mind me stealin' this crazy kiddo," David said. Then to me, he whispered, "I got us excused from our fourth periods so we'll have plenty of swinging time."

"How'd you manage that?" I asked.

"Never underestimate the power of prayer," David said with a solemn air.

I raised my eyebrows. "You prayed for us to be excused from fourth period?"

"In a matter of speaking," he said. Then he whispered, "I told our teachers we were having an emergency prayer session," in my ear and I couldn't help but laugh.

"She's all yours," Mary Jane said, and David gave me his wolfish grin.

Everybody seemed to be staring at us as David escorted me through the lunchroom. Any second now, the Mary Jane Portman, Whitney Nickels, Bridgette Josephs, and Poppy Browne Scandal would make its debut at Calvary High Gossip Central.

Right before we walked out the lunchroom doors, I grabbed the preacher's son by the collar and pulled him in for a long, delicious kiss. He gazed at me with a mixture of surprise and amusement. (And, at least I hoped, a smidge of lust.) "That will give them something to talk about," I said. And as I smiled at that sexy face of his, I felt a rush of adrenaline sort of like what I got from shoplifting, but even better.

Photo by Dimitria Van Leeuwen

Born in Texas, raised in Colorado, and now living in Utah, **Wendy Toliver** has successfully eliminated "y'all" from her vocabulary. However, she still managed to marry a pickup man. They have three young sons and an assortment of furry, scaly, and slimy pets. This is her third novel. Visit her online at www.wendytoliver.com.

Turn the page for a sneak peek
at Lauren Barnholdt's new book,
One Night That Changes Everything

7:00 p.m.

I lose everything. Keys, my wallet, money, library books. People don't even take it seriously anymore. Like when I lost the hundred dollars my grandma gave me for back-to-school shopping, my mom didn't blink an eye. She was all, "Oh, Eliza, you should have given it to me to hold on to" and then she just went on with her day.

I try not to really stress out about it anymore. I mean, the things I lose eventually show up. And if they don't, I can always replace them.

Except for my purple notebook. My purple notebook is

completely and totally irreplaceable. It's not like I can just march into the Apple store and buy another one. Which is why it totally figures that after five years of keeping very close tabs on it (Five years! I've never done anything consistently for five years!) I've lost it.

"What are you doing?" my best friend Clarice asks. She's sitting at my computer in the corner of my room, IMing with her cousin Jamie. Clarice showed up at nine o'clock this morning, with a huge bag of Cheetos and a six-pack of soda. "I'm ready to party," she announced when I opened my front door. Then she pushed past me and marched up to my room.

I tried to point out that it was way too early to be up on a Saturday, but Clarice didn't care because: (a) she's a morning person and (b) she thought the weekend needed to start asap, since my parents are away for the night, and she figured we should maximize the thirty-six-hour window of their absence.

"I'm looking for something," I say from under my bed. My body is shoved halfway under, rooting around through the clothes, papers, and books that have somehow accumulated under there since the last time I cleaned. Which was, you know, months ago. My hand brushes against something wet and hard. Hmm.

"What could you possibly be looking for?" she asks. "We have everything we need right here."

"If you're referring to the Cheetos," I say, "I'm sorry, but I think I'm going to need a little more than that."

"No one," Clarice declares, "needs more than Cheetos." She takes one out of the bag and slides it into her mouth, chewing delicately. Clarice is from the South, and for some reason, when she moved here a couple of years ago, she'd never had Cheetos. We totally bonded over them one day in the cafeteria, and ever since then, we've been inseparable. Me, Clarice, and Cheetos. Not necessarily in that order.

"So what are you looking for?" she asks again.

"Just my notebook," I say. "The purple one."

"Oooh," she says. "Is that your science notebook?"

"No," I say.

"Math?" she tries.

"No," I say.

"Then what?"

"It's just this notebook I need," I say. I abandon the wet, hard mystery object under the bed, deciding I can deal with it later. And by later, I mean, you know, never.

"What kind of notebook?" she presses.

"Just, you know, a notebook," I lie. My face gets hot, and I hurry over to my closet and open the door, turning my back to her so that she can't see I'm getting all flushed.

The thing is, no one really knows the truth about what's

in my purple notebook. Not Clarice, not my other best friend, Marissa, not even my sister, Kate. The whole thing is just way too embarrassing. I mean, a notebook that lists every thing that you're afraid of doing? Like, written down? In *ink*? Who does that? It might be a little bit crazy, even. Like, for real crazy. Not just "oh isn't that charming and endearing" crazy but "wow that might be a deep-seated psychological issue" crazy.

But I started the notebook when I was twelve, so I figure I have a little bit of wiggle room in the psychiatric disorders department. And besides, it was totally started under duress. There was this whole situation, this very real possibility that my dad was going to get a job transfer to a town fifty miles away. My whole family was going to move to a place where no one knew us.

So of course in my deluded little twelve-year-old brain, I became convinced that if I could just move to a different house and a different town, I'd be a totally different person. I'd leave my braces and frizzy hair behind, and turn myself into a goddess. No one would know me at my new school, so I could be anyone I wanted, not just "Kate Sellman's little sister, Eliza." I bought a purple notebook at the drugstore with my allowance, and I started writing down all the things I was afraid to do at the time, but would of course be able to do in my new school.

They were actually pretty lame at first, like French kiss a boy, or ask a boy to the dance, or wear these ridiculous tight pants that all the girls were wearing that year. But somehow putting them down on paper made me feel better, and after my dad's job transfer fell through, I kept writing in it. And writing in it, and writing in it, and writing in it. And, um, I still write in it. Not every day or anything. Just occasionally.

Of course, the things I list have morphed a little over the years from silly to serious. I still put dumb things in, like wanting to wear a certain outfit, but I have more complicated things in there too. Like how I wish I had the nerve to go to a political rally, or how I wish I could feel okay about not knowing what I want to major in when I go to college. And the fact that these very embarrassing and current things are WRITTEN DOWN IN MY NOTEBOOK means I have to find it. Like, now.

The doorbell rings as I'm debating whether or not the notebook could be in my parents' car, traveling merrily on its way to the antique furniture conference they went to. This would be good, since (a) it would at least be safe, but bad because (a) what if my parents read it and (b) I won't be able to check the car until they get home, which means I will spend the entire weekend on edge and freaking out.

"That's probably Marissa," I say to Clarice.

Clarice groans and rolls her blue eyes. "Why is *she* coming over?" she asks. She pouts out her pink-glossed bottom lip.

"Because she's our friend," I say. Which is only a half truth. Marissa is my friend, and Clarice is my friend, and Marissa and Clarice . . . well . . . they have this weird sort of love/hate relationship. They both really love each other deep down (at least, I think they do), but Marissa thinks Clarice is a little bit of an airhead and kind of a tease, and Clarice thinks Marissa is a little crazy and slightly slutty. They're both kind of right.

Marissa must have gotten tired of waiting and just let herself in, because a second later she appears in my doorway.

"What are you doing in there?" she asks.

"I'm looking for something," I say from inside my closet, where I'm throwing bags, sweaters, belts, and shoes over my shoulder in an effort to see if my notebook has somehow been buried at the bottom. I try to remember the last time I wrote in it. I think it was last week. I had dinner with my sister and then I wrote about what I would say to . . . Well. What I would say to a certain person. If I had the guts to, I mean. And if I ever wanted to even think or talk about that person again, which I totally don't.

"What something?" Marissa asks. She steps gingerly through the disaster area that is now my room and plops down on the bed.

"A notebook," Clarice says. Her fingers are flying over the keyboard of my laptop as she IMs.

"You mean like for school?" Marissa asks. "You said this was going to be our party weekend! No studying allowed!"

"Yeah!" Clarice says, agreeing with Marissa for once. She holds the bag out to her. "You want a Cheeto?" Marissa takes one.

"No," I say, "*You guys* said this was going to be our party weekend." Although, honestly, we don't really party all that much. At least, I don't. "All I said was, 'My parents are going away on Saturday, do you want to come over and keep me company?'"

"Yes," Clarice says. "And that implies party weekend."

"Yeah," Marissa says. "Come on, Eliza, we have to at least do *something*."

"Like what?" I ask.

"Like invite some guys over," Clarice says.

Marissa nods in agreement, then adds, "And go skinny dipping and get drunk."

And then Clarice gets a super-nervous look on her face, and she quickly rushes on to add, "I mean, not *guys* guys. I mean, not guys to like date or anything. Just to . . . I mean, I don't know if you're ready to, or if you even want to—oh, crap, Eliza, I'm sorry." She bites her lip, and Marissa shoots her a death glare, her brown eyes boring into Clarice's blue ones.

"It's fine," I say. "You guys don't have to keep tiptoeing around it. I am completely and totally over him." I'm totally lying, and they totally know it. The thing is, three and a half weeks ago, I got dumped by Cooper Marriatti, *a.k.a.* the last person I wrote about in my notebook, *a.k.a.* the person who I never, ever want to talk about again. (Obviously I can say his name while defending myself from the allegation that I still like him—that is a total exception to the "never bring his name up again" rule.) I really liked him, but it didn't work out. To put it mildly. Cooper did something really despicable to me, and for that reason, I am totally over it.

"Of course you are," Clarice says, nodding her head up and down. "And of course I know we don't have to tiptoe around it."

"I heard he didn't get into Brown," Marissa announces. I snap my head up and step out of my closet, interested in spite of myself.

"What do you mean?" I ask. Cooper is a senior, a year older than us, and his big dream was to get into Brown. Seriously, it was all his family could talk about. It was pretty annoying, actually, now that I think about it. I mean, I don't think he even really *wanted* to go to Brown. He just applied because his parents wanted him to, and the only reason *they* even wanted him to go was because his dad went there, and his grandpa went there, and maybe even his great-grandpa went there. If Brown was even around then. Anyway, the point is, the fact that he didn't get in is a big deal. To him and his family, I mean. Obviously, I could care less.

"Yeah," Marissa says. "Isabella Royce told me." She quickly averts her eyes. Ugh. Isabella Royce. She's the girl Cooper is now rumored to be dating, this totally ridiculous sophomore. She's very exotic-looking with long, straight dark hair, perfect almond-shaped eyes, and dark skin. I hate her.

"Anyway," I say.

"Yeah, anyway," Clarice says. She holds out the bag of Cheetos, and this time I take one. "Oooh," she says as I crunch away. "Looks like Jeremiah added some new Facebook pictures." She leans over and squints at the screen of my laptop. She's saying this just to mess with Marissa. Jeremiah is the guy Marissa likes. They hook up once in a while, and it's kind of a . . . I guess you would say, booty-call situation. Meaning that, you know, Jeremiah calls her when he wants to hook up, and Marissa keeps waiting for it to turn into something else.

"That's nice," Marissa says, trying to pretend she doesn't care. "Here," she says, picking a stack of letters up off the bed and holding them out to me. "I brought you your mail."

"Thanks," I say, flipping through it aimlessly. I hardly ever get mail, but sometimes my sister, Kate, will get a catalog or something sent to her, and since she's away at college, I can hijack it. But today there actually is a letter for me. Well, to me and my parents. It's from the school.

"What's that?" Marissa asks, noticing me looking at it. She's off the bed now and over in the corner, picking through the mound of clothes I hefted out of my closet. She picks a shirt off the pile on the floor, holds it in front of herself, and studies her reflection in the full-length mirror. "Are my boobs crooked?" she asks suddenly. She grabs them and pushes them together through her shirt. "I think maybe my boobs are crooked."

"Your boobs," I say, rolling my eyes, "are not crooked." Clarice stays noticeably quiet and Marissa frowns.

"They're definitely crooked," Marissa says. I slide my finger under the envelope flap and pull out the piece of paper.

"You should really hope that's not true," Clarice says sagely. She whirls around on my desk chair and studies Marissa.

"Why not?" Marissa asks.

"Because there's no way to really correct that," Clarice says. "Like, if your boobs are too big, you can get them reduced; if they're too droopy, you can get them lifted. But for crooked boobs, I dunno." She looks really worried, like Marissa's crooked boobs might mean the end of her. "Although I guess maybe you could get them, like, balanced or something." She grins, totally proud of herself for coming up with this idea.

"Hmm," Marissa says. She smoothes her long brown hair back from her face. "You're right. There's no, like, boob-straightening operation."

"You guys," I say, "are nuts." I look down at the folded piece of paper in my hand, which is probably some kind of invitation to Meet-the-Teacher-Night or something.

Dear Eliza, Mr. and Mrs. Sellman,

This letter is to advise you that we will be having a preliminary hearing on Tuesday, November 17, at 2:00 p.m., to discuss Eliza's response to the recent slander complaint that has been filed against her. Eliza will be called on to talk about her experience with the website LanesboroLosers.com including her involvement and participation in the comments that were posted on October 21, about a student, Cooper Marriatti.

Please be advised that all of you will be allowed to speak.

If you have any questions, please feel free to give me a call at 555-0189, ext. 541.

Sincerely,

Graham Myers, Dean of Students

Oh. My. God.

"What the hell," I say, "is this?" I start waving the paper around, flapping it back and forth in the air, not unlike the way a crazy person might do.

"What the hell is what?" Marissa asks. She drops her boobs, crosses the room in two strides, and plucks the paper out of my hand. She scans it, then looks at Clarice.

"Oh," she says. Clarice jumps up off her perch at my desk and takes the paper from Marissa. She reads it, and then Clarice and Marissa exchange a look. One of those looks you never, ever want to see your best friends exchanging. One of those, "Uh-oh, we have a secret and do we really want to tell her?" looks.

"What?" I demand. I narrow my eyes at the both of them. "What do you two know about this?"

Marissa bites her lip. "Wel-l-l-l," she says. "I'm not sure if it's true."

"Not sure if what's true?" I say.

"It's nothing," Clarice says. She gives Marissa another look, one that says, "Let's not tell her, we're going to freak her out too much."

"Totally," Marissa says. "It's nothing."

"Someone," I say, "had better tell me exactly what this nothing is." I put my hands on my hips and try to look menacing.

“I heard it from Marissa,” Clarice says, sounding nervous.

“I heard it from Kelsey Marshall,” Marissa says.

“HEARD WHAT?” I almost scream. I mean, honestly.

“Wel-l-l-l,” Marissa says again. “The rumor is that Cooper didn’t get into Brown because of what you wrote about him on Lanesboro Losers.”

“But that’s . . . that doesn’t make any sense.” I frown, and Marissa and Clarice exchange another disconcerting look.

Lanesboro Losers is a website that my older sister, Kate, started last year when she was a senior. The concept is simple: Every guy in our school is listed and has a profile. Kind of like Facebook, except Kate set up profiles for every guy—so basically they’re on there, whether they like it or not. Under each guy’s picture is a place for people to leave comments with information they may have about that guy and how he is when it comes to girls.

So, like, for example—if you date a guy and then you find out he has a girlfriend who goes to another school, you can log on, find his profile, and write, “You should be careful about this guy since the ass has a girlfriend who goes to another school.”

It’s pretty genius when you think about it. Kate got the idea when a bunch of the boys at our school started this list ranking the hottest girls in school. Only it wasn’t just like “the top eight hottest girls” or whatever. They ranked them all the way down to the very last one. Kate, who was number 1 on the list, was outraged. So she decided to fight back and started Lanesboro Losers. Even though she's at college now, she keeps up with the hosting and has a bunch of girls from our school acting as moderators. (I would totally be a moderator if I could, but again, another thing I'm afraid of—the moderators take a certain amount of abuse at school from the guys who know what they do.)

"What do you mean he didn't get into Brown because of what I wrote about him?" I ask now, mulling this new information over in my head.

"He didn't get into Brown because of what you wrote about him," Marissa repeats.

"I heard you the first time," I say. "But that makes zero sense."

"It totally makes sense," Clarice says. "Apparently the Brown recruiter Googled him, and when they read what you wrote about his math test, they brought it up at his interview and basically told him his early decision application was getting rejected."

I sit down on the bed. "That thing I wrote about his math test was true," I say defensively.

Well. Sort of. Last year before his math final, Cooper got a bunch of study questions from his friend Tyler, and when he showed up to take the test, it turned out they weren't just study questions—it was the actual test. Cooper had already given the packet back to Tyler, and for some ridiculous reason, he didn't want to get Tyler into trouble, so he didn't tell anyone. So see? He *did* cheat, even though it was unintentional.

"It was totally true," Marissa says, nodding up and down. "Which is why you shouldn't feel bad about what you wrote." She gives Clarice a pointed look.

"Totally," Clarice says. "You shouldn't feel bad about it." She keeps nodding her head up and down, the way people do when they don't really believe what they're saying.

I close my eyes, lean back on my bed, and think about what I wrote about Cooper on Lanesboro Losers. I have pretty much every word memorized, since I spent a couple of hours obsessing over what I should write. (It couldn't be too bitter, but it couldn't look like I was trying *not* to be too bitter either. It was a very delicate balance that needed to be struck. Also, I couldn't post the truth about what really happened between me and Cooper, since it was way too humiliating.) I finally settled on, "Cooper Marriatti is a total and complete jerk. He cheated on his final math test junior year just so he could pass, and he also might have herpes." The herpes thing was of course made up, but I couldn't help myself. (And, as you can see, despite my best efforts, I totally missed the balance.)

Anyway, the thing about Lanesboro Losers is that once you post something on there, they won't take it down. It's a fail-safe, just in case you end up posting something about a guy when he's being a jerk to you and then try to log on and erase it when you guys are back together. Kate set it up so that it's totally not allowed.

"Whatever," I say, my heart beating fast. "I don't feel bad." I hope saying the words out loud will make them true. And for a second, it works. I mean, who cares about dumb Cooper and dumb Brown? It's his own fault. If he hadn't done something totally disgusting and despicable to me, if he hadn't lied to me and been a complete and total jerk, I wouldn't have written that, and he would be going to Brown. So it's totally his own fault, and if he wants to blame anyone, he should blame himself, really, because it's no concern to me if he wants to—

My cell phone starts ringing then, and I claw through the blankets on my bed, looking for it. Some books clatter onto the floor, and Clarice jumps back. She's wearing open-toed silver sparkly shoes, and one of the books comes dangerously close to falling on her foot.

"Hello," I say. The number on the caller ID is one I don't recognize, so I try to sound super-professional and innocent, just in case it's someone from the dean's office.

There's a commotion on the other end, something that

sounds like voices and music, then the sound of something crinkling, and then finally, I hear a male voice say, "Eliza?"

"Yeah?" I say.

"Eliza, listen, I didn't . . ." Whoever it is is keeping their voice really low and quiet, and I'm having a lot of trouble hearing what they're saying.

"Hello!" I repeat.

"Who is it?" Marissa asks. "Is it Jeremiah?" Sometimes Jeremiah calls me looking for Marissa, if he thinks we might be together, or if he can't get through to her for some reason. Clarice's theory is that he does this so he can relay messages to me instructing Marissa to come over for a hookup, while not having to actually talk to her.

"Hello?" I say again into the phone. I put my finger in my other ear the way they do sometimes on TV, and it seems to help a little.

"Eliza, it's me," the voice says, and this time I hear it loud and clear. Cooper. "Eliza, you have to listen to me, the 318s and Tyler . . ." There's a burst of static, and the rest of what he's saying gets cut off.

"Cooper?" I ask, and my heart starts to beat a little faster.

Marissa and Clarice look at each other. Then in one fast springlike movement, they're on the bed next to me, huddled around the phone.

"Yeah, it's me," he says. There's another burst of commotion on the other end of the line.

"Eliza, listen to me . . ." he says. "You're going to have to—" And then I hear him talking to someone else in the background.

"What do you want?" I ask, my stomach dropping into my shoes. "If this is about you not getting into Brown, then honestly, I don't even care. It's all your own fault that you didn't get into Brown, and I don't regret—"

"Eliza," Cooper says. "Listen. To. Me. You have to meet me." His voice is low now, serious and dark. "Right now. At Cure."

Marissa and Clarice are falling all over themselves and me, trying to get at the phone, and Clarice's earring gets caught on my sweater. "OW, OW, MY EAR!" she screams, then reaches down and sets it free. I pull the phone away from my ear and put it on speaker in an effort to get them to calm down.

"Cure?" I repeat to Cooper incredulously. Cure is a nightclub in Boston, and they're notorious for not IDing. I've never been there. But Kate used to go all the time, and most of the kids at my school have gone at least once or twice.

"Yeah," he says. "Eliza . . ." I hear someone say something to him in the background, and then suddenly his tone changes. "Meet me there. At Cure. In an hour."

"Tell him no," Marissa whispers, her brown eyes flashing. "Tell him that you never want to see him again!"

"Ask him if he really turned you in to the dean's office!" Clarice says. She picks up the letter from the dean's office and waves it in the air in front of me.

"Are you there?" Cooper asks, all snottylike.

"Yes, I'm here," I say. "Look, why do you want to meet me at Cure?"

"Don't ask questions," he says. "You'll find out when you get there. And make sure you wear something sexy."

I pull the phone away from my ear and look at it for a second, sure I've misheard him. "'*Wear something sexy*'? Are you *crazy*?" I ask. "I'm not going." This doesn't sound like a "Come to Cure so I can apologize to you and make sure you forgive me for the horrible things I've done" kind of request. It sounds like a "Come to Cure so that something horrible can happen that may involve humiliating you further."

Marissa nods her head and gives me a "You go, girl" look.

"Yes, you are," Cooper says.

"No, I'm not," I say.

"Yes, you are," Cooper says. And then he says something horrible. Something I wouldn't ever even imagine he would say in a million years. Something that is maybe quite possibly the worst thing he could ever say ever, ever, *ever.* "Because I have your purple notebook." And then he hangs up.